Praise for *Acceptable Risk*

"*Acceptable Risk* by Lynette Eason is another can't-put-down suspense thriller. Eason never disappoints me and *Acceptable Risk* is no exception. . . . You won't want to miss this one."

More Than a Review

"So buckle up, folks, because you are going on a wild roller-coaster ride, and you'll probably not put this book down until you are done."

Interviews and Reviews

"Readers will be kept on the edge of their seats."

Booklist

Praise for *Collateral Damage*

"Eason remains a force in action-packed inspirational fiction with this excellently paced, heartening tale."

Publishers Weekly

"Lynette Eason keeps getting better with each new novel, and fans of her work will absolutely love the start to this new series. . . . I am falling more and more in love with her writing as she releases each new book."

Write-Read-Life

"*Collateral Damage* by Lynette Eason is full of danger, suspense, and risks. . . . Every page had me sitting on the edge of my seat."

Urban Lit Magazine

"I believe it is one of the best books that Eason has written in a long time . . . and I love her books! It had a gripping mystery and was so suspenseful that she had me on the edge of my seat. If you want a roller-coaster ride with a thrilling ending, you'll want to read this award-winning author. . . . High praise for this new series."

Relz Reviewz

ACTIVE DEFENSE

Books by Lynette Eason

Women of Justice

Too Close to Home

Don't Look Back

A Killer Among Us

Deadly Reunions

When the Smoke Clears

When a Heart Stops

When a Secret Kills

Hidden Identity

No One to Trust

Nowhere to Turn

Nothing to Lose

Elite Guardians

Always Watching

Without Warning

Moving Target

Chasing Secrets

Blue Justice

Oath of Honor

Called to Protect

Code of Valor

Vow of Justice

Protecting Tanner Hollow

Danger Never Sleeps

Collateral Damage

Acceptable Risk

Active Defense

DANGER NEVER SLEEPS ③

ACTIVE DEFENSE

LYNETTE EASON

Revell
a division of Baker Publishing Group
Grand Rapids, Michigan

Published by Revell
a division of Baker Publishing Group
PO Box 6287, Grand Rapids, MI 49516-6287
www.revellbooks.com

Printed in the United States of America

Library of Congress Cataloging-in-Publication Data
Names: Eason, Lynette, author.
Title: Active defense / Lynette Eason.
Description: Grand Rapids, Michigan : Revell, a division of Baker Publishing Group, [2021] | Series: Danger never sleeps
Identifiers: LCCN 2020018602 | ISBN 9780800729363 (paperback) | ISBN 9780800739645 (casebound)
Subjects: GSAFD: Suspense fiction. | Christian fiction.
Classification: LCC PS3605.A79 A66 2021 | DDC 813/.6—dc23
LC record available at https://lccn.loc.gov/2020018602

21 22 23 24 25 26 27 7 6 5 4 3 2 1

CHAPTER ONE

SEPTEMBER
KABUL, AFGHANISTAN

Dr. Heather Fontaine strapped her feet into the sandboard and pushed off. There was nothing like the feel of the wind in her face and that peace-filled stretch of time from the top of the mountain to the bottom. It was a stress reliever like no other. With the Bamyan mountains located about three hours from Kabul and considered a relatively safe adventure, it had been a no-brainer to head there when they'd had the time off. She wasn't a runner or gym rat, but she could hold her own when sandboarding or skiing.

An encouraging yell came from Gina Wicks, her nurse, and Heather grinned, happy to see the young widow enjoying a moment of fun. Gina's husband, Brad, had been killed by "friendly fire" and she'd returned a couple weeks ago to finish her tour.

At the end of the run, Heather expertly shifted her body to bring the board to a halt.

"Way to go, Heather," Gina said. "No one would know you hate to exercise."

Heather laughed. "That's not exercise, that's sheer exhilaration."

The other two friends who'd joined her and Gina grabbed their gear and they headed to the Jeep.

While Gina drove, Heather leaned her head back against the seat and shut her eyes. She was tired, but in a good way. Not in a twelve-hour-surgery-only-to-lose-the-patient way. She'd needed this. They'd all needed it. But now it was time to get back and her brain was already shifting into work mode, mentally reviewing the patients waiting for her in the recovery tent.

She must have dozed off, because the next thing she knew, Gina was poking her in the arm. Heather opened her eyes and realized they were almost back to base. "Wow." She scrubbed a hand down her cheek and drew in a deep breath. "I must have sacked out."

"Girl, you sawed enough logs to last all winter in Alaska."

Heather rolled her eyes, but smiled. "Hey, can you stop by the hospital? I want to check on a few patients."

"Now?"

"Yeah. If you don't mind?"

"Um . . . sure."

The other two ladies in the back groaned good-naturedly and guilt swept her.

"No, never mind. I'll walk over after we drop everyone off."

Gina swung the wheel and headed for the FOB hospital. "It's okay. It won't take you long. I'll drop you off first and come back and get you when you're ready."

That seemed to work for the others and soon Heather found herself walking toward the surgery recovery ward. The huge tents that made up the hospital might look rough and ancient on the outside, but the inside held state-of-the-art equipment for those needing it. And so many did—Afghani civilians and American soldiers, both.

She'd enjoyed being with her friends and knew she needed the mental break, but her patients weighed on her mind and in her heart the entire time she'd been away. Not that the other doctors weren't perfectly capable of caring for them, but . . .

Heather spotted one of the doctors caring for her patients while she was gone. "Hey, Hank, hold up."

He turned. "What are you doing here?"

"We got back a little early so I thought I'd check in. Catch me up."

He did, then patted her shoulder. "Glad you're back, Heather," he said. "It's too quiet around here without you."

She wrinkled her nose. "I'm not sure how to take that."

He laughed. "Can I grab you a cup of coffee?"

"Sure, thanks."

"I'll be right back." He darted toward the cafeteria.

Movement in the distance stalled her. She stood between the tents—to her left was the operating suite, to her right the recovery area. She tried to get a better view of the approaching figure and noted he'd caught the attention of several others.

He trudged toward them, head down, T-shirt two sizes too big and flapping around his thin frame. He passed two of the Humvees, walked between two more tents, and headed for the recovery ward.

The closer he got, the more she knew. Certainty settled in her gut. "No," she whispered. "No!" She ran toward him. "Please! No!"

He stopped and locked eyes with her. She could see his desperation even at this distance. For a moment, he stood motionless, half a football field between them. Then he yanked off the shirt, and Heather froze as she saw the bomb strapped to his chest.

"Help me!" He grabbed at the bomb, struggled with it, trying to rip it from his body.

"No! Stop! Don't come any closer! Bomb!"

Heads popped out from the tents.

Heather's focus remained on the teen. He'd managed to pull the explosive partway off, the duct tape loosening, some of it tearing. He held it out to the right side of his body, and for a moment she thought he might succeed, let go of it, and run.

The explosion rocked him, lifted him, then dropped him onto his back on the hard-packed dirt. Heather screamed. She raced toward him, pulling gloves from her pocket, hearing others yelling at her to get back, that there might be a second bomb, but she couldn't leave him like that. She dropped to her knees next to him. His right arm was gone, his right side a mangled mess. Blood pumped from the shoulder where his arm had been, and she clamped a hand over it.

"Hold on!" she yelled at him. "Hold on!" He was conscious, his eyes never leaving hers. "What's your name?"

"Abdul," he whispered. "I am sorry. I—"

And closed his eyes.

Heather looked back over her shoulder. "Someone get over here and help me!"

Another doctor raced from the tent, and time blurred as Heather went to work on the boy, who couldn't be more than fourteen or fifteen years old. "Please hold on."

She was acutely aware of others arriving to help transfer him to a portable stretcher and then to the OR. She raced alongside him, keeping her hands clamped around his open wound. And finally, they were in the operating room. Minutes turned into hours as they tried to put the boy back together. Another doctor worked to reattach his arm. Heather did her best with his torso. She pulled the last stitch and sucked in a breath.

"That's it," she said. "Now, we wait."

○ ○ ○

Two hours later, in recovery, Heather dozed in the chair next to Abdul's bed.

The alarms on the monitor woke her and she bolted to her feet. His heart had stopped.

Feverishly, she pumped his chest. "Please, please, please, don't give up. You asked me to help you and I will, but you have to live." More pumping. Sweat rolled from her in waves.

She had no idea how long she worked until Gina laid a hand on her shoulder. "Heather . . ."

Heather stopped, panting, heard the flatline—and knew it was over. They'd lost him. She blinked up at her friend, trying to keep from breaking down. "What are you doing here?"

"I came back just after the explosion to see if I could help. To make sure you were okay. I'm sorry."

Heather let out a low cry and swung away from her, stripped off her gloves, and darted out the door. The sun was setting, turning the sky all kinds of beautiful colors. But she didn't want to see beauty when she was surrounded by death. Not tonight.

"Heather!"

"Give me some space right now, Gina, please."

The woman hesitated, then turned and went back inside with Abdul.

Heather paced near the trash heap, working hard to get her emotions under control. She wanted to weep, to scream, to lash out at the evil that had overtaken this country, but she didn't. She couldn't.

She took a deep breath and had turned to go back in when she spotted the full trash bag against the wall.

And the navy-blue T-shirt laying on top of it. She picked it up, noted the white paint stains on the left shoulder. Pictured it on the teen who'd come to kill them.

She buried her face in it and wept.

○ ○ ○

JANUARY
GREENVILLE, SC

Heather pulled to the curb of her best friend's house, put the SUV in park, and cut the engine. Brooke James lived in a middle-class neighborhood in a cottage-style home with a perfectly groomed yard. Even in the dead of winter.

But that was Brooke, a woman whose friendship Heather deeply appreciated. Most of the time, she couldn't wait to get together with her. But at the moment, Heather wasn't in the mood to put on her party face. Her left leg jiggled up and down—a sure sign she was anxious and stressed. She didn't even bother to try and stop it. "Just go home," she muttered. "If you go home, you can curl up on the couch and read a good book." While intermittently checking the alarm system, windows, and doors to ensure no one could get in.

No one, meaning the stalker she seemed to have acquired. Four months home from active duty in a war zone and she still wasn't sleeping much. She found herself ducking at loud noises, avoiding crowds, but managing to function at work without too much trouble. Which was weird, but she'd come to accept that was the way her brain was going to work at the present and deal with it. Only this stalker thing was about to send her over the edge, back into that dark mental pit that had sent her running home at the first opportunity.

She sat tense and knotted while scanning the surrounding area for *him*. Seeing nothing that set off her alarms, Heather allowed herself to relax a fraction.

But she still wanted to go home. She cranked the car. Hesitated. And shut off the engine. "Ugh."

She'd promised Brooke and the others she'd come. They were welcoming Gina home from Afghanistan.

But doing that required getting out of the car. She pressed her thumb and forefinger to her eyes. Gina's arrival home had sparked all the memories Heather had worked so hard to suppress. To overcome. To ignore. Gina had been home a little over two weeks, and Heather had managed to avoid seeing the woman, much to her shame. But the truth was, Gina was a walking reminder of that day, and Heather didn't want to remember.

"Because avoiding Gina's working really well for you so far, right?" Her self-directed sarcasm didn't help. It was time to pull on her big-girl panties and go welcome home a woman who'd been nothing but a friend to her. She stuffed her keys into her bag. She had enough on her plate dealing with the mess in her head; she didn't have time to play games with a stalker.

The longer Heather sat, the faster her anger boiled. Seriously. A stalker? No . . . more like a watcher. He would watch her but not approach—or would act like he was going to, then change his mind at the last minute.

It was unnerving. Even when she'd been serving at the hospital base in Afghanistan, she hadn't been this jumpy. Going back to Kabul after an extended period of time home was not on her radar until the Army deployed her again, thanks to a shortage of physicians in FOBs. Once her time was up—right after the bombing—she took an honorable discharge, with the hopes it would help with the nerves and the nightmares. And it had. She'd been making progress. Had been going about her life just fine. Until this guy had shown up. And Gina had come home to stir up memories of that day at the hospital four months ago.

Another glance in the rearview mirror didn't help. Neither did checking the side mirrors.

There was nothing and no one there.

But she'd seen him. Several times. She just couldn't get a good look at him. Once, at work, she'd thought he might attempt to speak with her, but she had been approached by a colleague. When she turned back to the place she'd seen him, he was gone.

But . . . the short look she had gotten had reminded her of someone. She'd seen him before. In the past. But where?

Her phone buzzed and she snatched it from the holder. "Hello?"

"Are you going to sit out there all evening or come in?"

Heather closed her eyes and pulled in a deep, cleansing breath. "Sorry, I was just thinking about something. I'm coming."

"You brought your suit, right?"

"Yes, but—"

"Great. We're in the pool. Get changed and join us."

"Bossy today, aren't you?"

Brooke simply laughed, and Heather couldn't help the smile that curved her own lips.

"You do realize it's two measly degrees above freezing out here?"

"That's why my husband put the heater in. Plus, we have the hot tub now. Trust me, you'll love it. It's really relaxing." She paused. "And *relaxing* sounds like it might be beneficial for you."

Heather laughed. "I'm on the way." She hung up and grabbed her bag from the floorboard.

When she looked up, her gaze zeroed in on a shadow of movement on the street in front of the neighbor's house. A fleeting glimpse of someone in a ball cap, scarf, and plaid jacket. The same outfit she'd seen when she walked out of the hospital yesterday and the day before. He disappeared behind the van parked on the street, then reappeared, hands shoved into his coat.

She threw open the door, bolted from the seat, and raced in the direction she'd seen the person.

"Heather!"

The shout from behind her reached her ears, but she couldn't stop to acknowledge it. Just ahead was her stalker. Watcher. Whatever.

Her feet pounded the asphalt. "Hey! You!"

The man froze, then he turned and ran, hopped into a dark sedan, and sped off down the street.

A hand landed on her arm. On instinct, she spun and lashed out with a fist that connected to flesh. A harsh grunt escaped her attacker while pain exploded from her knuckles to her wrist. Her victim stumbled backward.

"Heather!"

She floundered to a stop, panting, heart thundering in her ears. "Travis?" Heather flexed her fingers to make sure she hadn't broken anything. When they moved freely, if painfully, she breathed a sigh of relief.

Travis Walker was bent at the waist, one hand covering his cheek. "Holy cow, you have a mean right."

Horrified, Heather gaped. "Oh, my word . . . oh no. I'm so sorry. What were you *doing*?" She'd hit him. The first guy she'd been interested in since . . . forever. But had been too leery to let him know it. And she'd hit him.

"I pulled in behind you and saw you sitting in your car," he said. "I was coming to walk inside with you, when all of a sudden you were racing down the street."

"So, you decided to chase me?"

"And *catch* you, much to my regret." He straightened and winced. "What were you running from?"

"Not *from. To.*" She glanced back in the direction she'd seen the figure. Gone now, of course. "And I . . . I'm not sure. I think someone is . . . watching me."

"Watching you?"

"That sounds so freaky and paranoid, doesn't it?"

"A little, without an explanation to go along with it."

"Heather?" Brooke's concerned call from her front porch sent a deep sigh shuddering through her.

"Be there in a minute!" She groaned. "I'll explain later. I don't want this to be a big thing tonight." The urge to share her fears and concerns nearly overpowered her. However, while she'd gotten to know Travis over the last four months, thanks to her friendship with Brooke, his best friend's wife, she swallowed the words and stepped closer to him. She studied his wound. He still looked amazing to her even with a slightly red eye. "Let me see it."

"It's fine. It was a glancing blow. I just want to know what you don't want to be a big thing."

Heather leaned closer. "Travis, come on." She caught a whiff of that cologne he used. A scent she'd come to associate only with him.

"Nope." He actually backed away from her, the expression on his face grabbing her curiosity. He rubbed just under the wound, his green eyes glinting at her, a mixture of admiration and . . . fear?

She raised a brow. "What in the world is wrong with you?"

He flushed. "Nothing. Doctors make me nervous." He bent and picked up the black Stetson that had flown from his dark blond head when she'd belted him.

"Doctors make you . . ." She sputtered to a stop. Then laughed. When he didn't join her, that trailed off too. "You're serious?"

"Now you know my deepest, darkest secret."

"Somehow, I doubt that. Are you going to explain?"

He raised a brow. "Are you going to tell me about this person you think is watching you?"

"Heather? Travis? Is everything okay?" Brooke called from the porch again, her voice a mixture of curiosity and concern.

"We're coming, Brooke." Heather figured Brooke's rabid curiosity—which was part of what made her such a great psychiatrist—would get the better of her and she'd come to investigate if they didn't hurry up. She waved toward the house. "Why don't we go join the party and put some ice on that eye?"

His eyes narrowed, and for a split second, she thought he might insist on further explanation for her odd behavior, but he agreed with a quick nod.

With one last glance behind her, she shook off the ominous feeling that her watcher was escalating and vowed to have a good time tonight.

Even if it killed her.

○ ○ ○

Travis leaned his head back against the edge of the hot tub and let the jets pound his body while his left eye and cheekbone throbbed. He'd shucked his cowboy boots and Stetson in favor of a bathing suit and old T-shirt from his college days at Baylor University. Caden Denning and Brooke's husband, Asher, sat opposite him while Gavin Black manned the grill.

Heather, Brooke, Sarah, Ava, and Gina had opted for the heated pool. Shortly after his wedding to Brooke last year, Asher had convinced his friends to join him in the DIY project of converting the existing pool into a pool and hot tub combo. They'd painted oversized game boards on the concrete, including chess, backgammon, and shuffleboard. It was a gorgeous entertaining space.

At the time, Travis had been certain he and the others were nuts for agreeing to help put it all together. Right now, he decided it was the best idea any one of them had ever come up with. Mainly because of the hot tub adjoining the pool. He settled back in the tub, elbows resting behind him on the ledge between the two. The ladies had migrated to the shallow end steps to chat. Travis closed his eyes and let the hot water relax him.

"How are you doing?" Heather's soft question whispered past his ear. Opening one eye, he turned his head to discern she'd aimed the question at Gina.

"Okay today," Gina said. She had her auburn hair pulled on top of her head in one of those clip things women liked. The floodlights from the pool illuminated her face. She was pretty in a girl-next-door kind of way, but the stress of losing her husband had stamped a grief onto her fragile features that would only be softened by time.

"Tomorrow I might not be," she said. "I try to stay busy. I joined a chess club here before I left Kabul and the first meeting is tomorrow night, but it's hard to work up any enthusiasm for it."

Travis grimaced at the pure sadness in her voice and shut his eye. Gina's husband had been killed in Afghanistan about six months ago. She'd come home to bury him, then returned to finish her tour. A courageous choice.

"It doesn't help that my mother-in-law keeps posting stuff on Brad's social media page, ranting about the military and everything wrong with it," Gina said. "Including me. She blames me and everyone involved for his death. She thinks I should have done something. Everyone should have done something to keep him from dying."

"Oh, how awful," Brooke said.

"I'd simply delete his profile, but his friends still post on there as a way to honor his memory, and I hate to take that away from them. Or . . . I could simply block her, but that doesn't seem right either. I can see it now, can't you? #worstdaughterinlawever." She rubbed her eyes. "And, truthfully, I don't want to lose the content that he posted."

"I've seen a few of the posts," Heather said, "and I can imagine those are really hard for you. Can you ignore her or snooze her?"

"I've been ignoring her. Or trying to. It's not working very well." Gina shook her head. "I need to stay off social media until she calms down—and she will. Eventually."

Heather rubbed her friend's shoulder. "I'm sorry."

Travis glanced over at Caden and noticed his eyes were on the ladies.

Most specifically, Ava. Caden and Sarah's childhood friend, but it was obvious Caden wanted to take that to a new level.

Travis lifted a brow and caught the man's eye. Caden gave him a deadpan look and rolled so his back was to Travis. He crossed his arms on the hot tub ledge and rested his chin on them. Travis filed the information away. So, Caden was interested in Ava. That was a relief. He'd thought for a long time he might be attracted to Heather.

He would understand it, of course. Heather had the looks of a runway model with her long wavy blonde hair, creamy complexion, and eyes that reminded him of his mom's sapphire pendant she wore only on special occasions. And while he had initially been attracted to her good looks, it was the heart that beat within her that kept his attention snared.

Travis had a healthy self-esteem for the most part, but when it came to women, he sometimes felt like a fish out of water—especially since his last relationship had gone south. Heather was so out of his league she didn't even have a league. He often found himself paralyzed when in her presence. It was stupid, but it was also reality.

". . . friendly fire," Gina was saying. "What's so friendly about it? It still kills."

"Aw, Gina . . ." Brooke's voice was soft, sympathetic, and raw with hurt for her friend.

Gina waved a hand. "Sorry. Being home and trying to adjust to this life without Brad has been hard." She paused. "So, here's some good news. I start my new job tomorrow."

"New job?" Heather tilted her head and frowned.

"It's part-time right now with a construction company, but it could turn into full-time. A friend of mine told me about it. I talked to the manager and he said he'd give me a chance."

"Construction?" Brooke asked. "What happened to nursing?"

"I . . . I'm not ready to go back to that yet. I just—" She looked away. "I'm not sure I'll ever want to return to medicine."

Heather and Brooke exchanged a glance, and Heather gave a slight shrug.

"Well, are you all right financially?" Brooke asked. "Because we can help, you know."

Gina blinked. "That's really sweet, but no, I'd never take your money. I'm fine right now, but the money from Brad's life insurance and the death gratuity won't last forever, so I have to start thinking about the future and making plans." She paused. "And . . ." She drew in a deep breath. "As part of those plans, I'm putting our house on the market."

A small gasp slipped from Sarah, and Gina gave her a sad smile. "I know. It may seem extreme, but I simply can't live there without him."

"Understandable. Where are you going to live?"

"With my parents. For now. I'll look for something else soon, though. As much as I love them, I'm not sure how long I'll be able to handle living with them." Gina shoved a few stray strands of hair behind her ear.

"How long were you married?" Ava asked. "I feel like I should know this, but I don't remember."

"A little over a year, but we dated for two."

"Brad was a wonderful man," Heather said. "I always enjoyed his stops at the hospital to see you. I appreciated his humor and obvious love for you." She shook her head. "It never should've happened and I'm sorry I couldn't save him. I tried, Gina, I promise, I tried."

"I know you did. But you and I both know it wouldn't have mattered who his doctor was," Gina said. "He barely lived ten minutes after he got to the hospital—and it was because of you that he had those minutes." The ladies gathered closer around Gina, who grimaced and gave a humorless chuckle. "Well, I'm a downer, aren't I? Let's talk about something else."

"Hey, Gina," Caden said, "how about a game of chess? I bet I can beat you. I've been practicing."

Gina actually laughed, her face softening as the strain of grief lifted for the moment.

"Beat me?" Gina smirked. "That's just delusional."

The two of them wandered over to the giant-sized chess set next to the pool, and Travis closed his eyes once more, glad to see Gina smiling.

"Cowboy, you gonna soak your skin off or come finish barbecuing these ribs? It's my turn in the hot tub."

Gavin's question made Travis smile. "I'm coming." He and Gavin had formed a friendship when they'd gone through boot camp together and stayed in touch in spite of the fact their lives had gone in different directions. Gavin had stayed in Afghanistan for a couple of years, Travis had been there for one tour, then opted out at the first possible opportunity to work as an EMT. He'd gotten bored with that and headed to the police academy. After working his way up to detective and the SWAT team, a restlessness he hadn't been able to shrug off had made the decision for him. He'd opened his own security firm and became his own boss, hiring Gavin and Asher, who were more partners than employees.

"You'd better hurry," Caden said with a lazy southern drawl, looking up from the game, "or someone's liable to punch you in the other eye."

"Don't know what you're talking about. It's just allergies." Travis ignored Asher's and Caden's quiet laughter—and Gina's quizzical look—and hauled himself out of the water. He grabbed one of the robes from the hook on the wall before the chill could chase away the warmth of the soak.

Brooke and Asher treated their guests well, and he was always happy to be included in any invitation from them—especially when it involved cooking and the pool.

And Heather.

At the grill, he grabbed one of the barbecue bottles he'd brought. A light laugh rang out from the hot tub.

Heather's.

Chills slipped up his spine. Chills that had nothing to do with the weather, but everything to do with the fact that the more he was around Heather Fontaine, the more he liked her. But something was definitely bothering the pretty surgeon and Travis wanted to know what it was.

She'd been chasing something—or someone—and the pinched look to her mouth and flare of fear in her eyes when she'd thrown that punch told him a whole lot.

He touched the bruise beneath his left eye. She hadn't broken the skin, but based on his glance in the bathroom mirror, it was already an intriguing shade of red. Dodging the immediate questions as soon as he'd walked into the house had required some quick thinking. Allergies. Yeah. Right.

Caden's comment during the chess match made him wonder if the man had actually witnessed the whole thing or if he was just a good guesser. No way to know without asking, and Travis didn't plan on doing that.

Once he had the ribs slathered with another layer of his special sauce, he stepped inside to find Gavin pulling more sodas from the refrigerator. "Ribs should be done in about another fifteen minutes."

Gavin nodded. "Thanks for bringing them."

"Do you know how hard it was not to finish cooking those suckers and have a feast? Even my parents came over hoping to score some."

"They could smell it from their house?"

"Them and every ranch hand on the place." That's what he got for living in close proximity to his entire family and the people who worked for them. And he wouldn't change it for anything. "They hate me now, but I refused to share. Only my promise to cook them some in the near future has kept me in the will."

Gavin smiled. "Glad you managed to protect them—and stay in the will."

"Barely."

"How are things on the ranch anyway? Haven't heard you mention it much lately."

"Not too much to mention. Things are mostly good. Some bad. Got a horse we're going to have to put down before too much longer. It's going to devastate my sister."

Gavin winced. "Ouch. I hate that. That the one she's had for a while?"

"Over twenty years." He didn't even want to think about it. "Dad's doing well. He's doing some contract work for the Marshals when he's not taking care of the ranch. He has to stay busy or go nuts." One would think the ranch kept him busy enough, but Travis knew the man missed his law enforcement days. "Mom just shakes her head." He paused and glanced at his phone. "I got a request from that senator who's getting married next month in Asheville. Are you and Asher up for it?"

"Sure."

"Might take all of us to cover it."

"Then it's a good thing you brought three more people on board. We've needed them."

"Thanks." Travis sent an acceptance email that would automatically log the event on his calendar. "How's Sarah doing?" A few short months ago, Caden's sister, Sarah, had been kidnapped by the Taliban and held until Gavin and his team had managed to rescue her. She and Gavin were now engaged and making wedding plans.

"Doing well. She and Brooke talk a lot and she's come a long way. She's more at peace with herself, her father . . . everything."

"She's still enjoying the job?" Sarah had been offered an investigative journalist position with a local newspaper once she'd been discharged from the Army. She'd finally caved after taking several months to decide if that was what she wanted to do. It said a lot about the respect she commanded in the profession that they were willing to wait for her.

"She is. It's a little different from what she was doing in Kabul, but she likes it. *I* like it because it's not near as dangerous."

"I get that. She's crazy talented. Some of her articles have left me reeling."

"You're preaching to the choir, man."

Travis chuckled and glanced at the ladies, who'd slipped into robes and gathered under one of the tall propane patio heaters. "Have you talked to Heather much?"

"I talk to her when I see her, which is every once in a while. Sarah sees her a lot more than I do. Why? Something going on?"

"I'm not sure." Travis told Gavin about her race down the street—leaving out the part about how he got the bruised eye. "She said she wasn't running from anything, but *to* something."

"To what?"

"I don't know. She started to tell me, but Brooke interrupted, so Heather said she'd explain later."

Gavin stroked the five o'clock shadow on his chin. "You know, she does seem a little more tense than usual."

"How so?"

"Just . . ." He shrugged. "The last few times I've seen her, she's just seemed . . . off. *Tense* is the only word I can think of—or strung tight."

"Yeah." Travis fell silent, processing. "I guess she'll share with us when she's ready."

Gavin gave light scoff of disbelief. "Heather *might* share with Brooke, and that means you'll never know what's going through her head."

True. Brooke would never betray a confidence. Which meant Travis would have to do his own digging. "Those ribs are probably done by now. You ready?"

"Been ready even though you made me stand here and talk instead of getting a good soak in."

Travis laughed and led the way back out onto the deck. With the three heaters, the grill, and the firepit, the chill wasn't too bad. Asher had already started handing out the plates.

Once they'd piled the food high and had gathered around the firepit, Travis waited for Asher to say grace, then shot a look at Caden. "So, who won?"

"Shut up."

Gina grinned and Caden scowled before giving a rueful smile and a shrug. Conversation shifted to small talk until Brooke turned to Heather.

"What were you running from earlier?" she asked.

Heather froze and her lips tightened a fraction. "Nothing."

"Running?" Sarah asked with a raised brow. "Since when does Heather run voluntarily?"

The others snickered. Heather's aversion to physical exercise was anything but a well-kept secret.

Gina leaned in. "Come on, Heather, spill it."

Heather rolled her eyes, then sighed. "I'll sound like I'm crazy. Y'all will think I'm flat-out losing it."

"Now you have to tell us," Sarah said. "No way you can say that and then just shut down the topic."

Travis caught the darkening of Heather's blue eyes and the furrowed brow along with the minuscule flash of fear. He frowned. "What's going on, Heather? We're your friends and want to help."

Heather scowled. "Y'all . . . really. It's *probably* not that big of a deal."

"But?" Travis asked.

"But . . . I think I might have something of a stalker."

CHAPTER TWO

"A stalker!" Travis's feet hit the ground with a thud and Heather refused to look at him. He'd just had to play the "we're your friends and just want to help" card, hadn't he?

"What?" Brooke cried.

Gina's eyes had gone wide. "You mean like a stalker . . . stalker?"

Heather held up a hand. "I said *something* of a stalker. Actually, *stalker* might be too strong a word. He's more like a watcher." But maybe not.

All eyes were on her, making her want to squirm. Instead, her left leg started the jiggle like it did when she was stressed. She crossed her right leg over it to keep it still. Sarah's knowing gaze homed in on the movement. "Explain, will you?"

"I've seen someone watching me and it's putting me on edge," Heather said. "So, when the guy showed up here, I wanted to confront him. But he disappeared on me."

"That's not nothing," Gina said.

"If someone's watching you, it could have something to do with that video." Sarah leaned forward and snagged her drink from the table, her gaze intense.

Travis tilted his head. "What video?"

"You're kidding me. Where have you been hiding?" Sarah asked.

"It's all over social media. It's the one of Heather and the team operating on the Afghan teen who blew himself up at the hospital. Caden's been trying to get it taken down but hasn't had much luck."

"Some of us don't spend every spare minute on social media," Travis said.

"Well, *some* of us have to know what's trending because *some* of us have a job that requires it." Sarah scowled at him, then smiled.

Travis rolled his eyes. Being friends with Sarah was like having another sister.

Caden frowned. "I'm making progress. It's not exactly my specialty area, so it's taking a little longer than I'd hoped." He'd called in a favor from his tech guru at the FBI, but she hadn't had spare time to devote to it yet.

Heather let out a low sigh. "It's probably a moot point by now. It has over six million views and is climbing. Talk shows are calling me. Can you believe it?"

Four weeks ago, someone had posted a video of Heather performing surgery while in Kabul. It had gone viral within hours. When it had gotten to the point that people were stopping her in the grocery store to either lambaste her for trying to save a suicide bomber or regale her with praise for her "saintly" heart, she'd had enough. For a week, she'd worked to get it pulled from the internet—all to no avail. Heather had finally asked Caden to intervene.

"And the bomb went off before he actually got inside the hospital," Heather said, her voice low. "I really don't think he wanted to do it."

"The boy? What makes you say that?" Travis asked.

She hesitated. "The hospital is in a rural area where a lot of fighting was going on. We were filled to capacity, working sixteen to twenty hours a day to help the troops and local Afghans caught in the middle. I was in charge of the operating room. We'd just gotten back from a short sandboarding trip and I wanted to check on some patients. I was walking toward the recovery ward when I saw him. He looked right at me, took his shirt off, showed us the bomb, and asked me to help him. That's when it went off. And I don't think the guy watching me has anything to do with the video." Although it *had* crossed her mind.

Sarah narrowed her eyes. "Why did we not know this?"

"I don't like to talk about it. It was four months ago. I'm trying to move on."

The others stared at her, and like a flash of lightning splitting the dark sky, the truth hit her. She closed people out. No matter how much she might crave the closeness she observed between the others, she didn't let herself have it. She'd thought she'd overcome that, but the reality was, she couldn't figure out how to do it. To change herself and what had been ingrained in her since childhood. *Don't trust anyone. Especially someone who offers to help you. They don't want to help you. They just want something from you.* The words of one of her foster siblings echoed in her head. She wanted the intimacy the others shared. She did. But not this way. Not by being needy. Then again, if she allowed them to help, it would be a real test of their . . . steadfastness? Loyalty? Trustworthiness? Guilt hit her that she even questioned that at this point in their friendship.

Brooke touched her hand, bringing her back to the conversation. "If you don't think it has anything to do with the video, what do you think it has to do with?"

Heather huffed a short sigh. "I don't know. Just forget I said anything. I'm making a big deal out of this. He'll get tired and move on."

"*He* will? Do you know who it is?" Gavin asked.

"No."

"Anything else we need to know about this situation?" Travis's quiet—lethal—tone sent goose bumps popping up on her arms. He'd gone still, his eyes narrowed, like a hunter who'd scoped out his prey and was simply waiting for the right time to pounce.

Heather blinked at the easygoing cowboy's transition, then shook her head. "I really don't think there *is* a situation." At least not one she was ready to admit to. Yet. "I'm taking some precautions and watching my back, but I'm not worried." *Liar. Why* had she said anything?

She was competent, used to being in control—of the operating room and her life. Always before, she'd handled her problems herself. She didn't go blabbing about them to other people. Not even her closest friends. But this *situation* had her off-kilter and had loosened her tongue way too much. "Seriously, I appreciate that you want to help, but I can deal with it. Really. If it escalates or I think I need help . . . I'll ask." No she wouldn't. She rose. "I'm going to get a refill." She took her three-quarters-full glass and headed for the kitchen, kicking herself for ruining the lighthearted atmosphere they'd finally managed to achieve after the despondent conversation in the pool.

Gina followed. In the kitchen, her friend grabbed another soda from the refrigerator while Heather waited, mind tumbling with thoughts of leaving.

"What's with you and Travis?" Gina asked.

Heather blinked. "What do you mean? We're friends."

A light laugh tripped from Gina's lips. "I think his feelings go a little beyond the 'just friends' thing."

Heat crept into Heather's neck and up into her cheeks. "I'm sure you're imagining things."

"No . . . I'm quite sure I'm not." A wistful smile curved the woman's lips. "Brad used to look at me that way. Like I was the most beautiful and priceless treasure he'd ever seen. And when you mentioned you thought you had a stalker, Travis's eyes went black. If you *do* have a stalker and Travis gets his hands on the man, it won't end well for that dude. I'm just sayin'."

"Oh, come on, Gina. Travis is just—"

"Why are you protesting so hard? I'm not blind, my friend."

Heather stilled. "You're right. You're not. We've been friends a long time and survived some crazy stuff. If you say he looks at me like that, then . . ."

"He does."

"Huh. Okay, then." So, she hadn't been imagining the spark of interest there. It both thrilled and scared her. All her life she'd longed for a family. She'd decided as a child she wanted a man who'd love her. Someone very different than her abusive father. But she'd also decided that if that didn't happen, she'd be fine alone.

Gina lifted her soda can in a "cheers" gesture. "I'm going to get back to the ribs. They're really good."

At the freezer, Heather added two cubes of ice and considered leaving once more. Gina's observations and her own loose tongue had served to throw her off her axis. Now that she'd been confronted with the reality of Travis's interest, she had to decide what to do about it. She'd only dated men she knew she could control—or at least maneuver like pieces on a chessboard. Her friends called them wimps. Travis was no wimp and he wouldn't be maneuverable. If that was a word. Not that she would ever plan on doing that with Travis, but . . . ugh! Dare she take a chance and encourage his interest?

"There's ice in the cooler on the deck," Brooke said from behind her.

"I know." Heather shut the freezer.

"Want to talk about it?"

"There's nothing to talk about," she said, turning to face her friend. "And I'm not saying that because I don't want to talk about it. I've truly told you everything. I'm probably overreacting."

"You don't overreact. It's not in your DNA."

A laugh slipped from her. "So we all thought." She shrugged, her smile sliding south. "I don't know, Brooke. Ever since the bombing at the hospital, and watching Abdul die, I just—" Why couldn't she turn the words off? "I can't even get rid of the T-shirt."

Maybe she did want to talk about it.

Brooke sidled closer. "What T-shirt?"

"The one the kid was wearing when he approached the hospital. I saw him and I knew, Brooke. I knew what he had planned."

"How?"

She took a sip of her drink. "I just did." She stared at the floor, reliving the day the bombing occurred. "I wasn't supposed to be there, did you know that?"

"You were sandboarding, weren't you?"

Heather nodded. "But we got back early from our trip and I decided to check on a few patients. I headed for the recovery ward, and that's when I saw him."

"And he saw you."

"Yes. I remember it like it was yesterday. The expression on his face was . . ." She looked away. "I don't even know if I can put words to it. A mixture of desperation and determination and . . . hope."

"Hope?"

"Hope that I would help him. Hope that there was a way out of his impossible situation. Hope that he wouldn't die. He didn't want to do it."

"What? Blow up the hospital? So you've said."

She nodded. "He tried to warn us."

Brooke frowned. "How so?"

Heather rarely talked about that day. Or Abdul. And she'd never told a soul about the T-shirt. Until tonight. "Like I said before, he took his shirt off and showed us the bomb strapped to him. He looked right in my eyes and cried out in English, 'Help me.'"

"Oh my . . ."

A tear dripped down Heather's cheek and she swiped it away. Why was she sharing this now? "And then the bomb went off. Far enough away that no one else got hurt. Just him."

"I had no idea." Brooke's sympathy—and shock—were tangible. "I knew you were there in the operating room—everyone knows that, thanks to the video—but I didn't know the details. Why haven't you told me this before?"

A gleam of hurt shone in her friend's eyes and guilt stabbed Heather. "Because it brings on the nightmares," she said, her voice soft. Sleeping tonight was going to be fun. Not. She was already mentally preparing for the nightmares heading her way. "After the bomb went off, I ran to him, not even thinking there could have been another bomb." Her friends' yells to stay back echoed in her memories. "He was still alive, even though he was missing part of his torso and an arm. His face was bloodied from the spray of his other wounds, but it was still beautiful, not damaged. I asked him his name and he said, 'Abdul.' Then he whispered, 'I'm sorry.' And passed out. He arrested a couple of hours later after surgery and we couldn't get him back. There was just too much damage." Heather shuddered, blinked. And found herself wrapped in Brooke's arms. "I'm sorry," she said and stepped back.

"I'm not. Well, not sorry that you told me. I'm very sorry for that poor boy and for you and everyone else who had to see the things they saw over there."

"Nothing you didn't see as well."

Brooke shook her head. "No, I was much more sheltered. I saw some awful stuff, but that . . ."

Heather swallowed and fought another rush of tears. "One question haunts me."

"Ask it."

"Why can't I throw the shirt away?"

Brooke frowned. "I'm still confused on the shirt."

"Abdul's shirt. After it was all over, I walked outside to get some air and found it on top of a trash heap, whole and untouched. Like his sweet face." She bit her lip and gave a slight shake of her head. "I grabbed it and kept it." She gave Brooke a sad smile. "It had been freshly washed and smelled like some kind of lemon detergent." She paused. "It still does. It was familiar, though, like I'd seen it before. It had kind of a unique design on it that made it stand out, but I can't remember where I might have seen it." She shook her head. "Not that it matters. I just want to know why I find myself unable to get rid of it."

"Well, I can offer my thoughts if you want."

"Sure, why not? What's the benefit in having a shrink for a friend if she can't analyze you every once in a while?"

"Haha." Brooke flashed her a small smile, then turned serious. "Seems to me that you're still hanging on to that shirt as a way of hanging on to the boy."

Heather pondered that. "But why? This will sound callous and I don't mean it that way, but the truth was, I didn't know him. He wasn't any different than any other patient I wanted to save. I've lost patients before, and while I've grieved them, it hasn't affected me like this."

Brooke touched her hand. "This *was* different. Very different. *He* tried to save *you*. *He* died because he decided to warn you and protect you. I think a lot of it boils down to the fact that you had no control over the situation."

That put a new perspective on things. One she'd have to think about. A lot.

A footstep behind them spun her around. Gina stepped into the kitchen and set her plate and cup on the counter. "I think I'm going to call it a day. This has been fun, and I appreciate everyone going to all the trouble to do this. It was a nice change of pace."

"Of course," Heather said, giving her friend a hug.

Travis walked in and raised a brow. "Everything okay?"

"Gina was just leaving." Heather rubbed her friend's arm. "We're glad you're home."

"Thank you. Home. That's the goal of everyone over there, isn't it? To come home?" Grief shattered her expression for a brief moment. "I just wish Brad could have made it too." She sucked in a breath and shot them a forced smile. "But it wasn't to be. I'll see you all later." She gave them another wave and headed for the front door.

"Gina—"

Heather started to go after her, but Gina held up a hand. "It's okay. I'm sorry for being so low tonight. This was incredibly kind of all of you, and I can't tell you how much I appreciate it." She sighed. "It was hard being without him overseas, but it's even harder being in our home with memories everywhere. I just have to hope the house sells fast. So, please, don't say anything more or I'll lose it."

Heather nodded, gave her another hug, and watched her leave. For a moment, her own grief was shoved aside while her heart hurt for her friend. Gina was right. Time would help.

"You've been gone awhile," Travis said from behind her. "I came to check on you."

"I'm all right," Heather said. "Starting to deal with some things that I've put off, but I'll be okay." Before her stint in the Army, she might have questioned his motives—or been defensive at the idea that someone thought she needed checking up on.

Growing up in the foster system had taught her some hard life lessons. But this was Travis. He was a modern-day cowboy raised by parents who'd taught him to appreciate women—and protect them. Whether they needed it or not. It was sweet. *He* was sweet. "Thanks for asking, though."

"Sure. If you need anything, just let me know, okay?"

Heather hesitated. She wasn't so sure she couldn't use a little protecting—or at least some help in figuring out who was following her. She prided herself in being independent, but everyone needed a little help sometimes, right?

"Get it through your head, brat. Don't be a nuisance. Don't ask for help. Don't be needy or clingy. No one likes that. Learn to handle things yourself and be invisible, or nobody is going to want you."

The words from the past echoed and she tightened her jaw. "I appreciate the offer. But I'm fine. Just overly tired and overthinking things. On that note, I'm going to head home. I have an early shift tomorrow."

He nodded, his eyes shadowed, concern on his handsome features. "You're more worried than you're letting on. I can tell."

He could? She forced a smile. "Well, worry never solved anything, did it? I'm going to go say my goodbyes." She hesitated, then touched his hand. "Thanks for being a friend. And I'm sorry for the nasty bruise you're going to have tomorrow."

His return smile was just as strained as she figured hers was. "You'll call if you need something?"

"Sure. I'll call."

She left to find the others, feeling his gaze on her back. And knew he saw through her lie. She wouldn't be calling no matter how much she might want to.

◻ ◻ ◻

Travis stepped back into the kitchen after watching Heather's taillights disappear. The urge to go after her was strong, but he wasn't sure she'd appreciate his interference.

Brooke shut the dishwasher and looked up. "Everything okay?"

"No. I don't think so."

She stilled. "What's wrong?"

"I don't know. Something's going on with her."

"We just had a pretty long conversation. Without betraying any confidences, I can say that she has quite a few bad memories from Afghanistan. A lot of stuff that weighs heavy on her."

He nodded. "I get that. Especially when that kid almost blew up the hospital. And I get that she talks to you about that more than she would me. I also respect that you won't say anything that might be a betrayal of her confidence. But this is more. It's this stalker thing she mentioned . . . *that* worries me."

"I don't like it, either."

"Don't like what?" Sarah asked, carrying her plate to the sink.

"The idea that Heather may have a stalker and she's not taking it seriously."

Sarah's gaze snapped back and forth between the two of them.

"So it's not just me who thinks she should be way more concerned than she is?"

Travis frowned. "No, it's not just you."

"When she was waving it off and saying it wasn't a big deal, she was pretty convincing, but she was . . ."

"Too convincing?" Travis asked.

Sarah nodded. "Exactly. Like she was working hard to not only convince us but herself as well."

"Then we need to do something."

"I agree," Asher said from the doorway. "But what? You guys know Heather better than I do, but even I know how private she is. She doesn't ask for help and won't appreciate interference. Not even from us."

"Unless she was asking for help in a very Heather way," Brooke said.

"By bringing up the subject, telling us the situation, then waving it off, all the while knowing we'd be concerned enough to do something?" Travis tried to relax the sudden tightness in his jaw. He'd already made up his mind that he was going to be her shadow whether she liked it or not. And if he was watching her, hopefully he'd catch sight of anyone *else* who might be doing the same.

Brooke nodded. "Doing it that way allows her to feel in control, feel like she's able to handle it on her own without actually asking. Even though she did. Ask, I mean. Even though . . . she . . . didn't." She drew in a deep breath. "Man, that's confusing, but you know what I mean."

Gavin walked into the kitchen wrapped in one of the robes, his dark hair and short beard glistening with water drops. "Oh good, you're all here. Listen, I can't relax. I think we need to talk about Heather. I don't like this whole bit about a stalker. We need to do something whether she likes it or not."

Short chuckles, devoid of humor, scattered through the room, and Gavin raised a brow. "Don't tell me. That's what y'all have just been talking about."

"Well, that settles it," Travis said. "We need to come up with a quick plan." He paused. "And then I'm going to head over to her house to camp out on her doorstep."

CHAPTER THREE

Heather pulled into the garage and sat in her vehicle while the door lowered behind her. Apparently, this was going to be her night for sitting in her car and thinking. Spilling her guts to everyone, especially Brooke, had stirred up the memories and was going to make sleeping difficult, if not downright impossible. She had three shows she could watch, she could scroll mindlessly through social media, or she could go into work and see if anyone needed her.

But she was tired and had a long day tomorrow, which would require rest. A headache started to form over her right eye, and she pressed against the spot. If she took her migraine medicine, she'd sleep until morning.

But what if her stalker came back and she was too drugged to know? A shudder rippled through her.

She took yet another moment to gather her thoughts and emotions while contemplating Brooke's observation that Heather didn't overreact—and the fact that she didn't like to be out of control of anything. Her life, her job, her emotions.

Okay, so that was true.

She pinched the bridge of her nose. *Lord, I'm at a loss here. Things are spinning out of control and I don't like it. I know you know that. I need your help to figure out who this guy is. And I need some sense of control. Please?* She paused. "But if you can't give me control, give me the ability to deal with it, because you and I both know I have control issues."

Denying that would be silly. The foster system had taught her no one was trustworthy and she couldn't rely on anyone but herself. That trait was so fiercely ingrained in her that it even overwhelmed reason at times. Like this one. And she'd let it bleed over into pushing Travis away when she wanted to pull him closer. A fierce rage welled from deep within. Rage at her father, at the foster system she'd hated, at life. Stunned at the wave of emotion, she swallowed it and did her best to focus on what she *knew* instead of how she *felt*.

Fortunately, over the years, the Army and her friends had shown her a different perspective than the voice in her head. They'd shown her how to rely on them—and God. However, that didn't mean she didn't occasionally fall into her old habits—or that expressing herself came easy. But she really did trust those in her inner circle, which was probably why she'd allowed herself to say so much tonight. Putting herself out there, asking for help, and being vulnerable was hard—practically impossible—for her. "Which is why you chickened out, you big baby."

Unable to find the words to express what she *really* wanted, she'd simply shut down. She chalked it up to being rattled from the race across the yard in the effort to confront the person now making her life one big basket of tension.

Which was *who*?

The one person she thought it might be was still in prison. She'd checked that first thing. He had a parole hearing coming up in a month, and she planned to be there just like all the other times to remind the board why the man should *not* be released. And he'd glare at her while muttering dire things she'd suffer when he *did* get out.

With a low growl of frustration, she shoved out of the SUV and slammed the door. The chill of the garage pressed in and she shivered. At least whoever was watching her didn't seem to be dangerous.

Yet.

In the kitchen, she disarmed the security alarm, then rearmed the system. She placed her purse on the counter and the emptiness smothered her. "I need to get a cat," she muttered. "Or a goldfish." With her hours at the hospital, a dog was out of the question, but a cat might be okay.

Next to the kitchen was the laundry room, and she tossed her wet suit and towel in the dryer before heading to the cabinet for a mug. Coffee would help. Wouldn't help her sleep, but she wasn't going to be able to do that anytime soon, so why not?

She paused as another chill passed over her. Why was it so cold in her house?

With a frown, she walked into the hall and found the thermostat still set on seventy-one. Warm enough to keep the house comfortable without being stuffy. The furnace was running—she felt the heat through a nearby duct—but the indoor temperature readout showed sixty-five.

Okay, then. Why wasn't the thermostat keeping up? "Great." Just what she needed. She made a mental note to call someone to fix it in the morning. She'd just double up on blankets tonight.

In the den, she stopped, goose bumps pebbling her skin—and not from the chill in the air. The lamp on the end table next to the sofa glowed with a soft light, inviting her to snuggle under a blanket and soak in the warmth and relaxation. So why was the hair on the back of her neck on end?

She looked at the clothes on her love seat.

They were . . . wrong.

She'd done the laundry yesterday, and while she'd been too tired to put it away, she'd folded everything. Neatly.

Now, they were not so neat.

Not exactly in disarray, but . . . moved.

Definitely moved.

With dread curling in the pit of her stomach, she crept to the entrance of the hallway that led to the back of the house. Her eyes traveled to the end where her bedroom and guest room were.

Her bedroom door was cracked, not wide open like she usually left it. Now the alarm crawled up her spine and settled at the base of her neck.

Keeping her eyes on the crack, she backed up until she had to round the corner into the den. She scanned the room once more while aiming for the kitchen.

Wait a minute. Her alarm had still been armed. She'd had to punch in the code to turn it off. She'd also reset it. Relief swept over her.

For a moment.

It faded when she noticed the picture on the mantel was too close to the edge.

Pressing a hand to her belly, trying to calm the roiling ball of nerves and rising fear, she strode to the kitchen, grabbed the box of cash from the top shelf over the glasses, then opened the second drawer.

She withdrew the Glock, checked it, then dropped an extra magazine into her purse.

Get out. Get out, get out!

Her second weapon was in the nightstand next to her bed. In the bedroom she wasn't going into.

More chills skittered up her spine.

Call the cops and get out.

Overreacting? Her gaze went back to the clothes on the sofa. The picture on the mantel. She couldn't chance it. While the alarm system and common sense said one thing, her nerves and churning stomach said another. And she'd always had pretty good instincts.

She kept the gun close and ready while she grabbed her purse. She'd call 911 when she was safely locked in her car. Once she had her phone in her hand, she turned, and her eyes landed on the picture on the refrigerator of her, Sarah, Ava, Kat, and Brooke.

A little red dot had been drawn on each of their foreheads.

Her blood stilled.

Her breathing hitched.

Heart pounding, Heather grabbed her keys, kept a firm grip on her Glock, and headed for her garage.

○ ○ ○

It had been a week since anyone had heard from Heather, and Travis was about to come out of his skin with worry. They all were. She'd sent a group text saying she needed to get away for a while and would be in touch later.

Heather

Don't worry. I'm fine. Or will be. You all may be in danger because of me. Please watch your backs. Talk soon. Stay safe.

Her supervisor at work had gotten a voice mail with a message requesting an emergency leave of absence. Then she'd shut off her phone and . . . disappeared.

Brooke had touched base with all of them to let them know she was looking for Heather in all the places she could think Heather might go and would be in touch as soon as she learned where she was.

Four hours after a fruitless search, she'd called each of them and together, Travis, Asher, Gavin, Sarah, and, and Caden, an FBI Special Agent, had gone into "Find Heather" mode. The few leads they followed had turned into dead ends.

Then twenty minutes ago, Caden had called Travis with news that he'd located Heather and had gotten eyes on her. "She's in Sunrise, North Carolina. A little town that's barely a dot on the map. I didn't speak to her," Caden said. "I didn't want her to know she'd been found and give her a chance to run again, should she be angry that I tracked her down. She has a room at a little hotel that she paid cash for, but, as far as I could tell, she looked physically fine."

"She's not fine," Brooke muttered after Travis and the others gathered at Brooke's home. "She's being Heather. She thinks she's protecting us by disappearing. That's the only thing that text can mean. I tried tracking her cell phone and got nothing."

"Caden found out she withdrew the ATM's daily limit two days before our party and then once again at 2:00 a.m. the night she disappeared," Asher said.

"Heather must have had a plan for what she'd do if the stalker escalated," Brooke said. "The fact that she dropped off the radar so quickly says a lot."

"Sounds like her," Travis muttered.

Sarah sipped her bottle of water and frowned. "So, how did Caden finally find her?"

Travis scrubbed a palm down his cheek. "Apparently, she drove to the hospital and Ubered to a rental car place. What took Caden so long was locating her vehicle, because she parked in one of the patient lots. Once he had that, he used hospital security footage to see her get into another vehicle, which turned out to be an Uber. He got the plate, then the drop-off location from the driver."

"Which was the rental car place," Sarah said.

"Yes. And from there it was easy peasy. She used a prepaid debit card, so there wasn't any kind of hit on her credit cards."

Brooke frowned. "And then drove off completely anonymous. So . . . how?"

"Nope, not anonymous. The car rental place has GPS trackers on their vehicles. He simply followed it to the little town of Sunrise, North Carolina."

"Ah," Brooke said, "of course."

"Well, if Caden found her and she seems to be fine, I have a bone to pick with her," Sarah said, cheeks flushed and eyes flashing. "I can't believe she'd do this to us."

Travis shook his head. "Come on, y'all. You know she wouldn't pull this kind of stunt without having a really good reason."

"She's hiding from her stalker and thinks she's protecting us at the same time," Brooke said, her voice soft.

"But why run?" Sarah asked. "Why not just ask us for help?"

"Heather?" Brooke scoffed with a raised brow. "Seriously? Have you met her? When has she ever asked for help?"

Sarah grimaced. "I know, but I would have thought we were past all that."

Brooke tapped her lips. "No, she won't ask for help if she thinks it'll put us in danger. Actually, she probably wouldn't ask for help regardless. She's so used to handling things on her own and being in control, she doesn't know how to do things any other way."

"Well, it's time for her to understand what it means to have friends," Travis said, "people who care about her and won't let her leave us in the dust."

Brooke stood and paced to the mantel to rearrange pictures that didn't need rearranging, then back. "I think we can agree that the withdrawal of the money two days before she disappeared means she was secretly afraid she might need it."

The others nodded.

"The fact that she disappeared means something happened after she got home that night."

Asher gave a slow nod. "The ATM hit at two in the morning would support that. She wanted to make sure she had plenty."

"I didn't realize it until later," Travis said, "but she was gone by the time I got there to watch her house." He pressed his fingers to his eyes and shook his head. "I can't believe I didn't notice, but the light was on in her kitchen and I thought she was there." He was still kicking himself that he'd let her drive off from Brooke's house without him. "I never saw evidence of anyone else, though. I never saw any indication of a stalker or that anything was wrong." His jaw tightened. How had he let her just vanish? He should have done something, noticed something was off while he was sitting outside her home. “Okay, here’s what I think we should do.”

The others exchanged glances and Asher raised a brow. “What?”

“It’s really simple, actually. We catch her stalker.”

“Well, that is simple—in a very complex way. Any brilliant ideas for how to do that?” Brooke asked.

“I might have one idea. And if it works, you’re free to label it brilliant.”

CHAPTER
FOUR

Mid-February
Thursday evening
Sunrise, NC

After three weeks of lying low and hiding out, Heather had finally convinced herself that she'd ditched her stalker. Tonight, she drove the winding back road in Sunrise, a small, practically off-the-grid town where no one knew her but had gotten used to seeing her around. Especially since she'd just started volunteering to deliver medications from the pharmacy this past week.

She was still watchful, still careful, still on edge, but she'd done what she'd learned to do as a child and later as a teen. Take care of herself, handle her problems alone—and depend on no one else to help her.

The thought left her strangely sad and empty. She missed her friends. She missed her job. She missed Travis. Which was completely silly because she hadn't given him—them—a chance. She'd let fears and insecurities send her scurrying. And it made her mad.

Mostly at herself.

In spite of that, she was ready to get back to her life, but was unsure of what that would mean. In the little town of Sunrise, she'd found a semblance of peace—and some volunteer work to pass the hours. The thought of staying there indefinitely wasn't completely unpleasant.

Headlights flashed in her rearview mirror and she adjusted it with a frown. Usually, before darkness fell, she'd finished her deliveries—and up to this point, none of them had been babies—and was tucked into the surprisingly comfortable hotel room, watching *I Love Lucy* reruns and sketching one "get back to life" plan after another. Plans that involved drawing her stalker out and catching him. Unfortunately, she'd tossed each one as ridiculous or stupid—or would require help. The one thing she was trying to avoid.

The headlights pulled closer. Three car lengths back, but definitely still there. "Stop freaking," she muttered. "It's a mountain road. One way up and one way down." The safe way. She didn't count the flimsy guardrail running along the edge, protecting motorists from the steep drop-off. "People have to travel this road every day at all hours."

Just because someone was behind her didn't mean he was *following* her. In spite of the mental reassurances, the hair on her arms spiked and she tightened her fingers around the wheel.

She hadn't thought about having to drive home in the dark, but a simple vitamin prescription delivery had led her to a woman in labor—a sweet young waitress who'd served her at the diner. When Heather had arrived, Kelly was too far along to make the trip to the hospital. Since cell reception was zero up on the mountain, Heather went into doctor mode. And she hadn't wanted to leave the new mother and baby too soon. Which meant she was finally on her way back, six hours later than planned.

And now the lights were right on her bumper. Closing in fast.

Certainty centered itself in her gut. If she was being paranoid due to a set of headlights, so be it, but she felt quite sure he'd found her.

Heather glanced at the phone clipped in its holder. Using voice commands, she said, "Call 911."

She breathed a relieved sigh when the call connected, despite the area's spotty reception.

"911, what's your emergency?"

"I'm on Tipton Road," she said, leaning over to open the glove box and slip the Glock from its foam-covered resting place. "There's someone riding my tail and driving recklessly. Could you send help?"

The keyboard clicked in the background.

Heather turned into the curve, tapping the brakes. The car behind her surged forward and rammed into her.

A scream escaped her as she spun the wheel to avoid shooting off the side of the road. Her tires churned on the shoulder, spinning gravel and slinging mud, but she made it back onto the road and gunned the engine. Then slammed on the brakes when she turned too fast into the next sharp curve.

The vehicle on her tail battered her bumper, sending her careening around the bend. The steering wheel spun beneath her palms, and she slid along the guardrail, firecracker sparks bursting at the metal-on-metal contact. Another hit from behind. The force of the motion hurled her against the seatbelt.

Her little rental car hit a post and spun, doing a one eighty, the back end smashing through a break in the guardrails and skidding over the edge of the mountain. Heather released another scream as she continued down, rolling and bouncing violently. No amount of brake stomping slowed her descent.

Another desperate cry strangled her and she held on, waiting for the impact that was going to hurt.

Jesus, help me . . .

○ ○ ○

Travis pressed the gas pedal, trying desperately to get to the scene in front of him. He'd followed Heather to the farmhouse, then stayed a good distance behind her when she left.

He'd rounded the curve just in time to see a dark SUV shoot out of a side street and into the single lane, causing him to slam on the brakes to keep from plowing into it. His nerves had tightened, his attention on the reckless driver, wishing he had blue lights to flip on.

Then the driver rushed ahead, crowding Heather's car in front of him, and finally, with one more burst of speed, sent it into a spin on the narrow mountain road.

Travis laid on his horn, blaring it long and loud. The driver who'd rammed the Mustang had surged past the drop-off and taken the next curve almost on two wheels, taillights disappearing.

Travis pulled to a fast stop on the shoulder and threw the truck in park. He opened the driver's door with his left hand and snagged his phone with his right, then bolted toward where he'd seen Heather's car drop out of sight, his stomach twisting as he looked down.

"Heather," he whispered.

The little white Mustang was wedged tail first against a large tree. The headlights pointed upward. However, the landscape leveled out near the tree that cradled the Mustang. If he could get her out, he would find a way to get her back up to the truck. Travis dialed 911 as he ran back to his vehicle. The call dropped. "No, no. Don't do this." He tried different locations until he finally got two bars and dialed again.

"MVA on Tipton Road," he said when the woman picked up. "Someone ran her off and she spun out over the side and down the embankment."

"What part?"

Not familiar with the road, Travis described it as best he could while grabbing his go bag and a long coil of rope. "There's no time to wait. I'm going down to get her."

Silence greeted him. A quick glance at the screen showed no bars once more. Praying she'd heard his scattered directions before he'd been cut off, Travis tucked the phone in his pocket, tossed the go bag over his shoulder, and hurried back to the scene. His former EMT days would allow him to give first aid until the paramedics arrived.

After tying one end of the rope to a thick tree trunk at the edge of the road, he tugged a length of it under his rear and started rappelling down the side, staying in the path the car had cut on its way down.

When he reached the vehicle, he assessed the scene and his stomach dropped. The area in front of the vehicle and on either side was level. The area behind the tree that had stopped the car was not. In fact, there *was* no area behind the tree except a sheer drop. His pulse pounded a fraction harder.

He gripped the driver's door and tugged. "Heather, can you hear me? Heather!"

The tree creaked and Travis froze, his adrenaline ramping up another notch. He gave the door another tug. When it screeched open, he froze, staring at the business end of a black pistol. "Heather. Whoa." He held up a hand. "It's me. Travis. Don't shoot."

Heather blinked up at him. A gasp escaped her parted lips, and she lowered the weapon, placing it on the passenger seat. "Travis? How . . . what . . . Travis?"

"I'll explain in a minute. We need to get you out of here. Are you hurt?"

"Um . . . no. I don't think so." She rubbed her chest and winced. "Stunned and with a heck of a seat belt bruise. A little whiplash, maybe, but surprisingly intact."

"Well, if you want to stay that way, ease yourself out of the driver's seat."

She paused. "What's behind me? Because the rearview mirror isn't telling me much."

"A tree."

"And?"

"Let's just get you out of here, okay?"

"Yeah. Okay, let's do that."

Heather had already released her seatbelt and grasped his outstretched hand.

A sharp crack sounded from the top of the hill. Something

whizzed past his ear, sending him ducking for cover in the narrow strip of ground between the open car door and the sheer drop-off. Heather, still in the car but with her legs out the door, locked her eyes on his, her fingers squeezing tight enough to cut off blood flow. "Was that . . . ?"

"It was. Come on."

The tree gave another groan and the car shifted. Her grip tightened and he pulled. The trunk gave one more massive crack just as Heather slid into his arms. He rolled, shoving her next to him and covering her head with his gloved hand. "Lie flat!" He pressed her cheek into the dirt as the car door passed over them with not a millimeter to spare. Travis froze, his heart thundering in his chest, while the vehicle bounced down the cliff. As it crashed its way downward, Travis scrambled to his knees, his hand still clasping hers. He placed his lips next to her ear. "Are you okay to run?"

Another crack of a rifle. Another bullet passing too close for comfort.

"I guess I'm going to have to be," she said, her breath wispy and faint, tinged with fear.

Travis bolted to his feet, pulling her with him. "Go."

CHAPTER FIVE

Pain lanced through her ribs, but Heather pressed on, praying she didn't have more serious injuries than bruises. Right now, adrenaline fueled her flight across the open ground, but she'd feel more aches and pains later. Travis's hand gripped hers, his fingers clamped tight. "Where are the cops?" she gasped.

"I don't know. It's a hard area to find. Keep going."

He didn't sound winded, and she thought she might keel over. "I hate running."

"Just go."

She held on and let him guide her to the tree line, expecting any second now to feel a bullet plow into her body.

But they made it into the protection of the trees with no more shots fired. Travis pulled up, and Heather bent double, holding her aching side.

"I lost my phone," he said, patting his pocket. "Great."

"And mine"—she panted—"went down with the car. So did my gun." More panting. She sounded bad and vowed to hit the gym more when her life returned to normal. *Please let it return to normal.*

"We'll find a phone somewhere. They'll have to get the gun when they pull up the car."

"Where do you think we're going to find a phone around here?" She caught her breath, then straightened, wincing as the action pulled her abused muscles.

"We'll head back to my truck and go straight to the sheriff's office in town."

She nodded. "Which way's your truck?"

"Up. But we've got to find a way to get up there without getting shot."

"Then that's not going to work. I don't think I could climb anyway."

"If I remember correctly from studying the map of this area, there's a road that leads down from Tipton Road. We just have to find it."

"In the dark?"

"Unfortunately."

The first raindrop splashed on her cheek and ran down to drip off her chin. "Travis?"

"Yeah?"

"It's cold. Like almost freezing."

"I'm aware, thanks."

"My point is, it's starting to rain. We need to find some shelter and wait it out, because if we get soaked, it's going to be extremely uncomfortable." Not to mention the possibility of hypothermia.

"Okay. Let's keep going. As long as we're moving, we're not freezing, right?"

She groaned. "Yes, we need to keep moving."

"Maybe we can find a convenience store or something."

She tromped after him, glad the rain was only a slight drizzle for the moment. "Convenience stores are usually on the main roads. You know . . . for convenience sake."

"You're awfully witty right now."

"It's a defense mechanism." What she'd really like to do was puddle onto the ground and have a good cry. But she wouldn't. She placed one foot after the other. "So, help me keep my mind off of all of this." Like that was going to happen, but it was worth the try. "How did you find me?"

"Caden did."

"How?"

"It took a few days, but he finally located your car in the hospital parking lot. Security footage helped get the plate off the Uber, and the car rental place has GPS trackers on their vehicles. Once he knew you had a rental, the rest was easy."

"Oh." She rubbed an aching temple. "I didn't think about a GPS tracker on the rental. Of course, it makes sense, but—" She stepped over a rotted log and stumbled.

He reached back and snagged her arm, pulling her against him. "You okay?"

"I'm fine." The automatic response slipped from her lips without thought.

"Sure you are." His lips quirked into a small smile, and she was tempted to lean her aching head against his chest and stay there forever. Safe. Warm. Wrapped in his strong arms. Yeah, she could be all right with that. Instead, she pulled back and let him take the lead once more.

"I still can't believe I didn't notice you weren't at your house that night after the party," Travis said. "The light was on in your kitchen and I thought you were there." He rubbed his eyes. "I never saw evidence of anyone else, though . . ."

"You were watching?" She was down to short statements at this point. It was all she could do to drag in the next breath.

He nodded, lips pressed together. "For all the good it did. Here we are. On the run. What were you doing at the farm for six hours anyway?" he asked.

"You were . . there . . the whole time?"

"Of course."

Another deep breath. "I made friends with the pharmacist." She stopped and lowered herself to the nearest old log on the ground. "Hold on a second."

"What is it?"

"I need to stop. Just for a minute." The pain in her ribs and across her shoulder was stealing what little breath she could find.

"All right." He paused and took the time to look back the way they'd come. "I don't think anyone was able to follow us. They'd have had to rappel down the side of the mountain like I did." He took off his beanie and settled it on her head, pulling it down over her ears. "Keep talking."

Keep talking? Really? "You don't have to give me your hat."

He took off his coat and wrapped it around her. "Push your arms in the sleeves."

"Travis, no, I can't—" But it was blissfully warm from his body heat. "You'll freeze."

"I have on a thermal shirt, a sweatshirt, and a hoodie. I'll be fine. And besides, I wasn't just in an accident. You need to stay warm. Now, be still so I can zip it."

Heather gave in. When she was adequately encased in the much-too-large warm Sherpa coat, he patted her on the head. "That's better."

It really was, but if he patted her on the head again, she might have to hurt him.

"You're good? Can we keep going?" he asked. "I don't like being out in the open like this."

"Sure." She could use a few more minutes but figured the light rain might be getting ready to morph into something heavier, and she'd really like to find a dry place to hole up.

"You can finish your story now that you can breathe." He held out a hand and she grasped it. "And explain how the pharmacist is involved in you being at the house on the top of the mountain."

He started off, and she once again found herself pushing through the wooded undergrowth, wishing she were back in her little hotel room, tucked safely in her bed. "So, a couple of days after I arrived in town, I was shopping and he—the pharmacist—had a sign in the window advertising for a delivery person. I asked him about it and said I'd volunteer."

"Let me guess. You didn't want to give him the information required for an actual paying job."

"Bingo. Anyway, he sent me out to the Gunderson farm to deliver some prenatal vitamins. When I got there, she was in labor, so I wound up delivering her daughter. Her sister got there about thirty minutes before I left."

"I saw her drive up." He looked back at her. "But I never saw an ambulance or anything."

"They wanted to stay at home." She was already tired again and feeling out of breath while her legs ached with the effort to keep up. The pain pulsing from her bruised body didn't help. She hadn't realized how out of shape she'd let herself get. There was going to be a lot of cardio in her future—assuming she lived through this.

"I guess the baby was okay?" he asked.

"She was slightly early, but healthy. And the mom was fine. There wasn't any reason either of them needed to go to the hospital. It was her third child, so she . . . knew what she was doing . . . And I'm going to have to"—she pulled in a gasp of a breath—"quit talking . . . if I'm going to keep walking."

After what seemed like an eternity, Travis stopped. "There's a cabin," he said, his voice soft in the night.

A shudder ran through her. The longer she was still, the more she felt the cold. The rain had started to fall harder, the wind picking up, whipping past her exposed cheeks. If she was cold, Travis had to be freezing.

"It's dark," she said. "You think anyone's in there?"

"Only one way to find out."

The rain fell harder as Travis tromped through the leaves to the gravel path that led to the front porch. He knocked, and within seconds the bottom dropped out of the sky. Heather gulped lungfuls of air while she huddled next to him on the small porch. It didn't offer a lot of protection from the rain that was now pounding the earth in a deafening roar, but it was better than nothing.

He knocked again. "Anyone home?" He turned the knob. "It's open."

"Then I'm going in." She slipped past him, stepped inside, and shivered harder. "It's as cold in here as it was in my house the night I left. There's wood on the fireplace. You think the chimney's open?"

He checked. "It's open."

Heather explored the small space while Travis worked with the fireplace. In the kitchen, she found peanut butter and jelly, a loaf of fresh bread, eggs, milk, and fruit that were still good. "Someone's living here, Travis."

"I gathered that from the stack of fresh wood. Hopefully, whoever it is won't mind us crashing until the rain stops."

She rubbed her hands together and returned to stand in front of the flickering flames.

He added another log and looked up. "Why don't you have a seat?" He gestured to the couch. "You probably need to take inventory and make sure you're not really hurt."

"I'm not. Bruised, jarred, angry, but relatively unscathed. I think. I'll be fine now that I can breathe." She sank onto the couch. "If you hadn't come along when you did, I wouldn't have made it out of there in time."

"You would have."

"No. I really wouldn't have. Thank you."

"You're welcome."

She crossed her arms over her stomach. "But I think you brought my stalker with you."

He frowned. "I don't know. He couldn't have known I'd be the one to come after you. He's never done anything violent before, has he?"

"No. In fact, I thought he might have disappeared. The last three weeks have been blessedly quiet and peaceful."

"Until today."

"Until today. Which is why I think you must have led him to me."

"I don't think so."

She raised a brow. "Why not?"

"Because, first, I've been watching you for the past two weeks and I've seen no sign of anyone else following you. Second, if someone *did* follow me, why wait this long to come after you?"

She didn't have an answer for that one. Wait a minute. "Two weeks?" She forgot about being chilled and stared at him. "You've been following me around for two weeks?"

"Yeah. Sorry."

He didn't sound very sorry. "But . . . why?"

He at least had the decency to look slightly embarrassed. "Once Caden found you and reported that you were fine, the group decided you'd disappeared for a reason. After all your talk about a stalker and your cryptic text, we deduced that you were probably hiding from him. I decided once we found you, I'd simply watch to see who was watching you—which is why I was at the scene where the person ran you off the road. I just wasn't quick enough to get to him before—" A muscle jumped in his jaw. "Well, *before*."

She nodded. "It's not your fault."

"I should have—" He paused and shook his head. "No sense in going down that road."

"I can't believe you've been watching me for two weeks and I never noticed."

A half smile curved his lips. "I'm in the security business, remember? Surveillance is part of that. I would have let you know I was there, but I wasn't sure how you'd feel about that. To be honest, we were all a little perturbed you didn't reach out to us and ask for help, but also realized that would be incredibly out of character for you."

She frowned. "Ouch." Her friends knew her well.

"What? I'm wrong?"

"No, not completely anyway." She paused. "Did you find the picture?"

"What picture?"

"The one on my refrigerator." She'd almost snatched it but had left it for them to find.

"There wasn't any picture on your refrigerator."

"What?" Ice settled in her veins, colder than any downpour that came from the clouds. "But the picture was supposed to clarify my text that Sarah, Ava, and Brooke were all in danger."

He held up a hand. "Hold on. Back up. What makes you think anyone was in danger?"

"There was a picture on my refrigerator of me with Brooke, Ava, Kat, and Sarah. Someone—the person in my house that night—drew red dots on all of their foreheads—like bull's-eyes."

He blinked. "Whoa."

"Exactly. They're all okay, right?"

"Yeah, they're fine."

She nodded. "I figure you'd have mentioned if they weren't. Anyway, I took that to mean everyone was in danger because of me. I mean, why else come into my house and draw bull's-eyes on my friends' foreheads? So, I . . . left. I thought if I disappeared, the person would have no reason to go after the others." She paused. "I kind of assumed you'd ignore my text and look for me. Leaving the picture was my way of hoping once you saw it, you'd understand why I had to disappear—and why you should let me."

"Of course we ignored your text. Especially after that stalker conversation at the party." He rubbed his forehead. "Did you really think we wouldn't move heaven and earth to find you?"

Finally feeling warm, Heather shrugged out of Travis's jacket and laid it over the back of the sofa. She then went to pace in front of the flames. "I . . . I don't know."

"Seriously?" He clasped his hands and leaned forward. "How long have you known us? How can you not see how much you're loved?"

"I . . ." She frowned. How could she explain without sounding pathetic? "No one's ever bothered to come after me before." No one had ever cared enough to worry about her.

Travis moved to kneel in front of her and gripped her fingers. She swallowed the surge of surprise mixed with hope and a touch of fear. The intensity of his stare stole the breath right from her lungs.

"You needed help. Whether you're willing to admit it or not. We'd—*I'd*—never turn my back on that. On you."

Heat crawled from her neck into her cheeks and she searched for the words to express her gratitude even while her mind was screaming at her to step away and keep her distance. *Don't ask for help. Don't let anyone see your weakness. No one helps you without expecting something in return.*

"Thank you," she whispered. She paused, then looked him in the eye. "I knew you'd come. Somewhere in my head—or maybe my heart—I knew you'd come."

"I'm very glad you knew that. Even if was only on a subconscious level."

The crackle of the flames and the steady roar of the rain outside filled the quiet space between them. Then she cleared her throat. "I have to say, I didn't think you'd find me this fast, though."

"They didn't give Caden that shield because he's pretty."

Heather snickered, then sobered. "I'd been thinking what I would do if worse came to worst with this stalker, and when I realized he was probably still in my house that night, I might have panicked a bit. I didn't know what to do. But I figured if he was still in my house, he wouldn't be able to follow me, so I turned my phone off and started driving. Ditched my car at the hospital, made my way to the rental place, hit an ATM, and kept going. That night, I knew I needed to get away to plan further and figure out what to do next. When I stopped for gas and to purchase a pay-as-you-go cell phone, there was a map of North Carolina on the wall. Sunrise sounded like a pretty place, so,"—she lifted her hands, palms up—"here I've been for the past three weeks—

which you already know about since you've been tailing me for two of them."

"Yeah, and during the two weeks I've been watching, I haven't seen a stalker. No one's paid you any extra attention or been overly watchful. Nothing. So, how did he find you tonight?"

She shook her head. "There's no sure explanation. Just like there's no explanation how someone got in and out of my house without setting off my alarm."

He eyed her. "You're sure someone was in there?"

"Absolutely no doubt in my mind."

"Where did you make the call to your supervisor from?"

She frowned. "My car. As soon as I started driving, I knew I wouldn't be at work the next day. Why?"

"Just wondering if someone could have traced that call."

"It wouldn't have mattered if they traced it. By the time anyone arrived at that location, I would have been long gone."

He tapped his chin, his frown deepening.

"What is it?"

"There's something about that picture on the refrigerator story that bothers me."

"What's that?"

"I don't know. And the fact that I can't put my finger on it bothers me too."

"I'll tell you what bothers me. The fact that it wasn't there when you searched my house."

A scuff on the porch propelled Travis to his feet. He lifted a finger to his lips, and she nodded just as the door opened and a figure stepped inside.

○ ○ ○

Travis wanted to pounce but waited. After all, they were the intruders. The newcomer was a young guy in his late teens. Eighteen? Nineteen? It was hard to judge with the dark hoodie covering a lot of his features. Scraggly blond hair peeked out from beneath the hood. He wore jeans, a quilted vest over the hoodie, and heavy boots.

Dark eyes flicked back and forth between Travis and Heather while rainwater dripped from his clothing. He held a hand against his left side. "I'm not going back, so you can just leave."

"Go back where?" Travis asked.

The kid's brow rose and he took a step back. "Who are you guys?"

"No one that plans to do you any harm. You live here?" Travis countered.

"Yeah. Sort of. This place belonged to my grandfather." Keeping an eye on them, the teen walked over and dropped a bag onto the small kitchen table. He slipped out of the vest and draped it over one of the chairs, then pushed the hood back from his face. His face was pale, but his cheeks held an unnatural flush.

Heather frowned. "Are you okay?"

"Fine." His eyes stayed on the two of them while one hand hovered near his right hip. And the knife he had strapped there.

"Sorry to intrude," Heather said. "We got caught in the rain and decided to try and stay dry while waiting for it to stop. I'm Heather. What's your name?"

"Ryker."

"Got a last name, Ryker?" Travis asked.

"I do. Do you have a first name?"

Okay, suspicious. Not that Travis blamed him. He'd be on guard, too, if he'd just walked in to find two strangers squatting in his home. "Travis Walker. Sorry to startle you like this, but do you have a phone we could use?"

The young man hesitated, then reached into his pocket, pulled out a device, and tossed it to Travis, who caught it one-handed. "It's an old flip phone," Ryker said. "Belonged to my grandpa—just like the cabin. I can't afford a smartphone just yet."

"As long as it'll dial a number, that's all that matters."

"No promises on that. The signal out here is spotty to nonexistent on a good day. Gets worse when the weather's bad."

Awesome. Travis glanced at the screen. No bars. He dialed 911 anyway and waited.

Nothing.

He tried Gavin's number. Again, nothing. He shut the phone and handed it back to Ryker. "Thanks. I'll try again in a bit."

"I'll keep an eye on the signal strength. When it gets to two bars, I can usually make a call." He hesitated, glanced at the fire, then back at the kitchen. "So . . . you guys hungry?"

"Sure," Heather said. "Want some help?"

"Uh, no. Thanks. I've got it." He kept his hand against his side and drew in a ragged breath.

Her gaze followed him, but she nodded and settled back with a wince while Ryker went to the refrigerator with one last narrow-eyed glance at the two of them. Travis frowned. Something was going on with the kid. Travis wasn't imagining things. Heather's gaze kept going back to him as well.

"How are you doing?" Travis asked her, his voice low.

"I'm all right. The soreness is settling in. I think you're right. I need to take inventory. I'm going to visit the restroom and assess the damage."

"Damage?" Ryker asked from the kitchen.

"Heather had a fight with a tree and the tree won."

"Car accident?"

"Yeah."

Ryker stepped to the counter that faced into the den, concern creasing his brows. His overly bright eyes blinked at them. "Do you need a lift to the hospital?"

Travis paused. "You have a car?"

"No, a motorcycle. You'll be soaked, but it'll get you there."

Heather raised a brow. "I didn't hear it over the rain, I guess."

"Same here." Travis rubbed his chin and studied the teen. "What'd you mean when you said you weren't going back?"

Ryker shrugged. Swayed, then caught himself on the refrigerator door handle. "Nothing."

"You have a fever," Heather said.

"Probably, but don't worry, I'm not contagious." He opened the refrigerator, pulled out some chicken, and turned. He shook his head and blinked.

"And you keep pressing against your side," Heather said. "Are you hurt?"

"What are you? A doctor?"

She smiled. "As a matter of fact . . ."

The kid huffed a short laugh. "You're kidding."

"Nope."

"Well, like my mama used to tell me, I just need to eat a good meal and everything'll be . . ." He coughed. ". . . fine." Ryker turned back to the stove, stumbled, and leaned heavily against the counter.

Travis frowned. "Dude . . ." He hurried into the kitchen to catch the kid as he went down. "Heather?"

"I'm right here." She rushed to press a hand against the teen's cheek. "You're burning up."

"I'm okay," Ryker said. "It's just a flesh wound." He stood with Travis's help.

"Flesh wound? I'll be the judge of that." Heather motioned them to the sofa, and Travis assisted him onto the cushions. "Lie down." Ryker didn't argue and Heather pulled up the kid's shirt. "What happened?"

"I got stabbed."

CHAPTER SIX

Heather paused for only a second, letting the words soak in. "Well, that had to hurt," she muttered.

A short, low laugh devoid of humor escaped him. "A bit."

Heather pulled the shirt up to expose a blood-soaked bandage. She used a fingernail to lift the edge of the tape away to reveal a three-inch gash surrounded by puffy red skin. "That looks seriously painful."

"It'll heal."

"Just like the other times?"

"Never mind. I shouldn't have said anything."

"Yes, you should have. Tell me what happened."

"No." Ryker swallowed. "Doesn't matter. It won't happen again."

"Why not?" Travis asked.

"Because, I'll be eighteen in a few months."

At first the response confused her, then reality slapped her. "Your dad or someone in your family do this to you? Someone you feel like you have to protect?"

Surprise—and fear—flashed before he covered it up. "No."

Heather glanced at Travis. "So, why not tell us?" he asked with a frown.

Ryker looked away.

"Okay, look," Heather said, "I get it. I had a dad who only knew how to communicate if it involved his fists. Eventually, I became intimately familiar with the foster system, so . . . trust me, if it was a family member who did this, I know exactly where you're coming from."

"It wasn't him."

"I also lied a lot," she said, her voice soft. "Lied about everything. Like I told my friends my dad was awesome and made up stories of how he helped me do my math homework or that he planned to take me on a cruise for my birthday."

"You did?"

"Yep. I was good at it too. I could pretty much make anyone believe anything." Even make a dying boy believe she'd save him. Tears surfaced and she blinked them away.

Ryker's gaze flicked between her and Travis. "You're not going to call the cops?"

"Will it change anything or make the situation better?"

"Definitely not."

"Then no."

"But you're a doctor. A mandated reporter."

"Yeah, and if we were in the hospital, I'd be calling them. This situation is a bit different." In so many ways.

After a brief hesitation, he closed his eyes. "Yeah," he whispered. "It was my dad, but if you tell anyone, I'll deny it."

"Not telling anyone." Yet. Heather's anger leaped into a full-blown rage. No one deserved this. No one. "You have any supplies around here?" The calm in her voice surprised her.

"In the kitchen in the bag on the table."

"I'll get them," Travis said, already turning. He grabbed the bag from the table and was back, one hand digging inside it before Heather could blink.

She finished pulling the dirty bandage from the wound to get a better look. "Go on."

"This is a first. I think this was an accident."

"How so?" Travis asked.

"We were arguing, and he took the knife out just to threaten me." He shifted and winced. "At least, I don't think he really meant to use it, but I wasn't sure, so I walked to the door to leave. Unfortunately, that just made him more angry, and he came at me, tripped over the rug, and . . . I felt the pain."

"When did this happen?" Heather asked.

"A couple of days ago."

"I'll need some kind of antiseptic," she said. "Is there any alcohol?"

"In the bag," Ryker said, his teeth gritting hard against the pain that no doubt had flared with her probing.

She took the alcohol from Travis. "I don't have any painkillers, but this is infected, and you need some antibiotics. Tell me which drugstore to call them in to."

Travis's eyes met hers and she flicked her gaze away. He couldn't have been easier to read than if he'd written his thoughts on the wall behind her. He wanted to go to the cops. To report the incident and see the father thrown in prison. She understood. That's the way it was supposed to work when someone abused a child—or a minor.

Or stabbed another person.

But Travis had grown up in a perfect family and wouldn't understand that reporting it could make things infinitely worse for Ryker. And while it was true she was a mandated reporter, she'd also learned to use her common sense. And she was in a whole different world at the moment.

At the hospital, she might not want to involve the cops in a similar situation, but she'd do it. Out here in the middle of the woods and a rainstorm with no cell service? She could think a little longer.

"All right," she said. "I'm going to scrub my hands. When I come back, you can use that pillow and bite down on it. Then I'm going to clean the wound and sew you up."

He groaned. "You sure you know what you're doing?"

"Quite sure. I'm impressed. You have all the right stuff here. Including a suture kit." She met his gaze with a raised brow. "Nice."

He flushed. "I want to be a doctor."

"Then I'd say you're on the right path."

He shot her a tight smile that morphed quickly into a grimace. "I graduated high school a year early. Now, I work part-time for the doc in town and take online classes to get my gen ed requirements out of the way. The doc teaches me about medicine and pays me to run whatever errands he needs. Mostly to the medical supply store that's about twenty minutes from here." He waved a hand at the bag of supplies. "I put that stuff on his tab. I'll have to work it off later."

"I think he might be the understanding type," Heather murmured. While he talked, she'd arranged the supplies in the order that she'd need them.

"He is."

She met his gaze. "I'll be right back." Heather scrubbed her hands and had Travis pour alcohol over them. Then she pulled on a pair of the surgical gloves Ryker had gotten and sat down next to him. "Okay, this is going to hurt."

"I know. Just do it."

"Okay, then. Brace yourself." She started to clean the wound with the alcohol, and he let out a harsh gasp, then clenched his jaw. Tears leaked down his temples, but no more sound escaped him. "I'm almost done, Ryker. Hang in there."

"He's passed out," Travis said.

"That's probably for the best." She finished the cleaning, then pulled the edges of the wound together and stitched it. After covering it with a surgical bandage, she removed the gloves, smoothed the teen's shirt down, and covered him with the blanket from the back of the couch. "Maybe he'll sleep for a bit."

"I'll finish the dinner. He was right when he said he needed a good meal."

Thirty minutes later, she and Travis had finished off their portions of the food. While Travis washed the dishes, Heather checked on Ryker. "The ibuprofen is working," she said. "His fever's not so high, but he needs those antibiotics."

"I can take his motorcycle and go into town to pick them up, but I hate to leave you two alone."

"Nothing's open at this time of night, I'm sure. The meds will have to wait until morning. Unless the doc has some samples in his office." Heather bit her lip. "But if you go into town, you could buy more groceries. I want to replace what we ate." And more. "Unfortunately, a lot of my cash went down the side of the hill."

"You'll get that back when they pull the car up." He scrubbed the stubble on his chin. "I have my wallet so I can get whatever we need. I just don't want to take the time to do it with a potential killer out there."

Heather sighed and rubbed her eyes. She was tired. Flat-out tired. And sore. "Yeah."

"I could go for my truck and come back and get you two. Then we could find a couple of hotel rooms in town, let the doc take care of Ryker, and get back to Greenville so we can figure out who this stalker turned sniper is."

She gave a slow nod. "It's not a bad plan. I can get my stuff from the other room and move it. I don't feel comfortable staying there anyway now."

"Right. But for that plan to work, I still have to leave you guys alone for a bit."

Heather paused, listening. "Has it stopped raining?"

Travis checked the window. "Looks like it." He paced to the other side of the small cabin, then back. "What do you think? Do we risk it?"

She glanced at Ryker, then back to Travis. "I think we have to. I need to get him to a clinic. I cleaned the wound as best I could, but he needs to be monitored."

Travis dug the keys out of Ryker's front pocket. He then removed his Glock from the waistband of his pants and passed it to Heather. "I know you know how to use that."

"I do, but what about you?"

"I'll be fine. But Ryker's not going anywhere without help." He glanced at the flip phone. "And this thing isn't going to be making calls anytime soon."

Heather placed the gun on the coffee table. "I think our only choice is to go along with your plan. Go get the truck and come back for us."

He gave her a short nod. "It may take me a few minutes to find it."

"That's okay, just be careful."

"Go up," Ryker whispered.

"What?" Heather leaned closer.

The teen cracked his eyes open. "Go up." He licked his lips. "I think I passed your truck on my way here. Lots of cops around the area?"

"Probably." Travis stepped into the kitchen and filled a cup with water.

"It's a winding gravel path that you can't drive a truck on," Ryker said, "but the motorcycle can make it. Once you're at the top, turn right and just go. You'll see it. With the truck, you'll have to turn off onto the paved road about halfway back down and wind around."

"Sounds easy enough."

He handed the cup to Heather, who held it to the boy's lips. "Drink."

He did and she lifted her eyes to meet Travis's deep frown. He finally gave a slow nod. "All right. Lock the door behind me. I'll honk three times when I pull up. If there's no honking, it's not me."

"Got it."

Travis threw another log on the fire, hesitated for a brief second, then grabbed his coat and hat from the back of the couch. With a short nod and a wave, he strode out the door.

Heather picked up the weapon, hefted it in her right hand, and let the calm descend. They had a plan. Whether it was a good one or not remained to be seen.

○ ○ ○

Following Ryker's simplistic directions, Travis gunned the motorcycle in the direction of "up." Fortunately, the worst of the rain had slacked off to a fine mist, and while it was cold and wet, at least he wasn't getting soaked.

In the beginning, the gravel road was more narrow, winding, and treacherous than he'd expected. If he slipped, he'd go over the side of the mountain, so his fastest speed was turtle for the first mile. Every so often, he glanced at the phone, hoping for a signal. So far, nothing. Finally, he hit paved road, and though it was still winding, he was able to speed up significantly—until he finally reached the top and turned right. Five minutes later, when he arrived at the place where he'd seen Heather go over the side of the mountain, every muscle in his body clenched.

But it was quiet now.

No cops.

No shooter.

Just a tow truck hooking up a vehicle. Travis braked and dropped his feet to the ground. "Hey! Stop! That's my truck."

The whir of the crank stopped and the driver stepped around the front grill to look back at him. "You got any ID on you?"

Travis showed the man his license.

He handed it back with a grunt. "Name's Wiley. Like the coyote. We've already gotten the other car up and it's at the shop. You know where the driver is?"

"She's all right," Travis said, "but we had to scramble out of here pretty quick. I don't suppose you heard if anyone found the shooter?"

"Shooter?"

"Yeah."

Wiley held his hands up. "Whoa. I don't know about any shooter. I was just called to come do cleanup. Sat here waiting for the rain to stop for about thirty minutes before we decided to get started."

"Right." Of course the gunman wouldn't have hung around. As soon as he'd heard the sirens, he'd probably taken off. "Hey, do you have a phone that works?"

"That's debatable." He checked his phone. "No signal right now. It comes and goes. Everyone who comes through here is like that chicken. They go as fast as they can to get to the other side." He laughed like he'd said something witty. When Travis didn't chuckle, he cleared his throat. "You have to go toward town to get any kind of consistent signal. About two miles thataway." He pointed and Travis nodded. He knew the way back to town.

"How do people out here communicate?" he asked.

"The old-fashioned way. With a landline or a CB radio. Some have satellite phones."

"Incredible."

"Oh, speaking of phones." He dug in his coat pocket. "I found this. Is it yours?"

Travis snagged the cell phone from the man's gloved hand. "Yes, thank you." Now the question was, would it work. Travis dug his keys from his front pocket and his wallet from his back. He passed the forty bucks. "Sorry, but that's all the cash I have on me. Can you unhitch my truck and help me get the bike into the bed? I'm kind of in a hurry."

"Sure thing. I tow bikes more often than you would think, so I've got a ramp you can use."

Within minutes, Travis had his truck back on solid ground and the bike safely strapped in the back. The tow truck driver gave him a sloppy salute as he pulled away, and Travis bolted for the driver's door.

He pulled the handle and something slammed into his back.

Pain arced through him and Travis went down to his knees. The surprise lasted only a moment before instinct kicked in. He lashed out with his left fist and connected with a hard belly.

A whoosh left his attacker, and Travis spun to face him. Dark eyes glittered for a moment through the holes of the ski mask, and Travis found himself facing the barrel of a gun. He stilled, adrenaline rushing, heart pounding. The only good thing about the man holding the weapon on him was that if he was here, he wasn't near Heather or Ryker. "What do you want?"

"You messed up the plan. Now you're going to fix it."

"How's that?"

"You're going to take me to Heather Fontaine."

And as soon as Travis did that, he was a dead man.

▢ ▢ ▢

Heather helped Ryker sit up a bit so he could eat some of the leftover chicken and rice. He ate more than she thought he would before he pushed his plate away. "How are you feeling?"

"About the same. Maybe a little better after the food."

She walked to the window and looked out. No sign of Travis. She returned to the couch and settled next to Ryker. "Tell me about your dad."

"Nothing much to tell."

"I'm sure there's something."

Ryker blew out a low breath and tilted his head to look at the ceiling. His eyes drooped and Heather thought he might fall asleep, but he shifted and rubbed his face with a shaky hand. "He didn't used to be this way. Not when my mom was alive. I mean, he never would have won the dad of the year award, but he wasn't mean like he is now. When she died, he just went over the edge." He shook his head. "I've got a few good memories of him, but only a handful. I don't even know what to think about him anymore. I keep waiting for the cops to show up and tell me he's dead."

"That's a tough way to live."

"It's the only way I know." His lashes fluttered against his cheeks. "Sorry, I'm sleepy."

"Sleep is good. How's the pain level?"

"About a six, but I can deal with it."

Like he had a choice. She wished she could make him more comfortable.

"You haven't asked me why I keep protecting him," Ryker said with his eyes still closed.

"I don't have to. He's your dad." She patted his hand. "I grew up in similar circumstances. You feel trapped no matter what you do."

"Yeah," he whispered.

"Get some sleep, Ryker. I'll wake you when Travis gets here."

"He should be back any minute."

"Yes, he should."

"I won't sleep long. Just for a few . . ."

He was out.

Heather glanced at the clock on the mantel. "Come on, Travis, where are you?"

▢ ▢ ▢

Travis allowed the man to prod him along the path in the direction he was ordered. "What do you want with Heather?"

"How many times have you asked that question?"

"Exactly. And I still don't have an answer." Or a weapon. He'd left his gun with Heather, knowing there was the possibility of running into the shooter, but playing the odds that the guy who'd bolted from the scene had most likely kept going.

He wouldn't underestimate the man again. Or his determination to finish his mission. "What did she do to you to make you come after her?"

"Nothing. She's just a paycheck."

So, there was someone else behind the scenes. "What happens if you don't deliver?"

"I don't get paid. And that's not an option."

"Who's paying?"

The guy chuckled. "None of your business. Now shut up and keep moving."

They continued to walk the edge of the road. No one had come this way since the guy had attacked him. And with the weather, he didn't expect anyone. Even if a passerby did catch a glimpse of them in the dark, the person probably wouldn't notice the weapon.

Travis's mind clicked with scenarios that would allow him to turn the tables and take the man down, but so far, the opportunity hadn't presented itself. What would Heather and Ryker do when he didn't show up in a timely manner?

Heather would start walking and Ryker would probably insist on going with her. He shuddered at the thought of the two of them trying to walk into town for help.

"What's your name?" he asked.

"Don't talk. Just walk. I'm not here to make friends."

"Don't you think I should know the name of the guy who plans to kill me?"

The pistol made contact with Travis's left kidney. He winced and kept going. He caught sight of the destination. A dark-colored van parked across the street off the road. "Where's your buddy? In the driver's seat?" *Think, Travis, think.*

A ringing sound split the night air. The guy behind him cursed and stopped walking. For a moment, the pistol was gone from his back, and Travis whirled, his elbow jamming into the man's chin. His head snapped back and Travis brought his left hand down against the forearm. The impact sent the weapon flying through the air. The man screamed and raced for it, fingers reaching. Travis launched himself forward and slammed a hand into the guy's back. The force of his shove threw the man off-balance and he stumbled, his hand slipping on the grip of the gun, sending it skittering away and under a tree limb.

The assailant whirled, kicked out, and landed a blow just beneath Travis's shoulder. It threw Travis back and he hit the ground hard. Even with the breath knocked from him for a brief moment, he still managed to roll, snag the weapon, and spin it around to aim it at the man making another come at him. "Stop!" The word came out on a gasp, but the guy skidded to a halt. More curses flew from his lips as he backpedaled and raced for the passenger side of the vehicle.

As soon as the door was shut, the engine gunned and the car sped away. Travis squinted but couldn't see a plate. Great. He dragged in several gulps of air, his lungs finally starting to work again.

With a grunt, he rolled to his knees and then his feet. Envisioning the epic amounts of ibuprofen he'd need for the aches and pains that would hit even harder tomorrow, Travis ripped a piece of his undershirt off and used it to wrap it around the weapon. Hopefully, the sheriff could send it off to whatever lab this little town used and get some prints off it. If he hadn't messed them up. Not only that, but his attacker had worn gloves, so he wasn't holding his breath.

He shoved the weapon into his coat pocket and headed for the truck.

CHAPTER SEVEN

Heather jerked and realized she'd drifted off, only to dream about Abdul. She rubbed her eyes and tried to push the images of the hospital in Kabul from her mind, but she kept seeing Abdul racing toward them, the T-shirt flying over his head as he flung it from him, the bomb strapped to his stomach.

His cry for help.

The terror in his eyes.

And the explosion.

The images were more clear tonight than ever, and she felt sure it had something to do with the young man on the couch.

At least she could help him. She paced in front of the door, checked the windows, checked the back of the house, then returned to perch on the edge of the couch, touching Ryker's forehead. Still warm, but not as hot as he'd been earlier. Her left leg started to jiggle and she let the action calm her while she thought.

Personally, she wanted to file a police report on his father but didn't hold out hope that Ryker would feel the same. She'd grown up in the system he was desperate to avoid. There was no way she'd send him into it. But she wouldn't do nothing.

So . . . what was she going to do? "I have no idea."

"About what?" Ryker asked, his voice low and thick.

She stood and spun. "Oh, sorry. Just thinking out loud."

"About me?"

"Not everything's about you, kid," she said softly, teasing. "Better learn that now."

He laughed, then coughed and shut his eyes. "It was about me."

Heather bit her lip on a smile, surprised she could even find one at the moment. "You okay?"

"Yeah, the couch was shaking. You wiggle a lot when you're anxious, don't you?"

When the laugh escaped her, she nodded. "Yes, it's a nervous habit. Sorry I woke you."

"It's okay."

The sound of an engine snagged her attention, and she darted to the window next to the door and pulled aside the curtain just enough to peer out. Her fingers flexed around the grip of the weapon, and she prayed she didn't have to use it.

When three honks sounded, she relaxed a fraction, and as soon as Travis was on the porch, she threw open the door.

"Any trouble?" he asked.

"No. None."

"How's he doing?"

"Better."

"Good. I've got the heat going full blast. Let me make sure the fire is out, then if you'll hold the door, I'll help him to the truck."

Once the fire was extinguished to Travis's satisfaction, Heather grabbed the remaining supplies and Ryker's wallet while Travis hefted the teen in his arms like he would a child. The kid might be young, but he definitely wasn't small. The sheer strength it had to take to deadlift him was impressive.

"I can walk, man." Ryker's protest fell on deaf ears.

Heather held the door and Travis carried Ryker to the truck, settling him in the back and making sure the blanket was wrapped around him.

"It's a good thing you two don't have phones or I'm sure I'd see this all over social media."

Travis laughed. "Not a chance, kid. I don't do that social media stuff."

"You living in the dark ages?"

"Something like that."

Heather took her spot beside Ryker so she could keep an eye on him. The fact that he was conscious was a good thing, but until she had him someplace safe—and inaccessible to his father—she wouldn't be able to stop worrying about him.

Travis drove away from the cabin and Heather kept an eye on the mirrors. Up to this point, she'd been distracted enough not to dwell on the fact that someone had tried to kill her. Now that they were mobile once again and Ryker was going to have help in a few minutes, her mind slid back to the moment when she'd realized she was going to die.

A shudder rippled through her and she closed her eyes.

Why, though? Why go from watching her to threatening her friends and trying to kill her? Who had she made so blasted angry?

She glanced out the window once more and noted they were on the main street of the quaint town she'd come to appreciate over the past month. "The doctor's office is the fourth building past the diner."

Travis pulled into the lot and parked in the handicapped spot near the door. He cut the engine and turned to look in the back seat. "Doesn't look like anyone's here."

"Well, this *is* a small town, remember?" Ryker rasped. "We don't have twenty-four-hour clinics. The doc lives upstairs so he has quick access to supplies in case there's an emergency. If the lights are off, the alarm system's on, but we can get in. Key is on the same ring as the bike's." He gave Travis the code to the alarm system. "He'll get a notification on his phone when you open the door, which means he'll come down to investigate."

"Does he have any weapons?"

"I've never seen any."

Heather raised a brow at Travis and he nodded, understanding her silent thought. Just because Ryker hadn't seen one didn't mean the man didn't have one. Most people in these rural areas did. "What's his name?" Travis asked.

"Dr. Erik Colson."

Travis pulled the motorcycle keys from his pocket and climbed out. When he returned, he slid an arm around Ryker's shoulder and helped him to the door while Heather slipped inside first.

"Dr. Colson?"

To the right and left of the entrance a row of chairs lined the walls facing the check-in counter straight ahead of her.

"Dr. Colson? Are you here?"

The door to the left of the counter opened, and an older African American man with gray hair and neatly trimmed matching beard stepped through. "What's going on in here?" He slipped a pair of glasses over his nose. "How'd you get in here?"

"It's me, Doc," Ryker said.

"Ryker!" His eyes widened. "Oh, my dear boy, what's he done to you now?"

"Doc . . ."

Dr. Colson stepped back through the door and held it open. "Get him in exam room one. There on the right."

Heather followed Travis. "He needs antibiotics and probably would appreciate a painkiller at this point. Do you keep any here?"

Dr. Colson eyed her for a moment and Ryker let out a dry chuckle. "She's a doc too, Doc."

The man gave a slow nod. "Guess questions can wait for a bit. Hold tight and I'll get you something for the pain."

"No narcotics, Doc."

"Ryker—"

"None. But I'm okay with Toradol."

"Not sure that's going to do the trick, but we'll start with it."

He left and Heather touched Ryker's hand. "Narcotics will take the edge off faster and better."

"My dad's a drug addict, an alcoholic, and everything in between. I won't do anything that he does. Especially not drugs."

Heather squeezed his fingers. "Come on, Ryker, let us help you."

Ryker's expression never wavered, and Heather gave up. She knew exactly how he felt. She didn't like anything that made her seem weak. Or not in control. Because if one appeared weak, someone might zoom in to take advantage of that.

She pushed the thoughts away as the doc returned, gloved up and with a syringe in his right hand. "Toradol coming up." He administered the shot. "Now, let me take a look at the wound."

Ryker's gaze met hers. "I let you help get me here, but no narcotics and no social services and no cops. I'll take the antibiotics and the Toradol, but that's it."

She hesitated, then locked eyes with Dr. Colson. The man frowned and gave a slight shake of his head. She nodded. "Okay. We'll do it your way, but we've got to talk to the local cops about what happened to Travis and me."

"Just leave me out of it."

"I can only promise that we'll say as little about you as possible."

"I guess that'll have to do." His scowl said he wasn't happy about it.

She glanced at Travis, who paced from one end of the small room to the other. "You ready to talk to the cops?" she asked.

"And a few other people."

"Like who?"

"Brooke, for one. And the others waiting to hear what's going on and how they can help."

She froze. "I really want to leave them out of it."

"They're your friends, they want to help."

"They also might be in danger if they try to help."

"Hey," Ryker called, "what happened to letting friends help you? Or was that just for me?"

Heather winced, the barb striking the bull's-eye. She sighed. "Ryker, this is a whole different situation."

"How?"

"Because if I let them help me, they might die because of it." And then how would *she* live?

"That's a bunch of . . ." Ryker glanced at the doctor. "Uh . . . what's that word you use, Doc? Hooey. That's it. No, it's a double standard. And that's wrong."

"Yeah," Travis echoed. "That's wrong."

Heather took a deep breath. "The sheriff might not even be in the office. After all, as Ryker pointed out, this is a very small town."

"We have a good sheriff's department," Dr. Colson said. "Just call the sheriff and he'll meet you there."

The doc rattled off the number and Travis punched it into his phone. "Good memory."

"I've had to call it more than once. We might be a small town, but we have our share of trouble."

"Like my father," Ryker said.

"Yep. And others too."

"So," Travis said, "you're fine with me rounding up help, right?"

Heather scowled and pointed to the door. "Let's talk about this on the way to the sheriff's office."

"Yes, ma'am, let's do that."

His hard-eyed stare sent her heart into her toes, and she didn't think the conversation had any chance of going the way she was planning for it to.

○ ○ ○

"She got away," Donnie Little said. He closed his eyes and scrubbed a hand down the side of his cheek. "I don't know exactly how, but she did." Why had he ever agreed to this stupid plan?

Oh. Right. He needed the money.

Silence.

"Then you need to get her back," the voice finally said.

"How? I was in her house, in her bedroom closet, and she never came back there. She left. And when we finally had a chance to get her on a back country road, she had a rescuer swoop in and ruin it." No way was he mentioning how they'd almost killed her when he'd run her off the road.

"Why did she run from the house? What tipped her off?"

Probably that stupid picture. It had been an impulse thing to draw the little red dots on the foreheads of her friends, but he hadn't expected it to send her running. He honestly didn't know what he expected. It had been a stupid, amateurish move, and his "boss" didn't need to know that either. "How am I supposed to know? Maybe the house felt different or something?"

A sigh. "Whatever. So, what happened tonight?"

"Sam and I almost had her and some guy came charging to the rescue." And no way was he admitting that he'd shot at the guy, trying to get rid of him so he could grab the girl. "I think you need to give up on this. Just let it go while you can. Why do you need her anyway?"

"Give up? There's no giving up. And it's not your business why I need her. I just do."

Why did he bother to argue? "Then what's next?"

"Plan B."

Donnie groaned. "What's plan B? Because from where I'm standing, you're going to have to act fast. They'll be leaving town soon."

More silence. Then a sniff. "All right, here's what you're going to do. In that go bag I gave you with the guns and other supplies, there's a chunk of Semtex in a box."

Donnie went still. "I'm sorry, what?" He'd noticed the small box but hadn't opened it. He'd thought it contained more food supplies. There'd been protein bars and fruit and several cans of beans. He'd ignored that stuff. All he'd been going for were the guns, the hood, and the rope.

"You heard me."

"You had us carrying Semtex? I could have blown us all up. Are you crazy?"

"Probably headed in that direction," the person muttered. "Look, there's not a lot of it, but it'll do what we need it for. Now shut up and listen."

○ ○ ○

The sheriff had answered on the third ring, groggy and cranky about being pulled out of a sound sleep since he was off duty. However, once he heard the reason why, he agreed to meet them as soon as he could throw on some clothes.

Travis shot silent glances at Heather, who hadn't said a word on the short trip to the sheriff's office. "I thought we were going to talk about this," he finally said.

"I'm procrastinating."

"No. Really?"

She scowled.

"The kid's right, you know," Travis said as he put the truck in park and turned to face her.

"Hmm."

"Don't do that," he said, his voice sharp. He didn't care.

Her jaw dropped and she met his gaze.

"I may be just a dumb cowboy, but even I recognize that 'Hmm' is a dismissive, cowardly response," he continued, "and you're not a coward. How would you feel if this was Sarah, Brooke, or Gina? Or Ava? Or any of the guys, for that matter? Would you let any of them get away with what you're doing to them?"

Her eyes narrowed, her breathing accelerated. The fury built and he braced himself for the explosion.

Only it never came. The fire faded into resignation and a weariness that she tried to, but couldn't, hide. "No. I wouldn't."

"Then stop doing it to them."

"I'm trying to protect them!"

"Maybe so, but you're just going to put them in more danger if you push them away."

"How—"

"Because you know as well as I do that they're not going to walk away simply because you refuse to let them help. The fact that I'm here should reinforce that they'll—*we'll*—do whatever it takes to ensure your safety. It would probably make that easier—and less dangerous for all of us—if you cooperated."

For a moment, she simply stared at him. He couldn't tell if she was thinking about punching him or opening the door and walking away.

"Well . . . wow," she said.

"What's that mean?" When a tear slipped down her cheek, Travis almost felt bad for pushing her so hard. Almost. When she still hadn't said a word a full ten seconds later, he sighed. "Think about it while we go file our report with the sheriff—assuming he's in the office. Then we're going home so we can surround you with protection and come up with a plan on how to find your stalker."

"I don't have to think about it," she said, her voice so soft, he nearly missed it. "Okay."

He stopped. "Okay, what?"

"I mean, you're right. So, okay, let's bring in the big guns. Asher, Gavin, maybe even Caden can help in his FBI kind of way. But they have to promise to take every precaution. If one of them is hurt—or worse—because of me, I don't think I'd ever recover from it."

"They'll be careful, but even if something happened, it wouldn't be your fault."

Heather raked a hand through her blonde hair, dislodging the messy bun she'd scraped it into back at the cabin. Absently, she redid it, and for some reason, her movements fascinated him. When she nodded, he blinked.

"Mentally, I know that," she said. "Just like I know it's not my fault that I couldn't save Abdul. I *know* it's not my fault when I lose *any* patient, but it still hurts." She rubbed her eyes. "I'm just not used to leaning on others for help."

He pulled her into a loose hug, and she surprised him by not resisting. "First of all," he said, "the fact that you hurt when you lose a patient is one of the prime things that makes you an excellent surgeon. Second, I know you're not used to asking for help or receiving it, but frankly, you don't have a choice, so try to adjust."

"You're awfully bossy."

"Only when I know I'm right."

A low chuckle escaped her, and she sat back with a small smile. "Come on, bossy, let's go get this over with."

Two hours later, the sheriff finally decided he was happy with the information he'd gathered from them. Travis had also turned over the weapon he'd confiscated from his attacker, and the sheriff had checked the number on it. Only to discover it had been reported stolen a week ago. Surprise, surprise.

"I'll send it off," the sheriff had said. "I'll let you know when I hear something."

So, now they'd wait.

Heather had asked him to grab her a soda from the machine while she collected the items from her rental and visited the ladies' room.

The television in the break room was turned to a news channel, and closed captions played at the bottom. He watched absently while he waited, wondering if the media would pick up on Heather's surgery story or if they could manage to keep it contained. No reason for them to know unless someone wanted them to. The television didn't distract him for long. His thoughts returned to the last part of their conversation before they'd met with the sheriff, and he was mortified. He owed her a huge apology.

The door to the bathroom opened. Might as well get it out of the way.

"You good?" he asked when she stepped out, purse over her shoulder and cell phone in her right hand.

"I'm fine. Tired of answering the same questions over and over, but fine." She took the Coke he offered and swigged it while he waited. "Thanks."

"Sure. Look, Heather, I'm sorry."

She raised a brow. "For?"

"Raking you over the coals back in the truck. I lost my temper a bit and I shouldn't have done that."

"That was losing your temper?"

"Yeah."

She laughed and patted him on the arm. "Wow."

"Wow?"

"That was just you being honest. I didn't get that you were having a temper tantrum."

He sighed. "I wasn't, I guess. Not really. I was ticked with you, though, because you have people who care about you, and you want to keep us at arm's length."

Heather slid her gaze from his. "I'm sorry. I don't mean to. It's just . . . habit."

"You know what they say."

"What's that?"

"Habits are meant to be broken."

A laugh slipped from her and she nodded. "Noted."

His phone pinged and he glanced at the screen. "Asher and Gavin are here."

"That was fast."

"It's only an hour-and-a-half drive, and they were on the way out the door almost before I hung up with them. They drove two vehicles. When we leave here, one will be in front and one behind."

She swallowed hard. "That's a lot of protection."

"Not really. Not as much as I would like, but it'll have to do for now." He paused. "They say anything about your rental?"

"Um, yeah." She rubbed her nose. "It's totaled, of course, but I purchased the extra insurance on it, so that's not an issue."

"All right. I want to go by and see Ryker one more time and make sure he has enough money to replace the groceries we ate."

A flush crept up into her cheeks. "I kind of already took care of that."

He raised a brow. "You did?"

"Yeah, when they brought my car up, they gave my stuff to the sheriff, including my purse. I gave him some cash for Ryker."

Some of the cash? She'd probably given him every last penny she had.

"Sheriff Dawkins is going to keep an eye on Ryker," Travis said. "I feel better knowing that between him and Dr. Colson, the kid is going to be taken care of."

"You didn't tell the sheriff about Ryker's father stabbing him, did you?"

"Didn't have to. That was the conclusion he jumped to. Said although he'd been doing his best to help get Ryker out of the home, Ryker wouldn't cooperate. Every time Child Protection removed him, he'd just run away and go back."

"Sad, but understandable. Ryker probably feels responsible for taking care of the man who can't take care of himself."

"The sheriff said he'd been waiting for the day he'd hear Ryker's dad had killed him. He's arrested him on numerous occasions, and each time Ryker finds a way to bail him out. Sheriff said he finally quit arresting him so Ryker didn't have to keep coming up with bail money."

Heather shook her head and frowned. "He shouldn't be in the home. He shouldn't be under that man's thumb, but interfering at this point will just send Ryker running again."

"But the law—"

"I know the law, but he's almost eighteen."

"Exactly. He's still a minor."

"Granted, but you don't understand, Travis . . ." She looked away.

"And you do, is that it?"

Heather nodded, and Travis's heart squeezed at the moment of vulnerability she allowed to shine in her eyes. Then it was gone, and her expression smoothed.

"I guess," Travis said, "the doc is watching out for him now. Not to mention, Ryker's hiding out in a cabin in the woods and isn't exactly living with his father anyway," Travis said. "Short of locking the kid up, they can't keep him from seeing his dad—or his dad from seeing him."

"I know." She paused. "You sure did get a lot of information from the sheriff."

"Only because he asked me a lot of questions, and I insisted on having my own answered." He shrugged. "Besides, he's a nice guy. Truly cares about this small county he's in charge of." His phone buzzed. "That's Asher. They're outside and ready to escort you home."

Heather stilled. Took a steadying breath. And nodded. "Okay, then. Let's go."

CHAPTER EIGHT

Once she was settled in the passenger seat with Travis behind the wheel, Heather let the memories wash over her. She'd found it better just to let them come when they wanted, deal with them, and move on. Only they seemed to be sharper, more in focus lately.

Maybe it was the stress of the stalker. Maybe it was Ryker who was only a couple years older than Abdul had been. At least she'd been able to help Ryker.

"Help me!"

I'm sorry, Abdul, I'm so sorry.

"You doing okay?" Travis asked.

"I'll be all right." Abdul's voice faded and she blinked. "I'm just really, *really* confused."

"Have you narrowed down the possibilities of who this stalker might be? Who the shooter could be?"

Oh, she'd thought about it all right. "Two people come to mind."

"Two? Who?"

"The first one is Jeffrey Steadman. We shared a foster home for three years. That was my fifth—and longest—placement."

"Okay. Why him?"

She'd been ten when she'd entered the system and fifteen when she'd landed in the Steadman household. Jeffrey had been seventeen and the local high school football star. He'd taught her how fun it could be to spend lazy summer days fishing in the local lake and to love Friday night high school football.

He'd also flirted with her from the moment she'd moved into the room above the garage to the day he'd left for college a year later. Fortunately, he'd never pushed the flirting too far, but then, she'd never encouraged him to. "He showed up at the hospital a few weeks ago and we had lunch in between surgeries. He asked me out, said he wanted to get to know me as an adult. I told him thanks, but no thanks."

"How did he take that?"

She smiled. A one-sided lift to her lip. "He seemed a little insulted. Wanted to know what was wrong with him. I just explained that I wasn't interested in dating at the moment and he finally left. I haven't heard from him since."

"I'll get Caden to look into him."

"Caden can't be everyone's personal FBI agent. He's got enough on his plate without me adding to it."

Travis's lips curled into a small smile. "He doesn't think we're asking too much of him. This was an attempted murder, after all."

"I know, but—"

"And when Sarah told him what was going on, he insisted on helping. He told us to let him know if we had anything he could go on. A name is something he can work with."

"I . . ."

He snorted. "I know. You don't like asking for help, but you agreed, remember? Do we need to rehash our earlier conversation?"

She grimaced. "No, no. I get it. I just don't have to like it."

"I know. Who's the second person?"

Before she could answer, Gavin slowed, his brake lights flashing.

"What is it?" Travis asked.

She frowned. "What?"

He tapped his ear. "Talking to Gavin and Asher."

For the first time, she noticed the earpiece tucked into his right ear canal. And her nerves settled. They were professionals, and Travis was right. She needed help. It was time to stop running and fight back.

With the decision made, her heart lightened, and hope penetrated the stress and worry that had gradually robbed her of her peace of mind. For the next couple of minutes, she simply enjoyed the fact that there was a plan. And she wasn't in this alone.

"Gavin, you see that?"

"What?" Heather sat up, tensing once again.

"Up ahead. There's a van parked on the side of the road."

Travis slammed on the brakes and the seatbelt cut into the bruise already there. Blinding pain shot through her. She gasped.

"Sorry, sorry. I didn't mean to hurt you, but I don't like—"

The explosion rocked his truck and Gavin's flew into the air.

"Hold on!" Travis looked over his shoulder and pressed the gas pedal. His truck roared backward.

Another muffled explosion sent her careening back to Kabul. To Abdul, to the thunderous sound that had rocked the ground beneath her. She blinked the images away as Gavin's truck came down hard on its side. "Gavin!"

Heather released her seat belt and scrambled for the door handle when a hard hand came down on her left wrist and jerked her back.

"Stay put!"

Her heart pounding in her chest and her temples, Heather obeyed. He was right, she couldn't get out yet.

The spurt of gunfire kicked up the dirt in front of Travis's truck. He shoved her down. The passenger door flew open. Travis fired over her head. The black masked figure grunted and stumbled back. Another one took his place. "Drop it, or she dies!"

Travis hesitated.

The attacker jammed the muzzle of his gun against Heather's

head and grabbed her arm in a viselike hold. She yanked against the grip, her heart pounding, adrenaline surging, while Travis held his hands where the man could see them. "Don't hurt her."

"Then don't do anything stupid." He gave Heather a hard jerk and she tumbled from the truck.

"Hurry up!"

The shout came from behind her.

"Travis!" Heather couldn't help the terrified cry that slipped from her throat.

From the corner of her eye, she saw him dive for her. Someone kicked him in the ribs just as a hood came over her head. Heather let out a scream and threw a blind punch. Her knuckles scraped mask material and then her arms were pinned to her sides.

"Don't let them get away!" Travis's shout was followed by gunfire.

She was shoved into a seat as more shots rang out. Someone yanked her arms behind her back and bound her hands together. "Stay there. Don't move if you want to live."

The driver gunned the engine and Heather planted her feet to keep from tumbling from the seat. Trembling, panting, trying to drag air into lungs that refused to expand. "Please," she whispered, "why are you doing this?" This didn't feel like a stalker situation. Did stalkers work in pairs? Or more?

Bound and blind, she fought the fear that threatened to send her into a total panic.

Breathe. Just breathe.

"He shot me, man," someone said, voice shaky, shocked. "Like for real shot me."

"Shut up. We'll take care of that after we get the girl back to the cabin."

Heather froze. *Cabin?* What cabin?

"Getting shot wasn't part of the deal."

"Shut your face," the driver said, "or *I'm* going to shoot you. For real. I told you there was always a chance for things to go wrong."

Silence. The vehicle swerved around a curve. "Please," Heather said, "just let me go. What do you want?"

"Right." The driver grunted. "Like you don't know. This is what you signed up for, sweetheart, so be quiet and let us do our job."

What she signed up for? A shiver racked her. Squelching the terror, she closed her eyes. *God, I don't know why this is happening, but please, please, let Gavin be okay. And please surround me with your protection. Please . . .*

◻ ◻ ◻

Travis bent, gasping, hands on his knees, weapon in his right hand. The dark Chevy work van had disappeared around the curve and they'd taken Heather with them. They'd *taken* her.

Right out from under his nose. Still reeling at the reality, he repeated the license plate over and over, then spun to jog back to the scene, tucking his weapon out of sight.

Patrol cars squealed to a stop. Travis ran toward Gavin's truck and saw the man crawling through the window. "You okay?"

"Yeah!"

Travis detoured to the nearest cop. "You need to put a BOLO out on a black Chevy van. I got the plate." He rattled it off. "They just took a woman. Heather Fontaine. Headed east on South Carlisle." The officer sent the message, finishing up just as an ambulance swung into the area. The sense of urgency at Asher's truck caught Travis's attention. Gavin waved the paramedics over and Travis hurried to follow. He grabbed Gavin's bicep. "What is it?"

"Asher's been shot."

His brain froze for a split second. "What?"

"He took a bullet in the side." Blood dripped from a gash on his forehead. Gavin raked a hand over his chin. "It's bad."

"Oh no."

"Yeah." His eyes sharpened. "Heather?"

"They got her, Gavin. They got her." His throat tightened and lungs constricted just saying the words. "You sure you're okay?"

"Yeah, I had to cut through the seat belt."

A muscle jumped in Travis's jaw. "Glad you're alive."

"Yeah, me too. You get any ID on who took her?"

Travis described the van and the fact that he'd passed the plate on to the officer. "There's a BOLO out."

"They'll find her." Gavin swiped the blood before it could drip into his eye.

"Of course they will." He tried to convince himself it was true, battling the statistics flashing in his mind.

The paramedics loaded Asher onto the gurney, and Travis hurried to his friend's side. The fact that his eyes were open sent a surge of relief through him. "We'll be right behind you," he said.

"Don't tell Brooke." The weak, raspy voice worried Travis.

Gavin snorted. "Right. She'll beat you to the hospital and be pacing the hall until you come out of surgery."

Asher swallowed and winced. "Tell her . . . it's . . . not that bad. I'll . . . be okay."

"Just do what the doctors say," Gavin said.

Asher groaned and closed his eyes.

The paramedics loaded him into the ambulance. Travis nudged Gavin. "Come on."

"Hospital?"

"Yeah." Travis tossed Gavin an old but clean T-shirt. "Press on that wound." Gavin did while Travis drove. "The cops will track us down at the hospital to get our statements," he said, "and we can keep up with their progress on finding Heather."

"You don't think we should be out there looking?"

Travis shot him a sharp look. "Of course that's my first instinct. I want to be looking, but that would be a lousy use of time and resources. It's time to use some of those military skills you've got that will allow us to work smarter, not harder."

"What do you have in mind?"

"Working with the cops is a good start. Seeing if there's any security footage out here is a hope, but I'm not holding my breath.

They picked the perfect spot for an ambush. I'm angry with myself for not studying the area more closely." He paused. "I was in a hurry to get her out of here. Get her home. I'm wondering what I missed." The words were bitter on his tongue. But true. And now Heather was paying the cost for his haste.

"You didn't miss anything. You know as well as I do that sometimes things are out of our control and just happen, so stop blaming yourself," Gavin said. "Let's get to the hospital and pray Asher's really going to be okay."

"Can you call Sarah and get her to come to the hospital with Brooke? Maybe Asher'll be out of surgery by the time they get here."

"Already thought of that." Gavin snatched his phone and punched in Sarah's number.

Travis drove with purpose . . . and a prayer on his lips.

CHAPTER NINE

Nausea swirled as the beginning of a migraine started to pound over her right eye. *Not now, not now.* She drew in a ragged breath of stale air. Occasionally, when her blood pressure spiked, a migraine would hit.

And she had no medication with her. At least they hadn't taped her mouth shut. She swallowed and held her head as still as possible until the van jerked to a stop.

A pained cry slipped from her lips. Lights danced under her eyelids—a sure sign that things were going to get worse before they got better. Rough hands pulled her from the van, then the hood from her head. She blinked at the brightness, her pain level ratcheting skyward.

She retched. "I'm going to puke." The hands released her. She bent and lost the contents of her stomach.

"You done?"

"Migraine," she whispered. "Don't have my medication."

A pause, then the one behind her to the right gave her a small shove. "Get inside and I'll find something for you."

Heather stumbled up the porch steps, trying to take in as much detail of her surroundings as she could, but her vision kept flickering and all she wanted to do was lie down and close her eyes. But the terror racing through her . . . *Oh God, please . . .*

Once inside, the taller man led her to a side room. "There's a bed in there." He aimed her at the door, and she bolted for it, wanting him to go away and let her suffer alone—and figure out how she was going to escape with a pounding head, wonky vision, and a churning stomach.

She eased onto the side of the bed, letting her squinted gaze roam the room. If she hadn't been a prisoner, she might have enjoyed the decor. A cabin with wood walls, a queen bed with a thick quilt. And an en suite bathroom. All the comforts of home.

The door opened. She tensed. "Here." The man still wore his ski mask. Blood crusted the dark jacket at his waist. He tossed a bottle of pills toward her and it landed on the bed next to her. "The best I can do. It's an over-the-counter migraine medicine."

She eyed the bottle, then her captor. Did she dare trust him?

"I'm not trying to poison you," he said as though reading her mind. "I think this was a big mistake and want this over with as much as you do."

"I doubt that."

He snorted. "My wife gets migraines. I keep a bottle of that stuff in the glove compartment. Take it."

"All right. I will. Thank you." Might as well make nice. "I'm a surgeon," she said. "Let me take a look at that wound."

He paused. Seemed to think about it before shaking his head. "It's fine. If I was going to bleed out, I would have done it by now. I'll hit a hospital after this is all over."

Heather frowned. "I don't understand why you're doing this. Who paid you to kidnap me?"

He snorted on a laugh. "Are you serious?"

"Of course I am."

He hesitated. "Wait a minute. What do you—?"

"What are you doing?" The gruff voice came from the other man. "No contact with the victim, remember?"

"She's got a migraine."

"Who cares? You wanna get paid or not? Get in here before you cost us both the rest of our paychecks."

The first man backed from the room, his gaze still on Heather. "She can look at this gunshot wound. She's a surgeon."

"I don't care who she is! Get in here!"

He shut the door without another word and Heather wilted. For just a moment. Then her eyes went to the bottle once more. She had no clue who could be doing this to her—and from the gist of the conversation, these guys were just the hired help. Someone else was calling the shots. Who? *Why?*

She jammed the heels of her palms against her temples. She needed the pounding to stop. More than that, she needed a plan of action. Unfortunately, the pain fogged her thought processes.

Letting out a low groan, she slipped into the bathroom to wet a washcloth and fill a cup with water. With those items in one hand, she grabbed the roll of toilet paper with the other and returned to the bed. After she set everything on the nightstand, she wrapped toilet paper around the pill bottle to preserve any fingerprints, then opened it to study the contents. They looked legit. She downed three, chasing them with the water. She closed the bottle, stashed it into the front pocket of her jeans, stacked the pillows, and leaned back.

With the washcloth covering her eyes, Heather allowed herself to relax, forcing her muscles to release their long-held, terror-induced tension.

But her ears focused on the voices beyond the door. She was desperate to know if Gavin was okay. The image of his truck flying in the air and landing on its side replayed over and over until she forced herself to move on to Asher and Travis.

Travis. He'd risked his life for her. They all had. Exactly what she'd been afraid would happen. She sent up a silent prayer for all of them even while one big question nagged at her. How had the two in the other room known exactly when and where to hit their little convoy? Had the sheriff said something to someone who passed the information on?

She forced herself to drift into a semiconscious state—a skill she'd learned to get her through medical school.

ooo

Heather's next conscious thought was that her head wasn't pounding nearly as hard and the nausea had faded. Her second thought was that no one had bothered her since they'd locked her in the room. She rolled her head, testing it. When no sharp pain returned, she swung her legs over the side of the bed to stand.

Okay, then. If they weren't going to tell her what was going on, she had to find out on her own.

Heather went to the window and looked out. Trees. Nothing but trees. And the setting sun. According to the skyline, it would be dark in about thirty minutes. That meant it was around 5:30 in the evening. She didn't recognize the area just beyond the window. Which meant she had no idea where she was.

But they'd driven approximately fifteen to twenty minutes. Maybe slightly longer. It had felt like forever with the migraine and the fear, so she could be off in her estimation.

She tried the window. Sealed shut, but no bars. Interesting. The nail holes looked fresh, but hope stirred. She could work with this.

Voices from the den area reached her. A shout. A door slammed. Another shout she couldn't understand echoed down the hallway. Heather walked to the door and pressed her ear against it.

". . . paid . . . did . . . job. I'm not . . . longer. What's the holdup . . . better be in . . . account . . . set her loose."

Well, part of that was clear enough, but she heard only one voice. And it wasn't the one with the bullet wound. The other captor on the phone?

Probably.

"Hey!" The one on the phone hollered to someone, his words

now clear. "Did you hear that? Check outside and make sure no one's snooping around here because they see lights in this place."

Heavy, slow footsteps sounded, then faded.

Heather pressed a hand against her head, praying the pain would stay away. From what little she'd heard, it sounded like they were waiting for the person who'd arranged for the kidnapping to pay them. Which explained why they'd left her alone. They'd done their job. Now they were going to get paid and be on their merry way.

And if they didn't get the payment, they'd turn her loose? Right. She wasn't holding her breath for that one.

It didn't matter.

She didn't plan on sticking around long enough to find out.

▢ ▢ ▢

Ryker hunkered down below the window, praying he hadn't given himself away. Dizzy, he'd lost his balance and slammed against the side of the cabin. When he'd heard shouting from the inside, he'd hurried to hide behind one of the large bushes. Trying to control his racing heart was harder than being quiet. He'd learned a long time ago how to sit for hours without making a sound.

Ryker curled into himself, hunching against the cold and ignoring it as he listened. Yet another skill he'd acquired at a young age. It had always been cold in their house in the winter since his dad was too cheap to turn the heat on.

Footsteps closed in on his position and a light swept over his head. *Don't see me, please don't see me.*

"Always gotta be the one to do the dirty work," a voice muttered, "me, with a bullet in him. 'Go check outside,'" he mocked in a singsong tone. "Go check outside yourself. Forget this." The man turned and stomped away, back toward the warmth of the cabin.

Ryker let out a breath of relief and pulled his phone from his pocket. No bars. He wanted to hurl the phone to the ground and pound it into a zillion pieces. But that was the way his father would handle his frustration. Ryker simply tucked it back into his pocket and mentally ran through his limited options. Break into the cabin and get Heather or go find a signal.

The clock was ticking for Heather. From what Ryker managed to overhear, those guys were waiting for someone—and that someone would be here soon.

Breathing a prayer, Ryker stood and walked toward the window of the room where Heather was being held.

○ ○ ○

Travis paced outside the door of Asher's hospital room, his heart pounding, thoughts racing. He'd finished his statement to the police and had done all the necessary paperwork about discharging his weapon, noting that he'd hit one of the kidnappers. Thirty minutes ago, Asher had been rolled into the surgery recovery room, and Brooke was back there with him. Sarah and Gina sat in the waiting room.

"You okay?" Gavin asked.

Travis turned. His buddy was leaning against the nurses' station, hands shoved in the front pockets of his jeans.

"No, I'm not."

Gavin frowned. "Asher's going to be okay."

"That's the good news I'm waiting to hear. The bad news is that I have no idea where Heather is or who took her. She could be about anywhere by now. Just before everything went down, she told me about a guy who came to the hospital and asked her out. Jeffrey Steadman. I sent his name to Caden."

"You think it's him?"

"I have no idea. Heather said he was insulted that she didn't want to go out with him, but that he finally left and she never heard from him again."

Gavin's eyes narrowed. "Hmm."

"Yeah. She also said something about one other person who might be responsible, but I never found out who because the attack happened."

A moment of silence drifted between them. Then Gavin rubbed his forehead. "I've been thinking."

"About?" The shiny white bandage on Gavin's head set off images of the explosion, the truck in the air. The crash. Travis blinked and gave his friend his full attention.

"Everything. Let's go over the timeline," Gavin said. "Heather seemed tense but fairly okay the night of the party, right?"

"Yes."

"Before she came in, she noticed someone watching her from the neighbor's yard, right?"

"Yeah. She ran after him, but he bolted."

Gavin narrowed his eyes. "You chased after her and—"

"When I caught up to her, she slugged me," Travis admitted.

"Why?"

"Instinct maybe? Her adrenaline was racing and she was reacting to her fear? Who knows?"

"Good to know the whole story."

Travis shrugged. No need to keep it a secret at this point.

"When she left," Gavin continued, "she went home. You weren't too far behind her and thought she was there."

"From my vantage point across the street, everything looked fine. Normal. I even drove around her block before parking there all night. I didn't see anything that set off my alarms." He ran a hand over his cheek. "If only I'd known she wasn't there . . ."

"There wasn't any way for you to know." Gavin narrowed his eyes. "You said there was a picture that indicated the ladies were in danger and Heather interpreted that to mean she needed to run in order to ensure their safety."

"Right."

"But we searched her home the next day—right after getting that text. There was nothing out of the ordinary. Her alarm system was set when we got there. Nothing to indicate there was any trouble in her house. It looked like she was just gone for the day and would be back at any moment."

"Yep."

"Caden pulled her phone records and there were no calls *to* her cell after she left the party, but she made one call to the hospital."

Travis nodded. "Which we now know was to her supervisor, letting her know she wouldn't be in the next day."

"Then her phone went dark because she shut it off."

"Exactly," Travis said slowly. "So, we can't say that we actually *searched* her house. We simply verified she wasn't there and it didn't look like anything was wrong on the surface."

"And the cops wouldn't search it," Gavin said, "because of the text saying she was going away for a while and would be in touch soon." He paused. "You think we missed something that could tell us who took her?"

"I'm saying I don't think it would hurt to take another look."

Brooke stepped into the hall and they fell silent. "He just woke up. Said y'all better catch the guy who shot him," she said as Gina and Sarah joined them.

Travis swallowed and a relieved weakness hit him. Sure, Gavin had said their friend would be okay, but the fact that Asher was awake and talking made it more believable. "Tell him we're working on it."

She nodded. "Any word on Heather?"

"Working on that too," Gavin said.

"We're going to go search her house," Travis said. "Like really search it this time and see if there's any kind of indication or clue as to who could have done this. Are you okay with us leaving?"

"Of course."

"Caden's pulling out all the stops to find her," Sarah said.

And that was the only reason Travis still had a shred of sanity left.

Gina twisted her hands. "Is there anything I can do to help? Today's my day off and I can be a part of a search team or something."

"Just keep praying for her right now."

"Of course." She frowned and started to say something, then stopped, her eyes still on his.

"What is it?"

"I don't know. It's probably nothing."

"Come on, Gina. Say whatever's on your mind."

She hesitated, then nodded. "Sarah and I stopped at a little café yesterday, and I thought I saw someone watching her. I asked Sarah if she saw the guy, but she didn't."

Gavin's eyes narrowed on Sarah. "Why didn't you mention it?"

"Because I wasn't sure anyone was there."

"I really wasn't sure about it either," Gina said, her voice soft. "I don't know if the person at the café was targeting her, but he followed us out the door. That's when I asked Sarah if she saw him. He must have seen me watching, because when Sarah turned, he slipped into the crowd on the sidewalk."

"Can you describe him?"

"Tall, looks like he works out. Goatee." She rubbed her nose. "He had on a red beanie hat, pulled low. I didn't really get a good look at his face."

"It could be the same guy that snatched Heather," Travis said.

"If I see him again, I'll try to get a picture, but I'd feel a whole lot better if someone were watching out for Sarah."

"You don't have to worry about that," Gavin said. "We'll have someone watching you, too, from now on."

Gina's eyes widened. "Me? No. He wasn't watching me. He was definitely watching Sarah."

"I think we may be overreacting. A little paranoid because of what's happened to Heather," Sarah said.

"I disagree." Gina placed a hand on Sarah's arm. "This is too serious to brush off or assume no one was there."

Sarah hesitated a fraction. "But why would someone be following *me*? I don't understand."

"When we figure out why someone snatched Heather, we may know the answer to that question," Travis said. He looked at Brooke. "Have you noticed anyone following you?"

"No. No one."

"Doesn't mean someone's not watching," Travis said. "How many favors can we call in to get some protection on everyone?"

"As many favors as it takes," Gavin said. "Between Caden and me, we can get it covered. I'm also going to ask Caden to pull video from the café and see if we can spot him." He pulled out his phone and stepped down the hall.

Travis watched the clock, his nerves ticking in time with the seconds. *Please watch over Heather, please don't let anything happen to her.* He continued the prayer until Gavin stepped back toward them. "All right. I've got two buddies headed this way. They're going to be bodyguards to Gina and Sarah for however long it takes." He glanced at Sarah, then back to Travis. "I'm going to stay here."

"No," Sarah said. "Travis needs you to do this with him. Heather needs you too. Go, we'll be fine."

Gavin frowned and Travis refrained from saying anything, knowing Gavin had to come to the decision himself. Finally, he nodded. "Okay, but we wait until my friends get here."

An hour later, with Gavin's buddies on guard, Travis hugged Brooke, then Gina. "Please keep texting updates. We'll do the same."

"Sure."

Travis and Gavin headed for the elevator. "It'll take us at least an hour to get to Heather's," Gavin said, "depending on traffic."

Travis gripped the keys to his truck. "Don't bet on that. You're sure you're comfortable leaving Sarah? I'd totally understand if you wanted to stay."

"I'm fine. I trust those guys with my life. I can trust them with my heart."

Travis's phone rang and he glanced at the screen. He didn't recognize the number but tapped the green button. "Heather?"

"No, this is Ryker, but I know where Heather is."

CHAPTER TEN

It was time.

The voices in the other room had fallen silent, and Heather thought she'd heard a door shut. Shut, not slam. That was good, right?

Unsure of their location, her fear at the thought of facing her captors—and what that might mean for her physical well-being—continued to grow. Shutting doors was definitely better than slamming.

She decided to try and make a break for it instead of wait around for whoever had hired the two to snatch her.

She yanked the pillowcase from the pillow and wrapped it around her hand and forearm. Once more in front of the window, she used her elbow to punch out the corner of the glass. The crash made her cringe.

And freeze.

Cold air rushed in through the gaping hole. She waited for the pounding footsteps, a yell, or the slam of a door.

And heard nothing.

Turning back to the window, she punched out the rest of the glass in the lower pane. When she was finished, she grabbed the blanket from the foot of the bed and tossed it out the window. Then snagged the comforter and placed it over the windowsill and remaining broken glass.

Without a backward glance, she climbed out and landed on the ground, glass crunching beneath her shoes. She let herself drag in a ragged breath, then grabbed the blanket from the ground and darted for the tree line.

"Hey!"

The shout nearly stopped her heart, but she churned her feet faster.

"Get her! I'll grab the van and cut her off!"

"This wasn't in the contract!"

Heather spared a quick glance behind her, ignoring the words but filing them away. One man was already in the driver's seat and the other—the wounded one—pounded her way. She wasn't concerned about being able to outrun him, but the one in the van worried her. And neither had on masks. She couldn't see the one in the van very well, but if they caught her now, they'd have no reason to allow her to live.

Please get me out of here, God. She hit the wooded area and kept going, shooting a look behind her. The van closed in. Much farther back, the wounded man went to his knees. Heather kept going, deeper into the trees, the underbrush crunching beneath her feet. The slamming of a door and harsh yell behind her sent terror shooting through her. She dodged limbs and jumped over dead trees, clutching the blanket around her.

She didn't like to run. Hated it, in fact. Would her loathing of exercise be the death of her? Taking the stairs at work probably couldn't be considered an exercise routine.

A limb scraped her cheek. She winced but refused to slow. Heather rounded the next tree and pulled to a stop, her breath coming in harsh pants. "Oh no, oh no."

The trees closed in, thick and dark, blocking out the light of the moon, making it impossible to discern which way she should go.

She darted behind the nearest tree to listen. The quiet of the darkness surrounded her. No engines, no footsteps, no curses. A shiver crawled up her spine, and she shuddered, clamping her teeth against the frigid cold. Why couldn't she hear anything? Because she'd lost them? Or were they simply waiting her out? Listening for her to make the next move.

She planted her back against the trunk of the tree and pressed her hands to her eyes. *Think. Listen. Listen and think.* She needed to find a way to the road. If she followed the road, she'd eventually come to a—

A rustle to her left. Her head snapped up and her blood went still. Footsteps reached her once more, coming closer. Muted breathing, low mutters.

Heather backed from the tree, slipping deeper into the woods, her sense of direction askew. However, going back the way she came wasn't an option.

A light passed over her head, and she sucked in a scream as she dropped to the ground.

"You might as well stop running," a voice said. The captor was calling the shots. "Make this easier on both of us, will you? There are only a few hours left, and I'm getting tired of this whole cat-and-mouse game."

Heather shuddered, her stomach clenching, threatening to release its contents even as confusion swirled. A few hours left? She clenched her hands into fists, then crept away from him, while her ears strained to pick up the slightest sound.

Behind her, underbrush crunched, and she stuffed one of her nearly frozen fists into her mouth to keep the scream from escaping. How did he get behind her? Had the wounded man recovered enough to be a threat once more?

Heart thundering, she whipped her head left, then right, and thought she spotted a slight opening in the tightly packed trees. But that's where the sound had come from. Right? Or had it been from the other side?

Clamping her lips, Heather closed her eyes to listen once more. The footsteps from the other direction grew louder, the low voice closer. "Come on, you stupid—" She closed her ears to the words and focused. He was in front of her, slightly to her left. Close enough to touch.

The light passed across her face this time. "Gotcha."

She darted for the opening, no longer worried about finding her way out of the woods—she just wanted to get away. His hand scraped her forearm and she stumbled forward, tripped on a log, and went to her knees.

A hand clamped around her ankle and sent her facedown. She twisted, kicked out, connected with something. His harsh cry brought her a split second of satisfaction—and blessed freedom.

She scrambled to her feet, racing for the obscurity of the trees. She rounded one, and a hand clamped over her mouth, yanking her to a sudden halt. "Shh." Harsh breaths escaped her nose in puffs of panic. Her terror spiked. "Be quiet," the voice whispered. "And I'll get you out of here."

Relief crashed into her. "Ryker?"

"Shh. This way."

With her cold hand clasped in his, he led her into the trees through an opening she hadn't seen—and now prayed her pursuers wouldn't spot.

Cursing blistered the air directly in front of her and she flinched. Ryker's reassuring grip and her military training enabled her to stay silent, to steady her breathing and stay in control. Light bounced off the trees in front of her. More cursing, then gunfire split the night, and she found herself facedown in the dirt once more.

○ ○ ○

"Almost there," Travis bit out. Ryker's call had immediately changed their plans. Gavin sat in the passenger seat while Travis floored the accelerator. "Cops should be on scene as we speak."

Caden was choppering in. He'd requested the case assignment, and his supervisor had handed it to him without argument.

The hospital was only thirty minutes by land from the location Ryker had given them, and Travis just prayed that Caden and local police would arrive in a timely manner. Like twenty minutes ago.

"I didn't have a signal with this phone," the teen had said. "I had to come down the mountain far enough to get one. I called the sheriff and figured you'd want to know, too, but I got to get back. I don't know what they're going to do with her."

"But she's all right?" Travis had pressed, not even caring that he sounded frantic. He was.

"Yeah. They've got her locked in a room. She opened the blinds but turned before I could get her attention. I was going to knock on the window, but one of the guys came out and started walking around the cabin. I thought he was going back inside, but he kept circling the perimeter. I think he was avoiding the one inside. They don't seem like they get along very well. Anyway, I didn't want to take a chance on getting Heather's attention because I was afraid she'd let on that I was out here and they'd leave. But I think they're waiting on something—or someone. One of them has a phone that actually works up there. He was talking to someone and he didn't look happy."

Probably a satellite phone. "Anything else?"

"I got the plate off the van." He rattled it off to Travis. "Gave it to the sheriff too."

"Good job. Stay put. We've got help on the way."

"I've got to get back there and keep an eye on her. I can't let them hurt her."

"Ryker—"

"Don't tell me not to go."

Travis understood the kid's worry and his deep desire to make sure Heather was safe, but . . . Ryker would do what he was going to do. "I won't. Just don't let them see you, okay?"

"Not planning to."

Ryker had hung up, and Travis vowed to buy the kid a phone that actually worked.

Gavin's phone rang this time. "Yeah?" He looked at Travis. "Hey, it's Caden."

"Put him on speaker."

When Gavin tapped the screen, the sound of helicopter blades pounded in the distance. "Can you hear me?" Caden asked.

"Loud and clear. What is it?"

"I just got word back about Steadman. He got out of prison about a month ago for forging checks. Big-dollar amounts too. He served three of a five-year sentence and got out on parole."

Travis raised a brow. "So, why would he be going after Heather?"

"He's not. When Heather was snatched, Steadman was meeting with his parole officer."

"Doesn't mean he didn't hire someone," Gavin said.

"We're still investigating, and we'll make sure without a doubt, but my gut says it's not him."

His gut. Travis had learned to trust it. Caden probably had too. "Then we need to figure out who it could be ASAP."

"Agreed. See you soon." He hung up and Gavin snapped his phone back on his belt. "How much longer?" Gavin popped four more ibuprofen and pressed a hand to the bandage covering his wound.

Travis could only pray the man was up to this chase. "Ten minutes."

"Can you make it five?"

Travis barked a harsh laugh. "I was hoping you'd say that."

○ ○ ○

The gunshots had stopped and Heather had scrambled to her feet, then pulled Ryker to his. "You're going to reopen that wound," she'd said with a gasp.

"You can fix it later if I do. At least you'll be alive to do it."

He had a point. She followed him, stepping where he stepped, stopping when he stopped. If she never saw a wooded area again, she would be okay with that. She listened, straining to hear. "I don't hear him, do you?"

"No, but that doesn't mean he's not back there."

Yet another good observation. "Do you know where you're going?"

He gave a short, low laugh. "I've been hiding out in these woods since I was eight years old. You know. To get away from my old man. I'm more comfortable here than in my own house, so, yeah, I know where I'm going."

And probably better than anyone who'd try to follow. But . . . *eight*? Her heart clenched, sorrow for the poor boy beating hard against it. "Okay then."

"There's a convenience store off the road. If we can get there, we should be all right."

Convenience store. That brought back even more memories of slogging through the woods with Travis. Tears pricked her eyelids, but she refused to let them fall. "I'm right behind you."

He touched her arm. "That convenience store that I'm aiming for is about another two miles or so. You okay with that?"

"I'd prefer an Uber, to be honest, but truly, I'm fine with anything that doesn't involve being shot at."

"I hear you."

Relatively certain the men were no longer behind them, Heather focused on putting one foot in front of the other, grateful her head throbbed with only an annoying headache and not a full-blown migraine. "I absolutely hate hiking and running," she muttered, "and yet, here I am again—hiking and running." She glanced up as though she could see God peering down at her. "If you're trying to teach me something," she muttered, "I'm willing to learn." Preferably from the comfort of her recliner, but— "Although, if you could just do it without woods and cold and the whole running-from-bad-guys requirement, I might get it faster."

"Sorry, did you say something?"

She grimaced. "Not really. Just complaining to God. You can ignore me."

"You think he's listening?"

"Of course."

"Interesting."

Ryker pressed a hand against his side and pulled in a breath. Now there was something to complain about. His own father had stabbed him, but she hadn't heard Ryker utter one whiny word. Not even with a stitched-up hole in his side. Shame burned a path straight to her heart, and she silently apologized to God and thanked him for sending rescue in the form of Ryker. Woods, cold, walking and all. It was much better than a warm prison with sketchy captors.

Time passed. A chopper swirled overhead, then disappeared. Hope flared. Could that be someone looking for her? But how? No one knew where she was. She shoved the despair aside and put one foot in front of the other. She also kept an eye on her rescuer. He seemed to be doing okay, but she was worried about him. "How'd you find me anyway?"

"My dad showed up at the clinic looking for me. I snuck out the back and wheeled my bike far enough away that he wouldn't hear it start. I was heading for the sheriff's office when I saw you guys drive past in your caravan. That was subtle, by the way."

Heather grimaced.

"Anyway, I decided to follow you."

Heather caught a glimpse of his pale face. Sweat beaded his brow. "Do we need to sit down?"

"No, we're not too far away. So, I followed you and I saw the whole thing. I stayed out of sight when the shooting started, but when they grabbed you and shoved that hood over your head . . ." He paused. "Well, I couldn't let them get away with that. When they took off, I went after them, but I hung back a ways to stay out of sight. I knew they'd be watching their rearview mirror."

"You followed us to the cabin?"

"Sort of. I lost them at one point and had to backtrack, trying to figure out which way they went. And, of course, my stupid phone wouldn't work. Not in that area in this weather."

At least it had stopped raining.

"Then how'd you find the cabin?"

"I made a gamble that they'd have a place fairly close by where they could hole up for a while. It was my only shot at finding you. If I was wrong, then I'd have to go find a signal and tell them the last place I'd seen the van."

"But you didn't give up. Thank you."

He shot her a tight smile. "Anyway, I remembered this cabin community that was usually closed this time of year and decided to check it out."

"There are a lot of cabin communities up here."

"Yeah. I know. That's why it took me so long to find you. I started driving through every one I came to, then decided to find the one that was the most isolated, because those guys would want as few witnesses as possible around. I spotted lights in four cabins. You were in number three." He shrugged. "And really, in the direction they were going, there aren't that many. Maybe six or so."

"I owe you big time, Ryker."

"Naw, you probably saved my life. I'd say we're even."

She laughed, a breathless sound that was borderline sob.

Just when she'd almost decided Ryker was delirious and leading her in circles, she spotted lights. Convenience store lights and the welcome blue lights mixed with red ones swirling in the parking lot. "Who called the cops?"

"I did," Ryker said. "When I found you. At first, I told them to go to the cabin but decided we needed a backup plan. I told them if we weren't at the cabin, we'd be here and to meet us. Guess they believed me."

Tears swarmed her eyes and she blinked them back. "Thank you," she whispered.

"Come on." He gripped her fingers and they made their way through the rest of the trees to emerge at the side of the small building.

Heather noted Ryker pressing a hand against his wounded side once again. The sheen of sweat had turned into rivulets that snaked down his temples. That and his flushed cheeks attested to the fact that he was still one very injured kid.

And yet, he'd come after her.

She didn't want to think about where she'd be if he hadn't.

"Heather! Ryker!"

She spun. "Travis?"

He broke away from a group of officers and raced toward her, his gaze flicking between her and the teen at her side. "You guys are all right?"

Heather nodded. "Yeah. We really are. Mostly. Ryker needs to get back to a warm bed and finish healing."

"I'm okay," Ryker said.

Heather ignored him and waved a paramedic over. After giving quick instructions on how to care for him despite the fact that they knew exactly what to do, Heather let Travis slip a heavy blanket over her, then an arm around her shoulders.

"I think you probably need to follow your own advice."

"I'll rest when those guys are in custody."

"They're working on that as we speak."

She nodded. "What about Gavin and Asher? Are they okay? I saw Gavin's truck flip and—" She shuddered.

"Gavin's fine. He's here."

She turned and scanned the organized chaos, spotted her friend in the midst of it, and let a wave of gratitude wash over her. "Did they get the guy who was shot?"

He frowned. "No, they don't have anyone in custody yet. Caden's here, though. He was assigned to your kidnapping. Now he'll probably be chasing the kidnappers. I know he's going to want to talk to you and Ryker."

"Of course." She paused. "And Asher? You didn't say anything about him." He hesitated and the fear returned. "Travis?"

"He was shot—"

She gasped and felt the blood drain from her face.

"But"—he hurried to say—"is recovering nicely. He should be fine in no time. Really. I should have led with, 'Asher is going to be fine, but . . .' Anyway, Brooke's with him and he's told us to find the guys who shot him."

Heather rubbed a hand over her eyes. "Okay. Then I guess that's what we need to do."

"Ma'am, we need to get your statement, please." An officer in his midthirties had slipped up beside her and now waited expectantly.

"Right," she said, "of course. I just want to check on Ryker."

"The teen who was with you?"

"Yes."

The man's brown eyes softened. "He's being transported to the hospital as we speak."

She hadn't noticed the ambulance leaving. "He went willingly?" He was a minor. The hospital would have to contact his father, and she didn't see him wanting that to happen.

"Somewhat."

Heather caught Travis's eye. "Will you call Dr. Colson and let him know where Ryker is?"

"I was just thinking I should do that."

"Thank you." She nodded to the officer. "I'm ready."

"Let's sit in the cruiser where it's warm."

That was fine with her. Once they were settled in the car, he opened his laptop. "All right. I'm Special Agent Hal Owens, by the way. I work with Caden."

"I'm Heather."

He smiled. "I know. Can you start at the beginning?"

Heather rubbed her head and started talking. Forty-five minutes later, she said, "The wounded one has a wife."

Hal looked up. "How do you know that?"

"He told me so. He tossed me the pill bottle. Oh . . . here." She dug it out of her pocket and, still wrapped in the toilet paper, passed it to him. "He said he kept them in his glove compartment because his wife gets migraines." She rubbed a hand over her eyes. "I'm not sure that means anything, but it's just one more random piece to add to this convoluted puzzle. And maybe there'll be some prints on the bottle."

"Any and all pieces are good." He continued to type, stopping when Caden rapped on the glass. Hal lowered the window. "Caden. Good. I'm going to email you the statement shortly. It should be in your inbox when you're ready to read it."

"Thanks, Hal."

"Sure thing."

"And Ms. Fontaine will need to work with a sketch artist. She saw them."

"I saw one of them," she said. "The other one was just a blur."

Heather climbed from the agent's car, shivering when the wind hit her in the face. She ducked her head against another gust as Travis walked up.

"Ready to work with the sketch artist?" he asked.

She shook her head. "I don't want to leave until I know Ryker's going to be okay. If it wasn't for him—"

"He's going to be fine," Travis said. "He's going to stay with the doc while he heals."

"What about Ryker's father? What if he decides to go after him again?"

"Ryker told them that the stabbing was an accident. That he was carrying the knife, tripped, and fell on it."

"I'm not surprised at the lie." How many times had she done the same thing as a teen? Like she'd told Ryker, she'd lied to her friends, her teachers, strangers on the street. If it had served her purpose to lie, she'd done so.

"We could tell the truth, but it's Ryker's word against ours. The good thing is, the sheriff's a smart man. He didn't buy Ryker's story and let me know he'd be watching Mr. Donahue—along with having his deputies do a lot of drive-bys. If Donahue steps out of line again in the slightest way, he'll find himself behind bars."

Well, that was something anyway. "I'm okay with him being behind bars."

"Yeah. That's the best-case scenario. I also left my number with them and told them if Ryker needed anything, they could call me."

Her heart stumbled a beat and she hugged him. "You're a good man, Travis Walker."

Now, she needed to get herself—and her emotions—under control before she made a complete fool out of herself. Then the terror of the last few hours rolled over her once more, and she decided she didn't care. She hugged him tighter, felt his hands on her shoulders. A sob ripped from her in spite of her effort to contain it.

"Let it go, Heather," he whispered against her ear. "It's okay to cry. I've got you."

"I don't cry," she muttered against his chest.

"Okay, then don't. But I've still got you."

And the dam broke. She let the tide of fear and worry and sheer exhaustion release in a torrent of sobs. And true to his promise, Travis simply held her. In fact, having Travis hold her was the only thing keeping her from shattering into a million pieces at his feet.

She wasn't sure how long they stood there, but she finally got her weeping under control, took one more shuddering breath, then stepped back and wiped her face. "Thanks."

His hand swept her hair away from her face. "It's okay, Heather. You needed to do that."

"I know. I'm mortified, but thanks."

A chuckle rumbled from him, but the humor didn't quite reach his eyes. "You can lean on me any time."

His words warmed her and chilled her all at the same time. Her leaning on others had gotten Asher shot. That weighed heavy on her, and she vowed to do her best to let the others help but find a way to keep them from harm as well.

Unfortunately, she had no idea what that looked like.

CHAPTER ELEVEN

"Where were you?" Donnie Little demanded. "Everything went exactly like we planned, and then you don't show up?" He pulled the knit cap from his head and raked a gloved hand through it. If his nerves got any tighter, they were going to implode. Why had he thought hooking up with this person was a good idea? Because he'd been blinded. Stupid and blind.

"I couldn't." A huff and a sound that reminded him of a low growl. "I can't believe this. If you'd grabbed her at her house that night, *none* of this would be an issue."

Donnie scoffed. "Well, that didn't work out, did it? The plan was to snatch her when the opportunity arose. So, that's what we arranged. *An opportunity*. Which I thought went relatively well for being a last-minute thing. Only Sam got shot—which was *not* planned—and then you don't show up? That's not what we agreed on. That's not how everything was supposed to go down." The silence on the other end of the line nearly sent Donnie's rage through the roof of the small, nasty bathroom twenty minutes from the little town he wished he'd never heard of. "Well?" he demanded.

The person's throat cleared. "Look, I'm sorry. I had a situation that I couldn't get out of. And who shot Sam?"

"The boyfriend she was riding with."

A pause. "Is Sam okay?"

"No, I don't think he is." Sam was the least of his worries right now.

"Okay. Okay. Let me think."

For the next thirty seconds, Donnie listened to pacing and muttering. Finally, the person said, "Why couldn't you just keep her there? A few more hours wouldn't have hurt."

"Are you not hearing me? She *escaped* and called the cops! There weren't supposed to be cops involved." He breathed in and pressed fingers to his burning eyes. "She saw our faces. My prints—and Sam's—are all over that cabin, of course. It's only a matter of time before they track us down, and I don't need this."

"Will you relax? You had the hood over her face, right? She couldn't see where she was going in the van. She won't be able to tell anyone where you were holding her, so no need to worry about prints."

"Are you really that stupid?" he snapped. "They'll search this area until they find it. And she *ran* from it, so she may have a pretty good idea how to lead someone *back* to it."

"It's pitch-black outside. She was panicked, not thinking clearly. Her only goal was to get away from you. I really don't think you have to worry about her being able to lead anyone back to it."

"This isn't good. In fact, this is very, very bad. You messed this up and now I need you to fix it."

A pause. "Unfortunately, I don't think there's going to be any fixing this. If you'd just—"

"If I'd just what? You were supposed to be there! If you'd been there like we agreed, none of this would have happened, and now I'm going to rot in prison for the rest of my life."

"Then I suppose you'd better disappear."

The words stunned Donnie into a moment of silence. "Disappear?" he finally managed to croak. "Seriously?"

"Yeah, seriously. This whole thing has gone sideways, and you didn't even do what I told you to do. You let her get away. So, consider us done. Again, you'd be smart to vanish while you can."

"Vanish? Are you even listening to yourself? You know what my life is. What about Liz and my kids? What about Sam's wife and kids? And Sam didn't even know this was the real deal. He thought it was all just a game and wound up taking a bullet. And you still owe me for killing that guy in Michigan."

"I'll wire you that money."

"When?"

"As soon as we hang up. Now, what about Sam? You didn't take him to a hospital, did you?"

"I'm not that stupid." He glanced back at the man on the floor and swallowed. "I think Sam's dead."

"Well, one less person to worry about talking then, right?"

What a cold-blooded— "Look, you know as well as I do that I can't just *vanish*! I need that money. My *kids* need that money for when I'm gone." For when he left them. He was sick of his wife, sick of his life. But he wouldn't leave his kids destitute. "I have kids. I'm not just disappearing."

"I don't know what to tell you. You didn't do your part, so you don't get the money."

If he could have reach through the line, he would have gladly wrapped his hands around the throat attached to the voice. "I'll go to the cops. I'll tell them everything."

"Then I guess you can say goodbye to Liz and your kids, can't you? Besides, what are you going to tell them? None of this connects back to me. Goodbye, Donnie. It's been a good ride, but don't bother contacting me again." The line went dead and Donnie gaped. With shaking fingers, he redialed the number, only to have it go straight to voice mail. The same thing happened the next three times he tried.

"No. No. No. This can't be happening." He refrained from throwing his own phone and stuffed it into the back pocket of his jeans. "What have I done?" he whispered to the empty room. He didn't mind killing. He didn't take pleasure in it like some people, but he didn't mind doing it. Especially if the price was right. But this . . .

He pulled his phone back out of his pocket, turned off his location services, and powered the device down. With another shaky breath, he inhaled the stale stench of the overused and undercleaned restroom and looked at Sam sprawled on the floor. Blood saturated the man's shirt.

Donnie nudged the nearest thigh with a toe. Sam didn't move. Idiot. Had to go and get himself shot, then let the woman get away. This was all his fault, and if he wasn't already dead, he soon would be. And as much as he hated to admit it, his "boss" was right. With Sam gone, there would be one less witness to spill everything.

Donnie drew in another deep breath, then regretted it when he gagged on the stench. However, his mind continued to grapple for a way out of this.

Now that he thought about it, if the cops did happen to find the cabin, his prints would be easy enough to explain away. So, maybe his "boss" was right. Maybe he was being overly worried about it. His tension eased a fraction.

He considered loading Sam's body into the back of the van but didn't have a clue what he'd do with it. He finally stepped over his former partner and friend, opened the bathroom door, locked it, and let it shut behind him. Wind and snowflakes battered his face, but he didn't even feel the chill. He was too busy trying to formulate a plan as he pulled his hoodie over his head and darted to the van.

Donnie needed that money he'd been promised. Desperately. If he couldn't get it one way, he'd have to get it another.

◻ ◻ ◻

While Heather wanted to forget the last few hours, she decided she needed to see the cabin where she'd been held. She had no idea why, but her gut pushed her to go.

The investigators were fine with her walking through it in the hopes that it would trigger another memory that might offer a clue to her kidnappers' identities. She wasn't so sure about that, but didn't bother arguing.

Heather climbed from the cruiser and pulled the blanket tight around her shoulders.

Travis walked with her to the front door. "You're sure you want to do this?"

"I'm sure. And no, I don't know why exactly." She paused. "I think, deep down, maybe I feel like this place is going to show up in my nightmares. Maybe by confronting it, seeing that it's simply a place, I can break any kind of stronghold my mind might be compelled to give it."

"I can understand that. I can see Brooke telling you to do it."

She laughed. "Funny, I think it was her voice in my head suggesting it." She drew in a deep breath. "How'd you find it?" she asked.

"Ryker."

"Of course."

One of the officers still on the scene opened the front door and led her inside. Caden hurried to join them in the living area.

"I haven't seen this area," she said. "I was kept in the back bedroom, so I don't know that I'll be able to add to anything I've already told you."

"That's all right," Travis said, "just take your time."

"They brought me in the front door, I guess, then led me through the house to the back. When they had me in the bedroom, they undid my hands and shut the door."

"And?"

"And I had a migraine." The pain still wasn't completely gone, but at least she didn't feel sick to her stomach. She looked around and noted it was a nice place.

For a prison.

Heather headed to the back bedroom, her anxiety growing with each step. The door was open. As soon as she stepped over the threshold, the terror rushed in.

Travis gripped her hand and squeezed. Her pulse slowed and her anxiety lessened. Travis. Always there when she needed him, whether she wanted to admit she needed him or not. "This is where they kept me." She frowned at the broken window. The curtains gusted according to the changes in the wind, and the temperature in the room had to be in the forties. A shiver skated up her spine. "It was awfully easy to get out of here. Wouldn't you think they would have kept me tied up or in a place that had bars on the windows?"

"Maybe they didn't think you'd try to escape, knowing you were in the middle of nowhere."

"But that's the thing," she said, "I *didn't* know." She moved to the window, then turned and looked back at the room. A baseball cap lay on the floor next to the bed. "That wasn't here when I was."

Caden motioned to one of the hovering officers, who hurried to bag the cap. "The crime scene unit has lifted all the prints they're going to, so we can start collecting items for DNA testing. They'll run this for hair and skin DNA right away," he said.

A tremor shook her, and Travis pulled her next to him. "You're safe now."

She nodded. "I know."

"You said you overheard them talking and that they were waiting for someone to show up."

"It's what it sounded like."

She found Caden studying her. "And you have no idea who that could be?"

Heather blew out a low breath. "I've been thinking about that."

"And?"

"Could you check and see where a man by the name of Roger Maddox is? I confirmed a few weeks ago that he's still in prison, but maybe we should double-check."

"Sure. Who's that?"

"My father."

○ ○ ○

"Your father?" Travis pulled her back into the den area of the cabin.

"Yes, I have one, you know."

He blinked. "Cute. Yes, I'm aware. I guess I just assumed he was out of the picture."

"Oh, he is. And has been for a long time, but he hates me and I wouldn't put it past him to come after me if he was out." She rubbed her eyes. "But he's not supposed to be out."

Caden dialed a number and pressed the phone to his ear as he walked out of the cabin.

"Why does your father hate you?"

"Because I'm the reason he's in prison—and hasn't made parole the last two times he was up for it."

"*You're* the reason?"

Heather eyed him. "Yes."

He wanted to hear that story. "Has he ever threatened you?"

"Not recently, but as he was led out of the courtroom, he made it clear he planned to come after me if he ever got out."

"What did you do to him?"

"I set him up to get arrested, but I can tell you about that later. For now, I just think it might be worth taking a closer look at him. Not necessarily his location—I know that—but who he's calling from prison or associating with there."

"When's the last time you saw him?" Travis asked.

"Before I deployed to Afghanistan five years ago. I showed up at his parole hearing and reminded them why they'd put him away in the first place—and the fact that my life would be in danger if he got out."

Travis pressed fingers against his eyes. "Why haven't you said anything before this?"

"Because, one, I checked and my father is still in prison. And two, I caught glimpses of the guy stalking me and it wasn't Roger. He looked slightly familiar, but I can't place him. However, since we now know these people are working for someone, it makes sense that it could be that Roger simply hired someone from prison." She paused. "Which would make sense because he's up for parole soon and if I'm not in the picture, he might actually have a chance of making it."

Caden stepped back inside. "Your father is definitely still in prison. I talked to one of the guards on his block, and he said Maddox hasn't had any uptick in activity or changes in behavior. That doesn't necessarily mean much if he's good at hiding that kind of thing."

She let out a shaky breath. "He'd be good at it."

"Then I think it might be wise to have a word with the man."

Heather crossed her arms and leaned forward. "I'll do it."

Travis raised a brow. "You want to see him?"

"*Want to?* No. Not particularly. But if you give me the questions to ask him, I'll be able to read him and see if he's lying."

Travis and Caden exchanged a glance, and Heather narrowed her eyes. "Brooke told me about that bro language stuff. If Asher and Gavin don't get to do it, neither do you two."

Travis laughed in spite of the seriousness of the moment. He and the other guys had known each other for so long, they could often communicate simply with a look. Brooke had been known to call them out on it. Apparently, she'd influenced the other ladies as well. "No bro language. We're just concerned."

"I know. I am too. We all know that I have control issues, so just humor me, okay? Confronting him will help me feel like I'm . . . being proactive. Standing up for myself rather than being a victim."

"You're not a victim, Heather."

"No, not anymore. Because I refuse to be one. So . . . when do we go see Roger?"

"I'll set it up," Caden said, "and we can head over there first thing in the morning if you want to."

"Sure."

"I'd say for now, you meet with the sketch artist and get that composite done. The faster we can get that to news outlets, the faster we'll catch these guys."

"That's fine." She rubbed her eyes. "So, sketch artist now. Sleep. Then prison in the morning, then my house. Right?"

"If you have the energy for that schedule."

"I'll find the energy."

"You need to sleep, Heather, and start recovering. This was a very traumatic thing for you. For all of us."

"I know." She grimaced. "The truth is, I doubt I'll sleep much, but I suppose I should try."

Travis caught her eye and could see the thought of the inevitable nightmares was more than she could deal with at the moment.

As they were walking out to the vehicle, he took her hand and leaned over. "You're strong, Heather, you can do this. And you can sleep too."

"I'm glad you think so. I guess eventually I'll find out. For now, adrenaline is keeping me going."

Yep. And when she crashed, he planned on being there to catch her.

CHAPTER TWELVE

Saturday morning
9:00AM

The prison loomed large and imposing, surrounded by chain-link fence, barbed wire, and patrolling guards. She'd been right. Sleep had been elusive, even though a female police officer had stayed in the room with her, and Gavin and Travis had been in the connecting room with the door open. After two hours with the sketch artist, she'd been wired, doubts about her descriptions plaguing her. But she'd dutifully climbed into bed a little after three in the morning and shut her eyes.

At 7:30 this morning, she'd never been so glad to have to get up and get ready for the day.

Only now this.

Heather pressed a hand against her churning stomach.

Throwing up wasn't an option. The first two times she'd attended Roger's parole hearings, she'd puked in the ladies' room after each visit. Today, flanked by Caden, Gavin, and Travis, she swallowed hard, walked up the concrete steps, and through the glass doors of the prison.

Stale metallic air hit her in the face, and she did her best to breathe through her mouth without being obvious about it.

Gavin stopped just outside the doors. "I'll be out here watching the vehicles. I don't want anyone getting near them." He'd also make sure no one had followed them.

After making their way through security, they were led to a private visiting area where Heather took a seat at the rectangular table. She wasn't so sure it was a good idea to meet her father without a wall of glass between them, but with Caden and Travis in the same room, she felt like it would be doable.

Besides, if Roger was on one side, he could simply hang up and walk out if he decided he didn't like the tone of the conversation. At least this way, it would be a little harder to get away from her.

The door clanged open, and Roger walked in, his wrists and legs shackled. When he saw her and the two men, he paused as though rethinking his agreement to meet with her. He'd aged a lot since she'd last laid eyes on him. His gaze never left her. "I'm so scary you need two bodyguards?"

"Hello to you too, Roger. And they're not because of you." At least not completely.

He snorted, then shuffled to the table and dropped into the nearest chair. "I don't have a parole hearing for you to sabotage, so what's this all about?"

No doubt he'd thought about refusing to see her, but since she'd never reached out to him before, it was most likely his curiosity had gotten the best of him. "Someone's trying to kill me. I need to know if you're behind it."

For a moment he stared, then laughed. Waves of laughter that brought tears to his eyes. Heather sat in stony silence, knowing her expression gave away nothing of her inner turmoil. She'd learned how to do that at an early age. Yet another thing that had only enraged him.

He finally calmed down and wiped his eyes. "Well, that's karma, ain't it?"

"Not really. Just a lowlife who seems to have something against me. You were the first person I thought of."

"Lowlife, huh?" He sniffed. "You ever think it could have something to do with you trying to save that terrorist punk?"

Rage bubbled beneath the surface. From the corner of her eye, she caught Travis's hand fisted at his side. For her. Some of her ire fizzled. "Yes, I've thought about it. This doesn't have anything to do with that."

"How do you know about the video?" Caden asked.

Roger rolled his eyes. "This is prison, not the Sahara." He looked back at Heather. "How do you know it doesn't have anything to do with the video?"

"I guess I don't for sure," she said, "but that's not where the leads are taking us."

"And they're bringing you here?"

"It was worth asking."

"You believe me?"

"Yes."

His brows rose. "Oh."

She stood. "He doesn't have anything to do with the attempts on my life."

"How do you know?" Travis asked.

"Because I always know when he's lying. He has a tell."

Her father huffed a laugh. "I do not."

"Sure you do."

"Then what is it?"

Heather simply smiled and walked to the door.

Roger stood, his chains clanking. "Hey! What is it?"

Caden and Travis fell in behind her. The guard opened the door.

Roger thumped the table. "Tell me!"

She turned. "Just so you know, I really do wish things were different between us."

That silenced him and Heather thought she saw a brief flicker of regret in his blue eyes. Then it was gone. If it was ever there.

"What's my tell!"

The guard shut the door and Heather blew out a low breath. However, she noted that her stomach stayed in place. Interesting.

Travis took her hand, and she curled her fingers around his, relishing the feel of his rough palm against hers. He might not realize it, but the little things he did to offer her comfort gave her strength. "What's his tell?"

"He blinks his left eye just before he lies. When I asked him if he was the one trying to kill me, it took him by surprise and he simply stared at me before laughing. He doesn't know anything."

Once they were back in his truck with Caden behind them and Gavin in front, he shot her a hooded look. "I couldn't tell if you were rattled or not."

"I was."

"You hid it well."

"It's something you learn in med school since there are times you never want a patient to be able to read your face. However, I'd already had a few lessons from Roger."

"Why do you call him Roger?"

"He doesn't deserve the title 'dad.'" The words slipped past her filters and she sighed. "That sounds harsh, I know, but truly, he's never been a father to me, and I've never been able to bring myself to use that word with him. At least not past the age of nine."

"I can see that."

"I sometimes refer to him as 'my father' when discussing him with other people, but to his face, he's Roger."

He stopped at a red light, then turned to study her. Long enough that she wanted to squirm.

"What is it?"

"Just thinking."

"About?" She glanced away. "The light's green."

He pressed the gas and kept his eyes on the road, but asked, "So . . . how did you become you? A doctor. A compassionate human being who cares about others?"

"Funny. I asked Ryker almost the same question as we were running through the woods." She paused to find the words to explain. "I tend to learn by example, then figure out if it's a good example or a bad one. I knew Roger was definitely a bad one, so I did my best to be the exact opposite of his personality. He treated people terribly, I tried to exhibit thoughtfulness and kindness. He hated God, so I learned as much as I could about God and grew to love him—and view him as the example of what a father should be. Roger loved money, I decided to give away as much as I could. The list is endless, right down to the fact that Roger loved working out, lifting weights, and using that acquired strength against anyone who got in his way."

"That's why you don't like to exercise!"

"My concession to exercise is the stairs at work whenever possible. And that's usually several flights multiple times a day. I know I need to do something active to stay healthy—I won't let him take that from me as well—but setting foot in a gym probably isn't in my future." Heather grimaced. "I don't know if I can blame that one on him, but I'm happy to do so."

He laughed and took the next left, following Gavin.

She yawned. "You know, just because you have a bad start in life doesn't mean you have to have a bad finish."

"That's a great attitude."

"Hmm . . . well, I didn't always have it, but all that matters is that I finally got it." Another yawn hit her. Riding in the car always made her sleepy—as long as she didn't have a hood over her head and was terrified she was going to die.

"Why don't you rest your eyes for a few minutes?" Travis said. "We've got another thirty minutes or so before we get there."

"I'm all right."

"Heather, take the opportunity to rest."

"What about you? I know you didn't sleep much last night."

"Gavin, Caden, and I took turns on guard duty. I actually got a few hours of good sleep."

"I'm glad someone did."

He shot her a knowing look. "Exactly."

She grimaced. "Fine. You're right. I won't sleep, but I'll close my eyes." Thirty minutes. There was no way she'd allow herself to fall asleep, because all the talking about her father brought back many unpleasant memories, while the thought of walking into her house might just bring on a few nightmares.

ㅁ ㅁ ㅁ

Travis pulled to a stop at the curb of Heather's house and cut the engine. Gavin and Caden flanked his truck with their vehicles. He glanced at his sleeping passenger and hated the thought of waking her.

Then again, her furrowed brow and occasional stifled whimper didn't suggest that she was resting all that well. And who could blame her?

Travis touched her arm, and she jerked, eyes snapping open, instantly ready for battle.

"Hey," he said, "it's just me."

She wilted, the nightmare fading from her gaze. "Did I cry out?"

"No. You were just really restless."

She gave a short nod, and he didn't discern any hint of self-consciousness that he'd witnessed her in such a vulnerable state.

Caden stepped up to the window. "Stay here while we clear the place. It looks undisturbed from here, but . . ."

Heather waved a hand in understanding, and Caden punched in the code to her alarm system. When her garage door went up, she let out a long sigh. "You do realize that I'm having trouble processing that my home needs to be cleared before I enter it. Even after everything. It's just . . . surreal."

"Yeah. I'm sorry about that. Better safe than . . . not."

"I know. I'm exhausted. All I want to do is climb in bed and pull the covers over my head." She paused. "Maybe a bed in a hotel, though. I don't know if I'll be able to sleep here anytime soon."

"I can understand that." He let out a slow breath. "Want to see how you feel once you're inside?"

"Maybe. Yeah. I can do that." She pressed her lips together, her eyes on the garage. "I have dreams," she said. "I guess you noticed."

"I did."

"It's mostly when I'm stressed that they find their way to the surface."

"I can't imagine what you'd be stressed about."

She shot him a small smile. "Right."

"Seriously. It happens to a lot of people. My cousin's husband used to be a cop. Four years ago, he had to shoot a guy who pulled a gun on him. He says he still dreams about that night."

"I'm sorry. That's an awful thing to have to do." She fell silent for a moment. She put her hand on the handle but didn't open the door. "What's taking him so long?"

"He's being careful. Hey." He waited until her eyes met his. "I hope this isn't a dumb question in light of the circumstances, but what's wrong—besides the obvious?"

Her lips flattened and she turned to gaze at her home once more. "It's my house, but it's not now."

"Sorry?"

She jabbed a finger at her home. "That *looks* like my house, but it doesn't *feel* like mine anymore. It feels . . . weird. And . . . scary. And not a place I want to be." She paused. "I feel like things are rolling out of control and I don't know how to make it stop. And it's just about to send me over the edge."

That was a real struggle for her to admit and he'd confess he was a bit surprised that she did. "Are you sure someone was in there? Because when we stopped by to look for you, everything appeared fine."

She scowled. "I'm sure. It was little stuff. Subtle things that you wouldn't realize were out of place, but yes, someone was definitely there."

When Caden appeared at the front door and waved a hand, Heather pushed out of the truck and Travis did the same. She shoved her blonde hair from her face, and the wind whipped it right back into her eyes. "He doesn't look very happy," she said.

"No, he doesn't." Travis glanced around the area. After everything that had happened, he wouldn't be surprised to see someone lurking in the bushes—or catch sight of a sniper rifle aimed her way. He stayed as close to her as possible, shielding her from anyone who might be out of his visual range.

She gave him a distracted glance as she stepped into her kitchen.

Caden stopped her. "Prepare yourself. It's been tossed," he said. "Mostly the den and the bedrooms."

"What?" Heather gaped at him for a brief moment, then pushed past him.

"Heather, wait!" Travis went after her and caught her at the doorway. "Don't go rushing in there. It's a crime scene."

Caden caught up to them. "I've already called the local police. They're on the way."

"They'll take prints and stuff?" Heather asked.

"If they don't, I will. I can't tell that anything was stolen. Looks more like the person was looking for something."

"But . . . what?" Heather asked. "I don't have anything worth stealing except for a few electronics."

"Television was still there and so was your laptop. That's why I think the person was looking for something. This wasn't just a thief breaking in to find something to pawn."

"A stalker would go for something more personal," Travis said, "if he was looking for a . . . souvenir."

She grimaced and anger surged at the invasion of her life.

When the officers arrived, they introduced themselves as Billy Norman and Marie Howell, then walked with Heather into the den. Travis followed silently. The room was a mess. Drawers pulled and dumped, sofa cushions on the floor.

Her breath caught and Travis touched her arm. She ignored him and continued to study her living area, her spine growing more stiff with each passing second. "I don't see anything missing in here." She spun and beelined for the refrigerator, stopping in front of it. "It's really not there."

"The picture?"

She nodded and wrapped her arms around her middle.

"I told you it wasn't here when we searched your home shortly after you disappeared."

"Right. So, the person who was here that night took it."

"And returned to do this after we'd already come here looking for you," Travis said.

"Why is it still cold in here?" Heather muttered.

"You pay the bill?" Gavin asked from the doorway. Officer Norman waited behind him, eyes bouncing from one person to the next.

"Of course," Heather said. "It's on autopay."

Gavin headed for the thermostat, and Travis walked through the kitchen into the den. He paused, returned to the kitchen, then back to the den.

Heather followed him this time. "What is it?"

"It's noticeably colder in here than the kitchen. By several degrees."

Gavin nodded. "The thermostat's set on seventy. The door to your bedroom was closed, and when I went in there, it was comfortably warm—also trashed, but warm. I don't think anything's wrong with your furnace."

"Great." She paused. "I never shut my bedroom door. When I got home that night, besides the chill in the house throwing me off, when I walked toward the hallway, my bedroom door was cracked. I knew I hadn't left it that way, so that meant someone had been in there—or still was."

Travis squeezed her hand. "So you left."

"In a hurry. I still don't know how the person got in without setting off my alarm, though. I never got a notification on my phone about it being disarmed."

"I might have an answer for you." Travis stepped toward the French doors that led to her deck and looked out. Just beyond the deck was a backyard lined with trees that hid a wrought iron fence encircling the property. "The wind is really blowing out there today."

"You a weatherman now?" Caden asked.

"Shut up." Travis didn't change his tone from the calm thoughtfulness he'd started with. "Listen for a second."

They fell quiet. Then Gavin frowned. Cocked his head. "Hey, you hear that?"

Travis nodded. "A low whistle?"

Heather frowned. "I've never noticed that before. Where's that coming from?"

"Here." Travis stepped left and rapped on the window next to the French doors. He placed a hand on the edge of the glass. Cold air blasted his palm. "Wow. Feel that."

Heather stepped over to mimic him. She gasped. "What in the world?"

Travis dropped to his knees to study the pane. What he saw chilled him more than the cold air. "Well, I know how your intruder got in without setting off the alarm."

"What?"

"So, your windows are armed, but the alarm will go off only if the frame connection is broken. Your intruder knew that and decided to be clever. Gavin, you got your gloves on you?"

"Of course."

"Put them on and go outside and catch the pane."

Gavin met his eyes and understanding dawned. While Travis pulled a glove onto his right hand, Gavin slipped out the door and around to stand with his hand next to the glass. Travis gave it a light tap and the pane landed safely in Gavin's outstretched hand.

CHAPTER THIRTEEN

Heather gaped. "Someone cut the pane of glass out of my window and then just stuck it back in there?"

Even the two officers, still patiently waiting for her to finish walking through the rest of her house, had raised their brows.

"Yep." Gavin readjusted the pane back into place, then rejoined them. "We'll need to get that bagged and see if someone can get some prints off of it."

"I'll do it." Officer Howell headed to get the items she'd need.

"You have anything in your garage we can use to cover the window?" Caden asked.

"I think so," Heather said. "But you don't have to worry about that. I can take care of it."

He narrowed his eyes at her, and she held her hands up in surrender.

"That would be wonderful. Thank you." It was hard to let someone else do for her. But she was going to have to try. "There's some plywood, I think. Or we can use some of the plastic left over from when I painted my kitchen."

"I'll get the plastic for now. Hopefully we can get someone out here to fix the window before too long."

Caden left and Heather shook her head. "This is unbelievable," she muttered. She ran a hand over her hair and pulled the strands into a loose ponytail at the base of her neck. "I noticed the chill when I got home that night." She closed her eyes, going back to the moment she'd stepped into her house from the party. "It was colder in here. Much colder. I checked the thermostat and walked through the house. Most of it anyway." She paused and opened her eyes. "The windowpane had to have been out when I got here." A shiver danced up her spine. "But wouldn't I have noticed a missing window?"

"Maybe," Travis said. "Maybe not. What was your state of mind when you got home?"

Heather grimaced. "I was . . . unsettled, irritated. Angry at myself for a few things. But I noticed the chill as soon as I walked in the door."

"So you were distracted, and your curtains were closed. Easy to miss, especially since you weren't here long."

Heather rubbed a hand over her face. "It doesn't matter at this point. It's clear that whoever took it out had to have been here when I got home."

"Which means it's a good thing you left when you did."

"My nerves were screaming at me. I had to get away. I grabbed some cash I had hidden in my kitchen cabinet and bolted. I hit the ATM for more once I decided no one had followed me."

Travis narrowed his eyes. "And you didn't call the cops about the picture."

Her gaze slid to the refrigerator. "Yes. The one that's not there anymore."

"The person who took it had to know someone would come looking for you," Travis said. "Guess they didn't want anyone else seeing it."

"Guess not."

"Excuse me," Officer Norman interrupted. "I'm actually finding all of this fascinating, but do you think we could finish the walk-thru?"

Heather blinked. "I'm sorry. Of course." The officer led the way to her bedroom. Travis and Gavin followed. The door was now open, and she entered the room that had once been her haven. Her escape from the pressures of a high-stress job. Someone had been in here when she'd arrived home from the party that night. What if she'd ignored her instincts? Would she have found the person?

Probably.

And might not have lived to talk about it.

Travis stepped up behind her.

"He was trying to isolate me," she said, her voice low. "He's been following me, letting me catch a glimpse of him every now and then. Making sure I was off my game, trying to unsettle me, make me think I was crazy or overreacting. Then he planned to strike. Isn't that what stalkers try to do to their victims?"

"Sometimes."

"It worked. I fell for it. He didn't want me asking for help, so he threatened my friends." She paused. "But you know what's really scary? He knew I wouldn't involve you—the people I was close to. Which means he's gotten to know me." How long had he been watching her before planning to break into her house?

"But he didn't know you'd run."

She stilled. "No. He expected me to walk into my bedroom." A shudder rippled through her at the images that sprang to mind.

"But you didn't." He rubbed a hand up and down her arm, and Heather took comfort in the contact.

"So, now that I'm back—and his little attempt to snatch me failed—I guess I get to keep looking over my shoulder."

"Well, the good thing is, now you have other people looking over it too."

She swallowed the sudden surge of emotion and tried to get everything back into the neat little mental box where she kept things like fear, worry, and anger. "I appreciate that." She pointed. "Someone opened the drawers and didn't close them all the way. I'd never leave them like that."

Officer Howell nodded to her partner. "Let's dust this room and the refrigerator for prints, along with the window frame and the French doors. I brought the kit in when I got the bag for the windowpane."

"I'll get it," Officer Norman said.

Caden's phone rang as Travis and Gavin escorted her from the house back to wait near his truck.

"So, if I lost my stalker by running, how did he find me after this long?"

Travis rubbed a hand over his chin. "Had to be Caden. Somehow, he led them to you."

A throat clearing caught her attention. Caden stood in the doorway. "I didn't lead them to you. Travis did." He held up a small button-shaped item clutched between gloved forefinger and thumb.

Travis sucked in an audible breath. "What?"

"I don't know how this person knew you'd be the one to track her down, but this is how they found her."

"You got that off of my truck?"

"I did." He held out his other hand, palm up. Two more matching trackers rested there. "And these off of Gavin's and mine."

"So it could have been you when you found her," Travis said.

"Nope." He looked at Heather. "I followed the GPS location from your car and spotted you at the hotel, but I didn't drive this vehicle. I was in my personal ride. There's no tracker on it. I had Zane go by and check it." Zane Pierce, Caden's partner.

Heather blew out a low breath. "So, who knows me well enough to know which of my friends' vehicles to track?"

○ ○ ○

The officers finally left after passing out their cards and offering their services should they be needed for anything. Travis asked them to drive by Heather's house on a more regular basis, and they promised to do so.

By the time Caden finished calling everyone else, they'd discovered they weren't the only ones who'd been tracked. "Sarah and Brooke found theirs," he said. "One was on Asher's car as well. On the off chance this person was watching the night of the party and keeping track of who Heather's been hanging out with, I called Gina. She found one on her vehicle too."

"Wait," Heather said, "then wouldn't there have been one on mine?"

"No, I had Zane check yours. It was clean. I don't think whoever it was put the trackers on the vehicles until later—but they sure took note of who you spent time with and which vehicles to target. They probably figured one of us would locate you."

"Maybe," she said, her gaze locking on his. "Unless, like you, he was just watching, letting me get comfortable."

Travis could see that happening. "And planning?"

She nodded. "I mean, it has to take a while to set up a kidnapping, right?"

"Yes," he said slowly. "But I never saw anyone watching you."

"Maybe they weren't. Maybe they didn't have to."

"Meaning they knew where you were and took the time to get everything arranged?"

"That's one scenario. But it failed." She chewed her bottom lip. "Trying to run me off the road wasn't the brightest idea in the box." She paused and tilted her head, brow furrowed. "I wonder if I was supposed to just kind of slide off the road and into the ditch instead of actually going over the side in a move that could kill me."

"So they could grab you? Makes sense." He rubbed his chin. "But the gunshots . . ."

"The bullets came close, that's true, but I think the person was aiming more for you than me."

Travis pondered that idea. "Okay, so they were trying to get me out of the picture in order to grab you?"

"It kind of makes sense in light of the fact that they did manage to kidnap me just a little while later—which brings up a whole slew of other questions. But for the moment, where my confusion comes in is that they could have killed me if that had been the goal."

"But they didn't mind taking out others who stood in their way of snatching you."

"Right."

"There's logic behind that."

"Thanks."

"So, let's talk about how they knew where to set the explosives," Caden said. His phone rang. "Hold that thought—or discuss it while I get this." He stepped into the kitchen.

"It had to start from the sheriff's office," Gavin said. "Or the attackers were just quick. Doesn't take long to bury an IED or set it off remotely when you're ready."

Travis nodded. "We know there were at least two men involved. One could have been watching the route we were going to take—which wouldn't be hard to figure out, even though we didn't take a direct one."

"Exactly." Gavin narrowed his eyes. "There are only a few ways out of that town, and whoever was watching Heather would know she was headed home and could simply radio ahead to the other person."

"So," Heather said, "not so hard to figure out after all. They simply watched to figure out where we'd eventually wind up to hit the interstate and picked a rather remote area along the way to set the explosive."

Gavin pursed his lips. "I think it sounds feasible."

"To me too," Caden said from the doorway. "Well, we know who the cabin belongs to. It's in the name of a woman named Tammy Powers."

"Who's Tammy Powers?" Travis asked.

"That's what we're trying to find out. Agents are on the way to her home as we speak."

Heather raised a brow. "She has two homes?"

He nodded. "The cabin is a weekend getaway place. Her primary residence—where she is now—is located about an hour from here. She said she's clueless who could have been in the cabin, but there's no alarm system and the door has a flimsy lock. It wouldn't have been hard for them to break in."

"But"—Heather frowned—"how'd they even know about it?"

"It's listed on a few rental sites," Caden said. "Or someone could have simply scoped the area and picked one that was empty." His phone rang and he snatched it to his ear. "Caden here." Travis and the others fell silent when Caden's eyes snapped up to his. "Right. Got it. We'll be there in about an hour." He hung up. "They found your wounded kidnapper on the floor of a gas station bathroom about an hour ago. EMS transported him to the same hospital where Asher is. Unfortunately, the guy's in rough shape and not really expected to live."

"They have a name?"

"No. There's no ID on him and he's obviously not talking right now. We'll get some prints and see if we can figure out who he is—and if they match up to the prints at the cabin. The crime scene unit said they pulled about ten different ones they'll need to run."

"Speaking of prints," Heather said, "have you heard anything about the ones off the pill bottle I gave to the agent?"

"Not yet, but I'll check on that."

"I think," Travis said, "you should come home with me until we can put all of the pieces of this puzzle together and figure out who your stalker-slash-kidnapper is. They might have one, but there's still another one out there."

She blinked at him. "Go home with you?"

"After we stop by the hospital to see if your kidnapper wakes up and is able to talk."

Caden nodded. "That might not be a bad idea. Are y'all ready to head out in about fifteen minutes?"

"If we can get there without getting shot at or blown up," Heather muttered.

Caden's lips twisted into a humorless smile. "I'm getting ready to make sure that's all arranged." He glanced at Travis, then back to Heather. "We have time for you to pack a suitcase. Sounds like you're going to be gone for a while."

CHAPTER FOURTEEN

Heather rode to the hospital in silence, fighting fatigue and the effects of everything that had happened over the last couple of days. Her snatches of sleep here and there hadn't been enough. She didn't ever remember being this tired—not even in med school.

Travis drove and a helicopter churned overhead below the gray clouds. "I wonder how many favors Caden had to call in to get that bird out here so fast."

"I think he has quite a reserve of them built up," Gavin said from the back seat, "so I wouldn't worry too much about it."

"Good to know." She leaned her head against the seat and closed her eyes. For the first time in weeks, in spite of her exhaustion, she actually felt safe. "How's Ryker?" she asked Travis. "Have you heard?"

"I got a text from Dr. Colson while you were packing. You're welcome to read it if you want."

"Sure." She snagged his phone from the vent clip and he gave her his passcode. She read the text aloud.

Ryker is doing well. Back in bed with a full stomach and a dose of Toradol. He's sleeping at the moment. Ryker's dad has gone missing.

No one seems to know where he is and Ryker's
worried about him.

"Having the man disappear might not be a bad thing," Travis said.

"Agreed, but he'll show back up. They always do." She slipped the phone onto the holder. "Dr. Colson says he'll touch base if anything changes, but for now everything is fine."

"For now. I'm just hoping it stays that way."

An hour later, Travis pulled into the parking lot of the hospital and rolled as close to the entrance as they could, then checked his phone. "Caden got the all clear from the chopper. No one followed us."

"Good," Gavin said. "I'll walk inside with her while you park the car."

Once inside the hospital, Gavin hovered, his stance tense in spite of Caden's reassurance that they hadn't been followed. Heather appreciated his vigilance but stepped to the side and scanned the area.

Sick children, worried parents, a young man with a bloodied towel wrapped around his hand—all waited for their turn to go back through the double doors. But no one who looked like they wanted to do her harm.

Still . . .

She kept her back against the wall and her eyes on the occupants of the area until Travis stepped inside. A fine white powder covered his black beanie hat.

"It's snowing?"

"Yep. Started as soon as I parked."

Caden appeared too. "The medicine bottle you gave the agent has been shipped off and is being processed for prints," he said, brushing flakes from his hair. "They were backed up, but I tried to push things along a little faster, so . . . we wait. On that anyway. I'm going to head up to get a status update on our John Doe."

Gavin nodded. "We'll go see Asher, then join you if that's all right with everyone."

"Sounds good to me," Heather said. She was just as anxious as the rest of them to see their friend. And Brooke. Would she still be speaking to her? Heather gave a mental scoff at the stupid question. Of course she would. Brooke wouldn't blame Heather for Asher being hurt. The only person who blamed Heather was Heather. She said a short prayer for wisdom instead of wasting time questioning why all this was happening.

"Heather?"

She jerked. Travis was looking at her, concern stamped on his features. "Right. I'm coming." She fell into step next to Travis while Gavin brought up the rear. Caden headed for the elevator at the end of the hall.

On Asher's floor, they found Brooke at the nurses' station filling a cup of ice water from the cooler.

Brooke gasped, passed the cup to Travis, and threw her arms around Heather to pull her into a breath-stealing hug. "You're okay."

Heather's eyes filled, and she blinked the tears away, grappling to corral her emotions once again. "I'm sorry, Brooke."

"Stop it." Brooke stepped back and looked Heather in the eye. "I mean it."

Heather nodded and smoothed her features. "Thank you."

"Now come say hey, but I'll warn you, he's antsy and ready to go home."

"When does he get to do that?" Gavin asked.

"Probably tomorrow. He lost a lot of blood so they're monitoring him pretty closely. Fortunately, I'm a universal donor, so I get to hold over his head the great sacrifice that I made to help save his life."

Heather forced a smile. She wasn't able to appreciate jokes about that yet. Brooke noticed, cleared her throat, and led the way to Asher's room.

He was sitting up in bed, pale and drawn, but with a smile on his face at their entrance. "Heather. Boy, am I glad to see you healthy and whole."

"I don't know what to say, Asher." Heather stepped forward and gave him a gentle hug.

Asher gave her hand a squeeze. "Nothing to say. All that matters is you're okay."

Heather nodded and cleared her throat. "So . . . you've got a good doctor?"

"I'm still alive. I'm assuming that says something about his skills."

"Cute." She glanced around.

Asher's gaze traveled from hers to the men behind her. "The gang's all here, minus Caden."

"Sarah and Gina went down to grab a bite to eat," Brooke said. "They'll be back shortly."

"Gina came too?"

"Yes. She was with Sarah and me when we got the call. Gina's still having a tough time, so we're all trying to be there as much as possible for her."

"Of course."

"But Sarah only has a couple of hours before she has to head over to do an interview with the mayor," Gavin said.

Asher cleared his throat and Brooke handed him the cup of water. After he took a sip, he raked a hand through his mussed hair. "How'd they know we were going to be there?"

"We've discussed that," Travis said. "Still don't have a real answer, just some speculation."

"Caden's working on it," Gavin said. "He and Zane were assigned the case."

Asher nodded. "Brooke told me."

For the next thirty minutes, they questioned Heather about who could be behind the attempts on her life—and if they were really attempts to kill her or simply take her. While rehashing the experience, Heather watched Asher for signs of fatigue. When his eyelids began to droop and he had to force them to stay open, she stood. "I think it's time for us to let Asher get some more rest."

He frowned. "All I've been doing is resting."

"Quit grumbling, hon," Brooke said. "Rest helps you heal."

"Aw, Brooke . . ."

She cocked an eyebrow. "I'll lay beside you and you can put your head on my shoulder."

Asher raised a brow and pointed to the door. "Right. Y'all need to leave so I can get some more rest." He turned and gave Heather a wink before pasting an obedient expression on his face.

Gavin snorted and Heather smothered a giggle. Brooke rolled her eyes and opened the door. They filed out and Brooke followed. When the door shut behind them, her amusement faded and tears filled her eyes, but she smiled through them. "Thanks for coming by. He was getting really restless. Now that he's had some company—and seen for himself that Heather is safe—he'll rest better."

Travis pulled his phone from his pocket. "Sorry, this thing's been going off for the last two or three minutes. I'd better check it." He glanced at the screen.

"Everything okay?" Brooke asked.

"Yeah. It's just Caden letting me know that our mystery man kidnapper has a name."

"They got the prints back that fast?" Heather asked.

"No, his wife identified him."

Heather frowned. "How'd they find her?"

"Not sure. Caden will fill us in when we get there."

"Go on," Brooke said. "Once Asher's asleep, I'll catch up on some reports I'm behind on writing or Sarah and Gina will keep me company before Sarah has to leave." She blew them a kiss and stepped back into her husband's room.

○ ○ ○

Heather yawned and fought the urge to pace a rut in the tile in front of the nurses' station, refusing to let her agitation show so clearly. Not while Travis leaned against the counter, hands jammed into his pockets, looking alert and watchful, but a lot more patient than she was.

She fought another yawn and dropped into the nearest chair, which happened to be just outside the kidnapper's room. She clasped her fingers in front of her . . . and waited. For all of thirty seconds. "Is he going to come out and tell us what's going on or what?"

"He will." He eyed her with an expression she couldn't quite put her finger on.

"What?"

He raised a brow. "What?"

"You're looking at me like I'm a bug under a microscope."

"Oh. Sorry. It's just I'm seeing a new side of you, and while I hate the circumstances, I have to say it's kind of interesting."

Her jaw swung loose for a fraction of a second before she snapped it shut. "What on earth are you talking about?"

He shrugged. "You're usually so calm and collected, it's intimidating."

She intimidated *him*? "Are you sure you didn't hit your head or something in all the chaos?"

He sputtered on a laugh. "I'm sure." Sobering, he shook his head. "Maybe *intimidating* is the wrong word, but you just never seemed quite human to me. Now, you're more *approachable*, I guess."

Uncertainty hit her. "Oh." What was she supposed to say to that? He hadn't thought her approachable? "What does that even mean?"

"It means . . . well, it's not like it's some kind of personality flaw. It's just how you come across."

"And I come across as intimidating and unapproachable?"

"No." He stopped. "Well, um . . . yeah. Somewhat. A little

unapproachable. Maybe a lot intimidating. It's not a bad thing," he rushed to reassure her, "but I think it's just because you're a doctor and you're used to barking orders."

She straightened. "I *bark* orders?"

Travis cleared his throat and pointed to the door. "You know what? I'm just gonna see if—"

The door to the room opened and Caden stepped out. "Sorry that took so long."

"I'm not," Heather said with narrowed eyes focused on Travis. "I learned a few things."

"About?"

"Something I'll deal with later." She turned her gaze to Caden. "What did you find out?"

"Your kidnapper's name is Samuel Powers."

She blinked.

"Wait a minute," Travis said. "The woman who owns the cabin is Tammy Powers. That can't be a coincidence."

"It's not. She's Sam's wife."

"His wife?" Heather asked. "He took me to a cabin owned by his *wife*? Is it just me or is that incredibly—"

"Stupid?" Caden asked.

"Sure," she said, "we'll go with that."

"Yes, stupid to you and me. But where's the rule that says all criminals have to be smart? That's why the majority of them get caught without too much of a problem. However, until Mr. Powers wakes up and talks to us, we'll just have to wonder why he'd do that. Zane's working on a warrant for the house. We'll search it and see if anything turns up."

"I'm sure his wife is going to love that," Heather muttered.

"I'm planning on being there during the search. Why don't you two go on to Travis's place, and I'll call when I learn something."

Heather frowned. "Did they say how long it might possibly be before Mr. Powers regains consciousness?"

"The doctor seemed hopeful by tomorrow morning. They had

to pump him full of donor blood and are keeping him sedated for now. Apparently, when EMS brought him in, he woke up briefly and was extremely agitated."

"Of course," Heather said. "Sedated makes sense. He needs to heal for a bit before they bring him out of it. If he wakes up and realizes he's under arrest, he could get violent and break open that surgical site." She drew in a breath and turned to Travis. "All right. I'm ready when you are."

Travis nodded. "When do you plan to search the home?"

"Depends on when the judge signs the warrant, but I'm guessing in a couple of hours. By the time you get to your place, I might have something for you. Hopefully a location on the second kidnapper and whoever hired them to snatch you. Once we find the second one and have them both in custody, we can play them against each other. Maybe one of them will spill how they knew where to plant that explosive."

Heather rubbed her eyes. "Fine. If I don't get some rest, I'm not going to be good for anything anyway." And she was used to long hours and sleepless nights.

Travis clasped her hand. "Come on. We'll come back in the morning—or whenever we learn that he's awake."

She chewed on her bottom lip, indecisive, her gaze bouncing between the two men.

"Heather," Caden said, "let us do our job. Your being here isn't going to hurry things along or change anything. You know I can't let you see the man until after we've finished questioning him anyway."

She grimaced. "I know."

"Then go get some rest and I'll catch you two up when I'm able."

Heather let out a low groan. "Okay, fine."

Travis led her toward the elevator. Heather was fine with the thought of getting some rest. Maybe once she could think straight, she'd be able to put all the pieces together for a clear picture on why someone was after her.

Maybe.

○ ○ ○

Caden met Zane on the front porch of the Powerses' middle-class home. It was a traditional two-story brick house that could use some attention to the yard. A soccer ball and a bicycle graced the driveway. Mrs. Powers was at the hospital but had asked a neighbor to open the home when she'd been told about the warrant.

"His wife didn't even hesitate to cooperate," Zane said.

"I think she's in shock. Where are the kids?"

"With the neighbor who let us in." Zane handed Caden a pair of blue gloves before pulling on his own. "You think Powers was dumb enough to leave evidence behind?"

"He was dumb enough to use that cabin, so I'm not above hoping."

"Good point."

Caden stepped inside and found the agents going through the home with methodical precision. "Keep an eye out for anything that might suggest this guy has ties to someone in Afghanistan."

"What makes you say that?"

"Just a hunch mostly. We've already run Heather's past surgical patient records, and none of them have thrown up any red flags. Not even the ones who didn't make it off the operating table alive."

"I bet that warrant was fun to get."

"Yeah, I jumped through a few hoops and called in a lot of favors. All that matters is we got it done." To no avail. "But the more I think about it, the more I'm convinced her problems really didn't start until after that video came out."

"You think someone's so mad about her trying to save a suicide bomber that they'd come after her?"

"It's not the dumbest thing I've ever heard of."

"Yeah, me either." His partner shook his head, and Caden threw himself into helping with the search, unsure of what he was looking for but fairly confident he'd know it if he saw it.

CHAPTER FIFTEEN

Travis pulled into his parents' long dirt drive, and the truck bounced toward the house that sat at the top of the hill. The drive ran along one edge of the property, and as he rounded the next curve, he could see the whole ranch.

Heather gasped. "It's beautiful!"

"Thanks. I feel blessed I get to call it home." The mountains in the distance surrounded the rolling valley, protecting both the livestock and the family. He and his dad had hiked over almost all the sixty-five acres in the time they'd lived there, discovering the secrets, the treasures, and yes, even the dangers of the land. Cliffs jutted from the majestic peaks, beckoning the more adventurous, a warning to the unaware and unprepared.

He never tired of seeing the "homestead," as his mother called it, but one day, he planned to pave the driveway and save the suspensions on all their vehicles.

He pointed to a two-story home on a smaller hill. "That's my sister and her family's place."

"The horses in the pasture make it postcard perfect."

"Wouldn't be home without horses." Four of them grazed in a nearby pasture, manes and tails blowing in the wind. "That's Herman, Iggy, Louie, and Marie."

"I love the names."

"Herman is the old man of the bunch. It's good to see him out there, but he probably won't be with us much longer. He's got cancer and is going downhill fast."

She frowned. "That's so sad."

"Yeah, it is. He's Sandra's horse. She's had him since she was fifteen."

"I've never had an animal other than the ones in the foster homes when I was there, but I know people love them like family members."

She drew in a deep breath, her shoulders relaxing, her tension seeming to ebb a bit. Good. The place did the same thing for him, lowering his stress level and blood pressure several notches.

"This whole area is breathtaking," she said. "I love the mountains. I bet the sunrise is incredible."

"It's indescribable." While he never tired of seeing the property, this time he pictured how it would look through her eyes and smiled. He loved all of it—the horses, the cows in the back pasture, the rolling hills that would be green come springtime, and the mountains surrounding the property.

She shifted her attention back to him. "Do you miss Texas?"

"Sometimes. Not as much as I used to. Having the family here helps a lot. When Joe, my sister's husband, got this job in Asheville, Mom and Dad couldn't resist moving to be close to both of their kids and grandkids, but they didn't want to live in the city. They wanted something that reminded them of Texas. Campobello was the compromise. They get country living close to city convenience."

"Sounds ideal. What does Joe do?"

"He's an electrical engineer and works very long hours." Travis rounded a curve and pointed again. "That's my home. I just finished building it about four months ago. Sandra and Mom helped me decorate it."

"I'm sure they loved that."

"They did. I'm just glad it's done. I can't tell you how many texts and phone calls I had to answer about paint color, fabric patterns, and picture themes."

She laughed. "I'm sure it's lovely."

Two barking dogs raced from the barn, their yips making him smile. "That's Bart and Dart. They're Australian shepherds and do a good job bringing in the cows when it's time."

"Cows? What cows?"

"In the back pasture. You can't see them from here." He parked the truck in front of his parents' house and shut off the engine before turning to her. "Do you ride?"

"Cows? Not recently."

He snorted, then chuckled. "Horses, silly, but if cows are your preference . . ."

She laughed. A deep belly laugh that caught and held his attention. Her mirth faded when she caught him watching. "What?"

"Uh, nothing."

"Not nothing. You were looking at me in a . . . *way*."

Caught. He cleared his throat. "What way?"

"You tell me."

"I don't think I'm intimidated by you anymore."

"No?" This time her laugh held a breathy quality. "I'll have to work on that."

He smiled. "You know I've been wanting to do something almost since I met you."

Her eyes sparked. "Oh?"

"Oh." He slid a hand around the nape of her neck, and she shifted closer, watchful, wary, but with apprehension mixed with a longing even a blind man would recognize. He leaned forward and kissed her on the forehead. Then her nose. Her eyes fluttered shut and he let his lips feather across hers in a brief, barely there touch. When he drew back, her eyes opened and he ran a thumb over her cheek, marveling at the softness.

"That's it? That's what you wanted to do?" she asked, amusement replacing her earlier trepidation.

"Not exactly, but it'll have to do for now. My mother is walking this way."

Heather's cheeks went bright red, and she tilted away from him. "Glad you noticed that."

He laughed and opened the door. The dogs attacked him with wagging tails and whimpers of delight. He scratched ears and rubbed bellies until he stopped to hug his mother.

"Glad you made it in time for dinner," she said.

His stomach rumbled in response. "Wasn't going to miss it."

"Your sister and the kids are coming too. Joe is working late tonight on that project."

"Surprise, surprise."

"Now, son, Joe's a good man."

"He's a workaholic, but yes, he's a decent guy. He doesn't deserve Sandra, though."

She chuckled. "No man would be good enough for your sister."

That was true enough. "I have someone I want to introduce you to."

"I've been wanting to meet her since I stepped out of the house."

So, she'd caught a glimpse of him kissing Heather. Even while the rush of heat climbed into his cheeks, a chill settled around his heart. Not that he cared if someone saw his affection for the woman waiting for him to introduce her, but he shouldn't have allowed himself to be distracted. That could be a costly mistake.

Making a mental note not to let it happen again, he made an effort to slow down his growing feelings for the pretty surgeon and held out a hand. When she slipped her palm against his, real terror threaded through his veins. He didn't want to lose her. He wanted a chance with her. A chance to explore what could be. After he made sure she was safe.

"Travis? Hello?"

He blinked. His mother stared at him half amused, half worried. "Sorry. Mom, this is Heather. Heather, this is Mom, but I'm sure she'll let you call her Debra."

"Of course." His mother clasped Heather's free hand between her palms. "Travis said you've been having some trouble. We've got plenty of room, watchdogs, and rifles. We'll take good care of you."

"Oh! Thank you, but I don't expect—"

Travis nudged her, and she shot him a wide-eyed look, then cleared her throat.

"Let me just leave it at thank you."

When his mom's gaze bounced between the two of them and her eyes narrowed, Travis nodded to the house. "We're going to stay with you and Dad. I think the more people around, the better."

"That works for us. It'll be nice to have the rooms filled up again. Heather, I think you'll like the sunflower room." She turned to head back into the house.

"Love the golf cart," Heather said to Travis.

"It's handy for them to go back and forth between the houses. Mom says she likes driving it better than her car." Travis took the small carry-on bag from Heather. "Let's get you settled, then we'll check in with Caden."

"Right. Sure. Let's do that."

He frowned at her. "You okay?"

"I'm just . . ." She smiled, but it looked forced to him. "Yes, I'm okay. Lead on, I'm right behind you."

◻ ◻ ◻

Heather knew she sounded dazed, but that was only because she was. Sideswiped. That was it. Among other feelings. Not to mention completely exhausted and running on fumes. But at least one of those feelings included safe. The house wasn't huge, but it was roomy and well laid out. The front door led to a two-story foyer. To the left was the dining room, to the right a living room that held a baby grand piano.

Travis led her straight through to the den, then turned left down a hallway. His mother followed, after snatching several towels from a linen closet.

She handed them to Heather at the bedroom door and Heather breathed in the fresh just-out-of-the-dryer scent. "If you need more, they'll be in the closet inside the bathroom. This room has an en suite, so you should have all the privacy you need."

"I can't thank you enough," Heather said.

"Happy to do it, hon. Make yourself at home. Don't be walking on eggshells around here."

"Yes, ma'am." Heather wanted to hug her.

The woman turned to Travis. "You know where to park your boots, son."

"I do. Thanks, Mom."

She hurried back toward the kitchen. "Dinner is in thirty minutes. Your sister's on the way and your dad is cleaning up in the barn. He's been spending a lot of time with Herman. That poor horse is down to his last few days, maybe hours."

Travis flinched. "I was afraid of that." He returned his attention to Heather, his eyes soft, but his posture stiff.

Heather frowned at the vibes coming from him. He'd kissed her not ten minutes ago and now he was distancing himself?

"Do you want to eat or sleep?" he asked. "I can always bring you a tray or you can raid the leftovers when you wake up."

She pulled her mind from her confusion about his weird behavior and debated. "Uh . . . yes, sure. I think I'd better eat something before sleeping. If I can actually sleep."

"You need to. So do I."

She gave a slow nod. "What's wrong?" she asked.

He blinked. "What do you mean?"

"You're distancing yourself from me. Mentally and physically. Why? If you don't want me here, I'll leave." She'd lived in too many places where she was unwanted. She wouldn't do it again.

"What? No. No, no, no. You're misunderstanding."

"But I'm right. You've got this"—she waved a hand between

them—"this I don't know what. But something's changed from the car to now."

He dropped his chin to his chest. "Yeah. I got scared."

Heather frowned. "Okay. Could I have a little more detail?"

He lifted a hand and traced it down her cheek. Heather swallowed, desperate to know what was going through his head.

"I got distracted. By you. By my . . . feelings for you. At that point, someone could have attacked and I would have been blindsided. My priority needs to be protecting you, not kissing you."

"I see." It wasn't that he didn't want her there, he was worried he'd fail her. The thought was enough to close her throat up and send cracks all through the wall around her heart. She needed to change the subject before she blubbered all over his shirt again.

"Good." He stepped back and stopped, his eyes on her face. "What is it?"

"What happens if someone managed to follow us?"

"No one did. And the truck was clean for trackers. I checked it before we left. My dad is a former Texas Ranger. I've filled him in a bit, and he's already arranged to have some of the hands patrol the property tonight."

Heather bit her lip.

"You're going to be all right, Heather, I promise."

"You sound really sure about that."

"There's no other option. There can't be."

She nodded. "I appreciate that, but you can't promise that."

"It's a promise to myself as much as you." He rolled the little suitcase inside the room. "Want to meet me in the den in fifteen minutes?"

"Of course."

His gaze lingered on her eyes, dropped to her lips, then back up. Her stomach flipped, and she swallowed, thinking about that kiss. "Travis?"

"Yeah. Um . . . yeah." He drew in a deep breath and shot her a tight smile. "See you in a few."

With that he left, and she dropped onto the bed, burying her face in the pillow. She was tempted to shut her eyes but figured if she did, she might not wake up for a week.

And she was hungry.

After freshening up in the bathroom, she headed for the den, where she found Travis hugging a young woman with dark hair. The woman held a baby in the crook of her elbow. When the baby caught sight of Heather, she kicked her legs, babbled, then let out a screech of excitement.

Travis turned. "Heather, come meet Sandra, my big sister."

"Hi." Heather walked closer to tap the infant on the nose. The baby grinned and held out her arms. Heather laughed and scooped her up.

"Oh, thank you," Sandra said. "She gets heavy fast."

"What's her name?"

"Lisa."

"Mama, Jackie touched my leg!" A small body zipped past Heather and hid behind his mother's legs. Another child just slightly older than the first rounded the corner and into the den, sliding on the hardwoods when she came to a sudden stop at the sight of Heather.

"And these are two more of my munchkins. Davey and Jackie." She detached the little one from her leg. "This is Davey. He's four. Jackie's six. Jackie, don't touch your brother." She glanced in the direction of the kitchen. "Martin's around here somewhere. He's ten."

"So very happy to meet you all." The children seemed to forget about their squabble as they stared wide-eyed at the newcomer holding their sibling.

Travis's mother entered the den, wiping her hands on a towel. "Well, we can go ahead and eat when y'all are ready."

The kids raced for the table. "I'm sitting by Uncle Travis," Jackie called.

"No! I am," Davey countered.

He looked at Heather. "I guess I'm sitting in the middle."

"Do you mind?" Sandra asked. "I know it's a cop-out to let them fight about it, then get what they want, but I'm too tired to worry about it."

"Joe's working long hours these days," Travis said.

Heather caught the look his mother shot him, and he pressed his lips together while Sandra rolled her eyes.

The two continued the conversation while Heather inhaled the scent of the baby and zoned to an inner place she didn't often let herself go. But this was the picture of the perfect family. At least what she'd envisioned when she was a child who longed for a stable home life and a family who loved her. *Really* loved her.

One memory stood out to her. At the age of nine, she'd arrived at one of her foster homes and had seen a pancake box in the pantry.

"Can we have pancakes for breakfast?" she'd asked the foster mother who was folding clothes into stacks.

"No."

"Why not?"

"Because I said no. Now go outside and play until I tell you to come in."

"But I don't want to go outside. It's hot."

"Go! Now!"

Then one of the older girls had grabbed her by the upper arm and pulled her outside. "Learn to be invisible," she'd said. "Don't ask for help. Don't be a pest. If you're too much trouble, they'll send you to a group home or something—and those are awful."

Heather had taken those words to heart. And just about every other word the girl had uttered.

Now those words of the past rose up to twist her heart into a lump of hurt. Sheer exhaustion was lowering her defenses. She passed Lisa to Sandra, cleared her throat, and grabbed hold of the emotions with a skill she'd learned in yet another foster home.

With Lisa settled in the high chair, Heather took her seat, still grappling with stuffing her feelings back into the appropriate box.

When she looked up from her plate, her eyes collided with Travis's, who sat opposite her. His furrowed brow and direct gaze silently questioned if she was all right. Heather forced a smile and nodded.

The door opened and a man in his midsixties stepped inside, slapping his Stetson against his thigh. "Snowing out there. Gonna be interesting come morning. Who's up for sledding?"

The cheers went up from the three older kids and Sandra shook her head. "It's not going to snow enough to sled, Dad."

"Don't be a party pooper, hon." He winked at the kids. "There's always hope." He washed his hands, then settled in the chair next to Sandra while his eyes locked on Heather. "Hello. I'm Parker. Glad to have you join us."

Travis said he'd filled him in on the situation. She was glad about that. The lines next to his eyes suggested he liked to laugh. The firm jaw, straight shoulders, and direct gaze said he'd be a good one to have on your side.

"Thank you," she said. "I appreciate it very much. I'm very sorry about Herman. Sounds like he's a beloved member of the family."

"He is. We're thankful God entrusted him to us."

Heather took the mashed potatoes from Martin and scooped some onto her plate. She looked around once more and a chill settled in her chest in spite of the cozy scene. What if whoever was after her found her here? Would that person hurt these precious people in his twisted desire to get to her? Could she take the chance? Tonight, she didn't have a choice, but when morning came, she'd have to insist Travis take her to a hotel.

Once again, she looked up to find his eyes on her and wished she could look into his mind and discern his thoughts.

At the same time, she was glad he couldn't read hers.

○ ○ ○

Caden raked a hand down his five o'clock shadow. Agitated didn't begin to describe the angst rolling inside of him.

After an all-night search, they'd found absolutely nothing in Sam Powers's physical files to indicate why he would be a part of Heather's kidnapping. "Powers was a model citizen." He reviewed the information again, hoping something would jump out at them. "Father of two, devoted husband, some debt, but nothing outrageous that required him to get his hands on some cash fast."

"You never know," Zane said, biting into a protein bar. He chewed slowly. "He could owe a bookie or maybe he's got another woman he's supporting somewhere."

"True, but none of the money leads to that assumption."

"Maybe he's good at hiding it. We've got his laptop. I have a feeling that's going to be the key."

"I sure hope you're right, because if he doesn't wake up, we may never know."

"Nothing on his accomplice, I guess."

"Nope. Without any security footage from the gas station, we don't even know if the man was there or not."

"Heather and the sketch artist did a good job—as good as can be expected when she said she didn't get a very good look at the driver. The picture is circulating. Hopefully, someone will recognize the guy and call it in."

"When did you start thinking so positive?"

Zane smirked. "I'm turning over a new leaf."

"What's her name?"

His partner's laughter rang out in the evening air. Then he slapped Caden on the shoulder. "Let's get some coffee and a big bar of chocolate. I have a feeling it's going to be another long night, and protein bars aren't cutting it."

"Who are they giving the laptop to?"

Zane frowned. "That new girl. Daria Nevsky. Annie finished training her a couple of months ago. Although, if you talk to Annie, she said she really wasn't sure who was training whom by the end."

Caden nodded. "Good to know. Hopefully, she's as ready as Annie thinks she is."

"If Annie says she's ready, she's ready."

"True. All right. Let's grab that coffee and hurry up and wait."

"Don't forget the chocolate."

"I wouldn't dare."

CHAPTER SIXTEEN

The minute Heather stepped into the kitchen the next morning, Travis knew that she was thinking of leaving. "No," he said.

She paused at the threshold and raised a brow. The fact that she didn't have to ask him what he was talking about spoke volumes. "I'm dangerous to them," she said. "To your family. How can you want me here?"

"I want you safe."

"I want that, too, believe me. I just want everyone else safe as well. Asher took a bullet because of me, and I can't have anything else like that happen. Especially not with kids around."

"We've already covered the topic of Asher's shooting and the fact that it's not your fault. It's the fault of whoever shot him. And Sandra and the kids are a good distance away."

"Except when they're here."

"Well, we've got a foot of snow outside and more coming down, so I doubt anyone's going anywhere anytime soon. Including whoever's after you. We won't assume that, of course. Every precaution will be taken, but I think we're okay for the moment." He paused. "Can I ask you a rather personal question?"

Wariness entered her eyes, but she nodded.

"Why do you find it so hard to accept help from people?"

She blinked. Then grimaced. "Wow. That answer might take a while."

"I've got time."

"Don't you have a business to run?" He simply looked at her and she sighed. "Fine."

"Wanna have a seat first?"

"Not really. Then I can't pace."

"So pace and talk."

Heather grabbed a cup of coffee in silence before turning to lean against the counter, hands wrapped around the mug. "I was in the foster system by the time I was ten. My parents were basically worthless, but I don't know that I completely blame them for their issues. They were products of their environment. However, at some point, I think a person has to come to the decision that if they want things to get better, they have to do something about it. My parents never did that." She sipped the steaming brew, and Travis was struck by the distance in her tone. Almost as though she was telling a friend's story instead of her own.

She walked to the refrigerator and turned to pace back to the counter, her hands still clasping the mug. "I can relate to Ryker so very well. My dad had a quick temper and a set of iron fists. If he didn't like something my mom or I said, he let them fly. He finally beat my mom to death one night when he was drunk. I was six. He went to prison and did about three years for it before his lawyer found a loophole and he got out on my ninth birthday."

Travis had never heard her whole story, just that she'd grown up in the foster system. "Your father killed your mother."

"Yes. Broke her nose, and a fragment went to her brain, which caused her to have a stroke and die. At least that's what I was told." She glanced away, but not before Travis caught a glimmer of the pain she carried with her.

"That's awful," he said. "I truly can't imagine and I'm so sorry."

"I am too."

"And what kind of loophole lets a murderer go free?"

"The kind where they finally realize he was never Mirandized."

"What! How is that even possible?"

"It's possible when you have a rookie who brought him in, was asked if he'd read him his rights, and not wanting to look like he messed up, lied and said he did."

"Oh, for the love of—"

"I know."

"How'd they find out? Did your dad tell them?"

"No, Dad later said he didn't even think about it. He figured he was just too drunk to remember. The rookie let that fact eat away at him for three years until he finally came forward. Dad's lawyer jumped all over it."

"Of course he did."

She rubbed her eyes and took a swig of her coffee. "Like I said, I was nine. I'd been staying with a family friend who'd taken me in. They were foster parents and had an opening, so moving in with them was like a new lease on life for me—and I never really considered myself 'in the system' until later. Anyway, my friend's father was in the video game business and wound up being transferred to Germany."

"And they didn't want to take you with them?"

She shook her head. "Legally, they couldn't. I was still a ward of the state and my father refused to give up custody rights. I do think Gabriella, my friend's mother, wanted to take me, but simply couldn't. I remember hearing her cry at night after that and heard her say she was going to miss me. Before they turned me back over to the system, she prayed with me and told me to do something with my life. That my parents didn't define me. And to do whatever it took to stay away from my father." She took a deep breath. "Anyway, when I heard my dad was getting out of prison, I freaked. I'd had almost three years of living with a family that didn't hit each other, I had known what it was like to have a mother and a sister who loved me and a dad who didn't hit. I was terrified of going back with a father I'd only known violence from."

He couldn't stand it anymore. He walked over and took the mug from her tight fingers. After placing the cup on the counter, he pulled her against him and rested his chin on her head. "I wish I could give you a do-over on the family thing."

A short chuckle rumbled from her throat. "I wish you could too."

"So, how did you wind up in the foster system—for real—if you went back with your father?"

She drew in a deep breath and stepped back. He let her go. Reluctantly. But stayed next to her. "I survived almost a year with Roger before I learned that a classmate was in something of the same situation as I was. I heard she'd been taken from her home and placed in a different one, so I asked my teacher how that could be. And she explained it very simply. She said, 'Children are to be protected, not hurt. When someone hurts a child, there's an organization that steps in to remove the child from the home.' Later that night, I put the landline phone in my room, and instead of being my invisible self, I mouthed off to my dad. He punched me in the eye and kicked me in the ribs a few times before I could get to my room, lock myself in, and call 911."

Travis's heart thundered in his chest. "You don't have to tell me any more. It's okay."

"I'm almost done. You might as well hear the rest of it."

He wasn't sure he could handle the rest of it. He wanted to go back to the prison and give Roger Maddox a taste of his own medicine. "All right."

"Anyway, the police arrived shockingly fast."

"You were a child in danger."

"Over the phone, they could hear him pounding on my door and screaming he was going to kill me. However, when they got there, my dad was passed out cold. He'd given up on me after about thirty seconds of his rant and sacked out on the couch, not realizing I'd called the police and was still on the phone with the dispatcher when they arrived." Her shoulders rose and fell with a deep breath. "I managed to come out of my room and open the door for them while my father continued to snore on the couch. One of the officers was a woman and she asked me what happened. I told her my father tried to kill me, then I blacked out. When I came to, my father was in jail and a nice lady from social services was sitting next to my hospital bed."

"And he went to prison?"

"He did. And I went into the system. Again, I suppose. It was one of the best and worst days of my life."

"You haven't addressed why you find it so hard to accept help from people who care about you."

She grimaced. "Right. I think it's because at my second foster home, two months after the first one, there was an older foster teen also in the home. She intervened during a moment with the foster mother and took me aside. Said she was going to give me some advice."

"Oh boy."

Heather nodded. "She basically told me that if I wanted to survive, I needed to be invisible, don't be a bother, don't call attention to myself, et cetera. She also said that anyone who offers to help you has an agenda. Never accept help from anyone unless you know what's expected in return. Long story short, I took that lesson to heart to survive, starting in that home and every home that came after it. I have to say, it served me well in the years that followed."

"Except when it comes to friends and people who care about you and want to help you—with no agenda."

She offered him a sad smile. "Yes, except for that. But I'm working on it."

He pulled her back into his arms once more and let her story wash over him. He lost track of how long they stood there. It could have been ten minutes or two, but he didn't figure he'd get tired of holding her for a long time.

"Good morning, young people." His mother breezed into the kitchen, heading for the refrigerator.

Travis loosened his embrace and Heather stepped back. Slowly, he thought. Maybe even a tad reluctantly? "Morning, Mom."

Her eyes twinkled a little more than usual, and he knew she was envisioning more grandchildren. For some reason that didn't bother him nearly as much as he might have expected.

◻ ◻ ◻

Heather refused to be embarrassed at being caught in Travis's light embrace. The truth was, she liked being in his arms. The fact that she was able to admit it to herself without having a complete breakdown was impressive. She'd never really pictured herself married and with children simply because if she allowed that longing to surface, she'd have to deal with all the emotions that came with it.

"Heather?" Travis was looking at her with a raised brow.

She blinked and realized his mother had said something. "I'm sorry. I think I'm still asleep. What did you say?"

Travis's mother chuckled. "I asked how you slept."

"Oh." She laughed. "Really well, thank you." She couldn't believe it when her eyes had popped open and she'd discovered she'd slept for nine hours without moving. "I guess deep down I knew I was safe and could rest."

"Of course you're safe," his mother said. "We had all kinds of security out there all night long. I slept like I haven't slept in ages just knowing people were watching over this house."

"Mom . . ." Travis gave his head a slight shake.

"Too much?"

"Just a little."

"Sorry." She turned serious. "Sandra called this morning. Herman took a turn for the worse and she can't get him out of the barn."

"Oh no. I was afraid of that. She's going to have to put him down."

"She knows and had already been making plans to do so." She gave a small sigh, then forced a smile. "What's on your agenda for today?"

"Keeping an eye on things. I've got a couple of potential clients I need to touch base with. And"—he turned to Heather—"Caden texted just before you walked in the kitchen."

"What did he have to say?"

"Mr. Powers is awake. Sort of."

"I see. Sort of?"

"He's in and out of it, but the doctors seem to think he'll be able to answer some questions before too long."

Heather refilled her mug and turned back to study him. "I want to go."

He nodded. "I figured you would."

"You're not going to try and talk me out of it?"

"Would it make a difference?"

Heather tilted her head. Would it? "It might."

Debra was busy in the background cracking eggs, pretending like she wasn't listening. Heather felt quite sure she was processing every word.

"Then I don't think you should go."

"Because you're absolutely sure that I'm safe here."

"No one followed us. No one knows where you are or has any way to find you. I think you should let Caden and the others do their jobs and lay low. At least until they finish questioning Mr. Powers."

He was right. She didn't like it, but he was right. What good would it do for her to go over to the hospital when all she might accomplish would be to draw the kidnapper's attention once again? And endanger those trying to protect her. "All right. I'll stay here."

He blinked. Then stared. "You will?"

She let out a low laugh. "I'm not completely unreasonable. I've even been known to use good judgment upon occasion."

He huffed a sigh. "That's not what I was implying."

"I know. It's okay. Like I said, I won't like it, but I'll do the smart thing."

"Well . . . good. Great. Do you want to go riding?"

"Horses, not cows, I assume." He rolled his eyes and she shot him a small grin. "Yes. Sure. But in the snow?"

"It's not icy and the horses aren't afraid of a little snow. It'll be fun."

"Sounds cold."

"That, too, but Sandra will have something you can wear. We can stop by her place and see what she's got."

"Okay, that might be fun."

"Might be?" His fake outrage made her laugh.

Then she sobered. "After I call Brooke and check on Asher."

"I'm going to go get my gear put together. You make your call and then we'll head over to Sandra's."

Thirty minutes later, with a full stomach and an appropriate amount of caffeine pumping through her veins, she found herself in Sandra's bedroom pulling on a pair of boots that actually fit. Of course, the woman had four different sizes, so odds were in Heather's favor. "My feet changed sizes with my pregnancies," Sandra had explained, "so, after my second, I just kept every pair of shoes and boots I had, knowing I was going to need them at some point."

Heather had laughed. "Well, it's a good thing for me you did." She'd ridden before, but not recently. "I hope I remember how."

"You'll do great. And Travis will probably put you on Iggy. He's a sweetheart and very calm."

"Iggy. He sounds perfect."

"He is." Sandra had plunked a black Stetson on Heather's head and declared her ready. "You look like you belong."

The words pierced Heather and went straight to her heart. Oh, how she wanted to belong. Somewhere. She swallowed the surge of emotion and pasted a smile on her face.

When she walked into the den, she found Travis on the floor building a massive LEGO structure with Davey and Jackie while Martin lounged in a recliner reading a book. "I didn't know kids still read books these days."

He looked up and grinned. "I do."

"Good for you."

When the baby, rolling from one end of the den to the other, got a little too close to the fireplace, Travis snagged her with one hand and pulled her to his chest. She squealed and kicked.

Sandra scooped her up. "Say goodbye to Uncle Travis and Ms. Heather."

"Aw, I wanna go," Jackie said.

"Not this time."

More protests followed them out the door, with Travis promising to play in the snow with them a little later.

In the barn, they tacked up the horses and he gave her a leg up onto the back of Iggy. The horse shifted beneath Heather's weight, and the comfortable feeling of being back in the saddle washed over her. "My third foster placement had a couple of horses. The daughter, Kendra, was about five years older than I was and rode in competitions, but she was kind and taught me how to ride. It was the first time in my life I can remember being excited about coming home from school. It's been a while."

"You'll do fine."

For the next half hour, they rode the land, with him pointing out details and telling her stories of exploring with his eldest nephew, Martin. "That kid may be only ten, but he's smart and is always looking for something to get into."

"You're referring to trouble?"

"Mostly." He laughed. "He doesn't have a mean bone in his body. However, all of his bones are infused with an insatiable curiosity. *Everything* is new and exciting."

"Just like a ten-year-old boy should be."

"Yeah, true, but he might drive his parents to an early grave because he has no fear." He pointed once more. "See that ledge up there? At the top of the hill?"

"No."

"It's kind of covered with snow, but you'll see something that looks like a black hole in the midst of all the snow. Let's go closer. You'll know it when you see it."

They walked the horses, and Heather scanned the area she thought he was talking about. Finally, it jumped out at her. "Oh! Yes, I see it."

"There's an opening behind it that you can't see from here. Sort of like a tunnel or a shallow cave that leads right out to that ledge. I found Martin sitting up there one afternoon, dangling his legs off the side of it."

She gaped. "You didn't!" She looked back. "That's at least a ten-story drop."

"No kidding. Scared me spitless."

"And his mother, too, I'm sure."

"Oh, Sandra doesn't know anything about it. She'd never let him out of the house if she did. But when Martin's being particularly ornery or stubborn and I happen to catch it, I only have to say one thing and he straightens right up."

Curious, she waited. When the silence dragged on, she frowned. "Well? What?"

"Oh, you want to know?"

"Travis . . . of course! Tell me."

He laughed. "I say, 'You're skating kinda close to the edge, aren't you?' He's scared to death I'll tell Sandra."

"You blackmail him into behaving?" She didn't know whether to be outraged or impressed.

"Hey, all he has to do is confess. I told him he needs to tell his mother what he did. He lied to her and to his grandmother about where he was. Each thought he was with the other. Instead, he was doing something foolish and dangerous."

"Oh my. So . . . you're letting his guilt eat him alive until it convinces him to come clean?"

"Something like that. I prefer to think of it as conviction more than guilt."

She liked the distinction. "Why haven't you put some kind of safety fence up there?"

"Well, see, that's something I'm struggling with. Martin promised me that he'd never do anything like that again if I would promise not to tell his mom about his little death-defying adventure. At first, I refused, but he asked me if he could earn my trust back."

"Oh."

"Yeah. I told him I'd think about it. It took me a couple of days to come to the decision not to tell his parents. I also thought about blocking that area off so no one could get to it. But look around." He swept an arm out and she followed the movement. "That's not the only dangerous place up there. The kid could go from that spot to another just as easy. And then, there was the issue of him earning my trust."

"Meaning if you blocked access after agreeing that he could earn your trust back, you'd be sending the message that you don't have faith in his ability to do that?"

The tender sidelong glance he shot her sent a warmth spinning through her veins.

"You get it," he said.

"I get it."

"However, he is an almost-eleven-year-old boy. I installed a motion sensor that pings my phone if anything sets it off. It's kind of like one of those remote doorbells. You can answer even though you're not home. The nice thing is, there's a small camera that lets me see if it's an animal or human. Because . . ."

"He's an almost-eleven-year-old boy and his safety comes first."

"Exactly. Like I said, you get it. And, true to his word, so far, he's not gone anywhere near that area. I also lectured him about other areas as well. The fact is, this is a ranch. It has its dangers. It's up to the adults to teach the kids how to be safe while protecting them at the same time. It can be a little overwhelming at times."

"I'm sure." She paused. "There's no power up there, is there?"

"No, it runs off rechargeable batteries. They're strong and last a long time."

"You're a good man, Travis Walker."

He shot her a small smile. "I try."

The horses had stopped and now grazed on hay bales that dotted the snow. Travis's phone rang and he snatched it. "It's Caden."

Any kind of relaxation she'd managed to achieve on the ride was now gone. Caden said something and Travis frowned. "Well, tell him that's not possible." More listening. "No."

He glanced at Heather from the corner of his eye, and she raised her brows. "What?"

"Hold on," he said into the phone. To Heather, he said, "Caden said the guy wanted to talk to you."

"Why?"

"Because he said you hired him to kidnap you."

CHAPTER SEVENTEEN

Heather sputtered a choked laugh of disbelief and stared at him. "He said what?"

Travis repeated it, but he didn't think it was necessary. She wasn't really listening, she was processing.

"Is he mentally ill?" Heather asked. "Delusional? Because if not, then he's flat-out lying. Why would I hire someone to kidnap me?"

Travis put the phone on speaker. "Heather can hear you now. Did you hear what she said?"

"I heard it. The man is practically hysterical and insists that he was just trying to earn some extra money. He said a friend of his is really big into some kind of weird reality game and asked him to join him in playing. They staged the kidnapping."

Heather gaped. "I can't tell you how confused I am right now."

"Join the club," Caden said. "Heather, he's insisting he speak with you face-to-face and that you'll corroborate his story."

"I most certainly will not."

"I hate to ask this, but he's refused to say another word unless you're in the room with us. He says someone's setting him up to be the bad guy and he's not having it."

Travis snorted. "He *is* the bad guy."

Heather studied the ground and Travis waited for her to think it all through. She finally looked up. "Fine. As long as you think it's safe for me—and everyone around me—to come to the hospital, then I'll come."

"I don't think I like that idea."

Heather raised a brow at him and he narrowed his eyes.

"But I'll bring her." He gave Caden the route they'd take. "I'll call Gavin as well. He can meet us there and lurk in the background to keep an eye on everything." And everyone. "Once we leave the property, it'll take us about thirty minutes to get there."

"I'll have local officers meet you at the end of your drive and escort you to the state line, then North Carolina officers can pick you up the rest of the way. Give me thirty minutes to get it arranged."

Travis nodded even though Caden couldn't see him. "We've got to head back and put the horses up. It'll take us at least that long, if not a bit longer."

"That's all right. Before I could question him further, Powers got so upset, he started setting off alarms. The nurse came in and kicked us out, so hopefully by the time you get here, they'll let us back in there and we'll learn the rest of it."

"Sounds good." Caden hung up and Travis gathered the reins to pull his horse's head up. "Ready?"

She nodded. "I really want to know what that crazy man is thinking."

"Then let's go find out."

An hour and a half later, flanked by two officers, Travis led Heather to a back entrance of the hospital. Hospital security met them at the door and ushered them inside.

Finally.

The short sprint from the truck to the door had seemed like an eternity, and Travis had almost expected to feel a bullet plow into him. "Thanks for the escort."

"Of course."

"We'll take it from here." The hospital security officer who spoke turned to Travis. "I'm Jim Estes. This is Laura Mann."

"Glad to meet you two."

The two officers who'd escorted them from the North Carolina state line left, and Travis slipped his hand around Heather's to give it a squeeze. "You okay?"

"Nervous about seeing this man, but okay too. I know he can't hurt me anymore. And I'll admit I'm raging with curiosity. That has to be the most ridiculous thing any criminal has ever said about a kidnapping victim."

"Yeah, that would definitely make the top ten list of dumbest criminals of all time. I'll have to send that one in." At her raised brow, he shrugged. "It amuses me."

"You have way too much time on your hands, Walker." She snickered.

"Hey, the baby was asleep on my shoulder and I was terrified to move. I couldn't turn the television on or do anything but scroll. It helped pass the time."

"Sure."

"What? You don't believe me?" His fake outrage lightened her spirit in spite of the circumstances.

"I believe you. I just think it's funny."

"Oh, come on, don't tell me you don't have some quirky little way you like to waste time on occasion." He paused. "Maybe waste time isn't the right way to put it. I guess I mean something you do when you need a brain break or just zone out for half an hour."

"Sounds like wasting time is exactly the right way to put it. And no, I don't waste time."

"Ever?"

"Ever."

He studied her. "I don't believe you. Are you actually lying to me?"

"Me? Lie?" A small smile curved her lips and she gave a light shrug. "You'll never know, will you?"

She did *not* just issue that challenge. "Heather . . ." He drew her name out in warning.

A sound escaped her and Travis almost did a double take. Was that a giggle? Had she actually *giggled*? "Did you just—"

A ferocious frown stopped him. "I did not."

"You did."

"I didn't because I *don't*."

"You two okay?"

Caden's voice jarred Travis back to reality. They'd arrived at the door to the prisoner's room. Her *kidnapper's* room. Her smile faded, and the instant return of tension hit Travis hard. He wanted to make her happy, to see her smile and hear her giggle—which she'd just done, whether she admitted it or not. Caden stood watching the two of them, his gaze bouncing from one to the other.

"Yes," Heather said. "We're fine."

"You sure you're ready for this?" Caden asked her.

"No, I'm not ready. Let's get it over with."

Caden nodded and rapped on the door. He pushed through and Heather followed, shoulders rising and falling with the deep breaths she dragged in. Travis gripped her cold hand and stepped after her. She came to a stop at the end of the bed. A shudder went through her and her fingers tightened to the point the circulation in his hand was cut off.

"Heather," Caden said, "this is Sam Powers and his wife Tammy."

○ ○ ○

Heather eyed the man in the bed. He looked . . . weak. Helpless. And agitated. But she was hit with the realization that seeing him like this was the best thing she could have done. All of a sudden, he held no power over her anymore. Her hand relaxed and Travis released her. She walked around to the side of the bed, her gaze never leaving the occupant. His eyes widened at her approach. The woman in the chair next to him wore a stony expression, and Heather could feel the anxiety mixed with anger rolling off her in waves.

"Tell them," he croaked. "Please tell them it wasn't real."

"It felt very real to me. Why would I tell them that I hired you to kidnap me when I didn't?"

"No." He shook his head. "No, it was a game. It was . . ." He closed his eyes and swallowed. His wife clutched her purse with a grip that would bend steel.

Heather snapped her lips together, then took a deep breath. "A *game*? What world are you living in that kidnapping and terrorizing someone is a game? Not to mention shooting one of my best friends!"

Caden cleared his throat. "The doctor let me back in a few minutes ago, so I've gotten some new information from him in the time it took you to get here. Let me just catch you up."

Heather crossed her arms. "All right."

"He said his friend Donnie Little was hired as some kind of participant in a game called Live Your Wildest Reality."

She stood there trying to process what he was saying. "Okay, but what does that have to do with anything?"

"Donnie said he couldn't pull off the 'assignment'"—he wiggled air quotes around the word—"without help. So, Donnie called and asked Sam here to take part and he'd split the money with him."

"But . . ." What did she even say to such nonsense?

"He also says he has your signature on a contract between Donnie, you, and the company hiring him, to give you the real experience of being kidnapped."

She held up a hand. "Wait a minute. Stop. I'm . . . just . . . stop." The room fell silent, and Heather forced her brain to cooperate. "Let me get this straight." She turned to Sam, who watched her through slitted eyes. "You're saying someone contacted that company, hired them to kidnap me. Donnie got the 'assignment' and asked you to help him out. You agreed to go along with it because you thought it was a game?"

"In a nutshell, yes. Only I thought you'd set the whole thing up and knew what was going on. When Donnie told me about it, I did some research. When I saw it was legit, I asked him for a copy of the contract. He had me sign up to be a part of the company—you know, fill out a profile and all that. Then they added my name to the contract so I would be protected in case of any legal issues that might arise."

"This wasn't in the contract!" The words echoed. Could he possibly be telling the truth? It was almost beyond her ability to process, but why did he yell those words as she was racing away from the cabin? And there'd been no bars on the windows or locks. Now that she thought about it, it had been relatively easy to escape. "This all happened so fast. How could someone put this together so quickly?"

He took a sip of the water his wife held out to him. "According to Donnie, it doesn't take long once you get the assignment. To get started, you fill out an online profile, saying what you're willing to do and that you can be ready to act at a moment's notice. Obviously, the more intense the job, the more expensive it is for the person doing the hiring. But we get paid well, too. I . . . I was laid off six months ago and have been having trouble finding work. We were in danger of losing the house when Donnie told me about this." He gave a light shrug. "I jumped at it."

"How much is the going rate for a kidnapping?" Travis asked, speaking for the first time since they'd entered the room.

"Thirty grand."

Holy cow. Heather couldn't fathom it. "How did I not know this was a thing?" Had she been living with her head in the sand for so long she was out of touch with current pop culture? "Go on."

"Anyway, they match you up with a compatible client—like someone who wants to experience a kidnapping—transfer half of the money to your account, minus the company cut, and then pay you the rest after everything is over with. Again, minus the company percentage."

Heather rubbed her head. The pounding had returned.

"I've verified the company," Caden said, "and it's legit. Donnie's worked for them for about two years now. However, they said they never sent him out on this specific job, but it looks like someone hacked into their system. The head of the company is investigating on his end while we keep looking into things on ours. We fast-tracked a warrant for Sam's and Donnie's financials and the amount Sam quoted was deposited one day before your kidnapping. Daria, one of our intelligence analysts, found the company contract on Sam's computer exactly where he said it was—with all of the signatures. Whoever hacked into the company site was probably looking for a legit contract with the signatures. Then simply added Heather's." He tapped the screen of his phone, then turned it around so she could see it. "That your signature?"

"I . . . don't know. I mean, no, it's not, because I never signed anything like that, but it's very close." Sickness welled in her gut, and she pressed her fingertips to her lips while her head upped the pounding. If she didn't know for a fact she hadn't signed that, she might think it was her signature. Right down to the little curl she used on her *H*. Unbelievable. "And they use real bullets?" That was the dumbest thing she'd ever heard of.

"N-no, of course not," Sam said. "They were supposed to be blanks. Everyone was supposed to have blanks."

"And the bomb that almost killed our friend?"

Sam shook his head, his rising frustration evident. "It was *supposed* to just be a smoke screen because everyone was *supposed* to be in on it and no one was *supposed* to put up any real resistance when it came time to take you. No one was *supposed* to get hurt—at least not seriously. Getting banged up might actually happen in the process—and that's stated in the contract—but definitely no one was supposed to get shot or . . ." He closed his eyes once more and groaned. "I thought something was wrong when everything was going down different than what we'd been told to expect but decided maybe I was just new to the company and things can sometimes go sideways a bit. It was so chaotic that it was hard to think much. I should have known," he muttered.

"Known what?"

"That it was too good to be true." He frowned. "What about Donnie? Didn't he explain all of this to you?"

"We can't find Donnie."

"Can't find him? Why not?"

Caden shook his head. "He's dropped off the radar. We pinged his cell phone to the gas station where we found you, but after that, it appears he turned his phone off. He hasn't been in touch with his wife since the morning of the kidnapping."

Someone had gone to an awful lot of trouble to get her out of the picture. "Wait a minute. Those bullets you were shooting after you ran me off the road were real enough."

Sam frowned. "No, they weren't. Donnie said he just shot the gun to scare you into running. He figured if you were on the run in the woods, it would be easier to find you when you surfaced back in town. And it was. When I saw you, I called Donnie to let him know."

"But the bullets were very real," Heather said. "The explosion was *very real*. The bullet that put our friend in the hospital was also *very, very real*." Her voice rose with each sentence. "So, explain *that*, because I'm still stuck on the real bullets thing."

The man raised a shaky hand to rub it over his lips. His wife glared at him. "Yes, Sam," she said. "Please explain that."

"Honey, please—"

"Don't. Just don't." She looked away and Sam flinched.

"Donnie and I did run you off the road," he said, "but we didn't shoot at you with real bullets. They were blanks. At least that's what I was told. Donnie said he just wanted to throw a scare into the guy with you. How many times are you going to make me say it?"

Heather choked on a bitter laugh. "So, they were blanks. Like the blank you got shot with?"

He blinked. "Well, no, I mean . . ." Sam rubbed a shaking hand down the side of his face. "I don't understand any of this. Donnie brought the bag with the equipment and asked if we could use the cabin as a secure location to hold the client."

"Victim," Heather snapped.

He grimaced. "I said sure, we could use the cabin. Because, why not? It was a game," he whispered. "Just a game. How did everything go so wrong?"

"When did Donnie ask you to do this?" Caden asked.

"About a week ago. He called me and asked if I wanted in. The money was good and I had the time, so I said yes. Donnie sent me the link to sign up online, then he said he'd handle everything else."

"Why bother with the whole reality game thing?" Heather asked. "And why you? Why not someone else?"

He winced and pressed a hand to his side. "I don't know. Probably because Donnie thought it would help me out and . . . I trusted him. He was my friend."

"Some friend," Travis muttered. "He left you on the bathroom floor to bleed out and die. If the owner hadn't found you when he did, you wouldn't be having this conversation."

Sam's eyes flashed anger—and hurt. "We've been friends since high school. I never in a million years thought he could do something like this. And I sure never would have agreed to be a part of it if I'd known it was the real thing." He shuddered. Sam locked his pleading gaze on Heather's. "I'm so sorry."

It made sense in a weird kind of way. Shockingly enough, she was leaning toward believing him. Could he be an innocent pawn in a madman's effort to take her? "So, if you ran me off the road in the hopes that you'd be able to snatch me, why didn't you stick around long enough to do it?"

His eyes slid from hers to his hands on the sheet. Fingers twisted the material tighter and tighter.

"Answer them, Sam," his wife said, her voice strained and thick with unshed tears.

"I . . . we . . . decided that we'd wait and try another time."

"You thought she was dead, didn't you?" Travis asked, his tone registering a lethal level of fury. "You thought you'd killed her, and you had to get out of the area before someone saw you."

"No, not at all. I mean, yes, we didn't want to be spotted, but not because we thought she was dead. We knew we'd have a lot of explaining to do if we were caught and we didn't . . ." He waved a hand. "We saw someone coming and it would be too hard to explain what happened."

"That someone was me, and if I hadn't been there, she probably would have died."

Heather wouldn't have thought it possible, but Sam paled even more, his skin a pasty white. He looked her in the eye. "I'm so sorry. I wish I'd never heard of that company, and even more, wish I'd never let Donnie convince me to sign up with them."

Now *that* sounded sincere.

CHAPTER EIGHTEEN

Travis felt like a sucker for even considering this far-fetched tale could have a grain of truth in it. However, the signed contract Daria had found on Powers's computer went a long way toward proving there might be something in his story that was true. And the weird reality company was real enough. Had this guy been a pawn in a very deadly game? If so, who had the skills to put all of this together?

"If I was going to actually kidnap someone, I wouldn't use a place that could be traced back to me. I do dumb stuff sometimes—as evidenced by my current situation. But I'm not that stupid." The man's gaze flicked from one person to the next. "Please, you have to believe me."

"I'm leaning that way," Caden said.

Heather drew in a sharp breath but nodded. "You were kind to me for the most part."

"Other than the whole throwing the hood over your face, shoving you into a van, and holding you hostage part?" Travis bit out.

Heather shot him a "be quiet" look, and he subsided with a scowl at the man in the bed.

"Thank you for the migraine pills," Heather said. "They helped."

Sam flushed. "I thought it was all a game, so I was playing the part. But I could tell you were in real pain. I couldn't let you suffer." His eyes drooped, but he forced them back open.

"I don't think this was a game to Donnie," Heather said.

"Of course it was."

"Sam," his wife said, her voice sharp. "You are not that dense."

The man flinched. "We've been friends for years, Tammy."

"And I've never liked him." She glanced at the others in the room. "Which is probably why my husband snuck around behind my back to hang out with him."

Sam didn't refute her statement. Instead, he focused on Heather. "I'm so sorry. I can't even begin to find the words to tell you how sorry I am."

Travis met Heather's gaze and he was surprised to see a flash of compassion in her eyes. Then she blinked and it was gone. "At the cabin, you stuck me in the room and left me, but I could hear someone on the phone. Who were you waiting for? Who hired you?"

"I assumed it was you, so I don't know. Donnie was the one who talked to the point person." He shuddered. "He was super intense and took this whole thing really seriously. I mean, I know it's a lot of money, but he was really into it."

"Because it was the real thing to him," Travis said.

Sam frowned, then gave a slow shake of his head. "Again, I don't know. It sure looks that way, but we were both playing a part, remember? Donnie's my friend and I have a real hard time picturing him doing this—and knowingly dragging me into it."

"Well, he did." Tammy glared at her husband. "And now he's missing, so that leaves you to take the fall. He set you up and you're too big of a fool to see it."

Sam gave a slight wince but kept his gaze on Travis. "I mean, obviously, I can't say for sure he knew it was the real deal. He sure acted like he didn't. At one point, he even told her to shut up and that she'd signed up for it."

"He played his part well," Heather said, "very well."

Sam glanced at Heather. Then Travis. "Maybe." His chin dropped to his chest. "And you were right."

"About what?"

Sam's gaze returned to Heather. "When you went over the side of the mountain, I was scared to death you were really hurt. Or dead. Donnie was driving and I yelled at him to stop, but he kept going. Said he'd call 911 as soon as we got to a safe spot—and could find a signal."

"We don't have any record of a 911 call other than from these two," Caden said, pointing at Heather and Travis.

"Why am I not surprised?" Sam sighed and shut his eyes, swallowed hard. "Again, I'm sorry. I wish I could rewind time and do everything differently, but . . ." He opened his eyes and focused on Heather. "I know I've said it, but I'll say it a million more times if I thought it would help. I truly am sorry."

Heather ran a hand down her face, spun, and exited the room.

Travis caught Caden's eye. "I'll check on her."

Tears leaked beneath Sam's closed eyes and he kept saying, "I'm sorry, I'm sorry," as Travis left the room.

He found Heather in the hallway leaning against the wall, shaking. Without speaking, he pulled her against his chest and simply held her.

"He's nice," she muttered. "And I believe every word he said. And on top of that, I feel sorry for him. What kind of idiot am I?"

"The same kind I am."

She stilled then looked up at him, her blue eyes glittering. "You're buying it too?"

"Yeah. I am."

"I still have so many questions. The main one being, who is the person behind everything? Who's going to so much trouble to rub me off the map, and why is it worth the boatload of money to make it happen?"

"All good questions."

Caden stepped out of the room and eyed them. "You two all right?"

"I just had to get away for a moment to catch my breath," Heather said.

Caden gave a short nod and disappeared back into the room.

Travis squeezed her shoulder. "Want to get some coffee?"

"I'd love some. And a doughnut. Maybe even two."

"Since when do you consume that much sugar?"

"Since someone tried to kill me and I discovered life's too short not to enjoy the occasional sugar binge."

He hugged her fiercely. "Come on, I'll buy you some coffee and a donut or two."

"Right now, you're my absolute favorite person on the planet."

"I was going for the universe."

She laughed and turned to head to the elevator. And stopped. A gasp escaped her, and she gripped his bicep. Tight.

"What's wrong?"

"That's him," she whispered.

Travis turned to catch a glimpse of a man at the end of the hall. He was dressed in a plaid jacket and a baseball cap. "That's him!"

Travis stuck his head in the door of the room. "Caden, need you in the hall. Now."

Caden bolted toward him while Travis jerked his gaze back to the man in the plaid jacket. Travis almost expected him to flee, but he stood his ground, then started walking toward them.

Travis pulled Heather behind him. "Stop right there."

"Keep your hands where I can see them," Caden said.

The man stopped and slowly removed his hat, clutching it in front of him. His dark eyes met Heather's, then quickly shifted away. But his stony expression morphed into softness. "*As-salaam alaikum*," he said. Travis recognized the Pashto greeting for hello. "Pardon me for interrupting, but I have been trying to speak with you for several weeks." Still he wouldn't meet Heather's eyes very long, instead transferring his gaze to Travis.

"You've been *watching* me for several weeks," Heather said, stepping around Travis to face the man she claimed was her stalker. "And you broke into my house? Chased me off the road? Hired people to kidnap me?"

His eyes widened and this time they connected with Heather's. He held up a hand. "No, no, no. That is not true. Not at all. You don't understand."

"Then why don't we take a ride to the police station," Travis said, his blood boiling, "and you make us understand."

"Hold up, people," Caden said, "he's done nothing wrong. At least nothing anyone can prove at the moment, so let's all take a deep breath and rein it in."

Heather's lips snapped together, and Travis could feel the slight tremors shuddering through her.

"Please," the man said, "can we go somewhere and talk?"

"Do I know you?" Heather asked.

"No, but you knew my son, Abdul." His voice broke on the name, his face tightening with the effort to hold back strong emotions.

Heather swayed and Travis moved his grip from her hand to her bicep. "Abdul?" she whispered. "Wait." Heather's eyes narrowed and she raised a hand to her lips. "I *do* know you. You're Musa Barakat."

"Heather?" Travis steadied her, taking in her pale features and shadowed eyes.

"I'm okay," she said.

The automatic response didn't fool him, and he glared at the man who'd brought even more trauma into her life.

"All right, Mr. Barakat," Caden said. He flashed his badge and eyed the newcomer. "Do you have any weapons on you?"

"No, of course not." He spread his arms. "Feel free."

Heather cleared her throat, turning toward Caden. "That's not necessary. I think we've jumped to some very big conclusions here. I know this man—by reputation only—from my time in Afghanistan. He's a good man, trying to turn his country around. He's no threat to me." She looked back at Mr. Barakat. "Sir, where's your security?"

"I came without them."

"I bet they're not very happy about that."

"It is one reason I have tried to keep a very low profile, worn the silly baseball cap and sunglasses. I do not want anyone to know that I am here."

"Let's head down to the cafeteria to talk. Feel free to put the baseball cap back on. Travis, you lead the way." She paused and cut her gaze to him. "I mean, Travis, would you be so kind as to lead the way? I wouldn't want to bark orders or anything."

Travis narrowed his eyes at the dig. Caden raised his brow and glanced at Gavin, who raised his hands in a "don't ask me" gesture.

"I'd be happy to," Travis said, biting his lip on a smile. At least she still had her sense of humor, even in the midst of confronting her possible stalker.

On the way to the elevator, Caden and Travis stayed behind Heather and Mr. Barakat while Gavin walked in front of them.

"You think he's legit?" Travis asked, keeping his voice low, eyeing the man's hands.

"I don't know. Heather obviously isn't worried about him, but I sent a text to Annie along with the guy's picture. She'll get back to me soon enough. Let's keep him busy until we find out."

"Good enough."

Once they were seated at a table in the cafeteria, Travis noticed Heather's haunted expression and figured she was reliving the moment the bomb had gone off. Or maybe her moments in the hospital with Abdul were playing through her memory.

Travis would admit he'd watched the video after learning about it, just to see what the others were so indignant about. The more he watched, the more his anger had risen. He'd been furious with the person who'd shot the video of her performing the surgery, but he had to admit, watching Heather in action had sent his admiration multiplying exponentially.

"First of all, Mr. Barakat," Heather said, "I hope you won't take offense at my accusations, but you *have* been following me. And with all the crazy things that have happened, I just assumed . . . I mean, before I realized . . ."

"Please, it's Musa." He flushed. "And yes, that is true. I have been following you. To be honest, I have been trying to work up the nerve to approach you. In my country, as I am sure you're aware, this conversation would not be happening. Not like this anyway."

"Of course."

"And while things are changing in my great land, I am from a very conservative part of the country, and I was not sure exactly what to do here. I may be very vocal about the progress my country needs to make in its treatment of women and what should be culturally accepted and thrown out, but to be here, in America, well, let us just say, it is one thing to shout it from a podium, it is quite another to see it happening here in person."

"I think I understand, but why not just call me?"

"Because I was afraid . . ."

"Afraid . . ."

"Afraid you would not want to speak to me. And if you refused to speak with me, I would be obligated to return home without accomplishing what I had come all this way for. No, it was better to speak to you in person."

Heather flinched. "Why would you think that I wouldn't want to talk to you?"

"Because of the grief my country has brought to yours. But I *had* to meet you. Each time I thought it might be the right time to approach you, something happened. Either someone would come talk to you or you would be on your phone and I did not want to interrupt. I was hoping to simply catch you alone, but you are almost never alone—except when you are at your home. I did not think approaching you in the hospital would be best as you were working, but knocking on your front door would not be appropriate either."

"You could have."

He offered her a wry smile. "I suppose, but, for me, that is not how things are done. When you disappeared for those few weeks, I almost gave up and returned home, but I could not." His eyes flickered. "Not until I had seen you face-to-face. Not until you knew the truth about Abdul."

Heather leaned forward. "Okay, tell me."

Travis couldn't help wonder if the man didn't want anyone knowing he was in the US because it would allow his opposition to strike while he was absent. Raid his home, take the rest of his family, whatever.

Musa frowned. "Abdul did not want to blow up that hospital. He was forced to put the bomb on."

"Who forced him?"

Caden had fallen silent, casting glances at his phone every so often, and Travis figured he was waiting for Annie or Daria to get back to him about Mr. Barakat.

"I have my suspicions, of course," the man said, "but no evidence to back those up. I did not find out about the whole plan until it was too late. But Abdul did what he did to protect his brother." He swallowed and looked away for a moment. When he lifted his gaze again, Travis flinched at the raw pain there. "Abdul left his phone behind. I know his password and I found that he had received a text message from someone. It was a picture of my younger son. He had been taken, with orders for Abdul to do as instructed or his brother would die." He pulled his phone from his pocket, tapped the screen, and turned it so they could see. A young dark-haired, dark-eyed boy stared tearfully into the camera. His hands were bound, and a knife rested against his throat. "Rayi is only eight, he will be nine next week," Musa said. "He and Abdul were very close. Ever since he was born, Abdul considered himself his protector. And so, he strapped the bomb on his chest as ordered, put on the shirt to hide the bomb, and went to blow up the hospital. He would have done anything for his brother—including die for him. Which he did." His throat worked and he looked away.

"I'm so sorry," Heather whispered.

"When I came here," Musa said, all expression gone now, "my goal was to thank you for working so hard to save Abdul. I wanted to see the woman doctor who did not seem to care that her patient was the boy who wore a bomb on his chest." He cleared his throat and met her gaze. "I wanted to meet the woman who heard my son's last words." He paused. "He was sent to blow up the hospital. No doubt to kill as many Americans as possible. Why did you try to save him?"

"Because that's what I do. If someone needs help, I try to help." She rubbed her eyes. "And Abdul asked me to help him." She leaned forward. "You're right, he didn't want to do it. He took off his shirt to warn us—to show me the bomb. I think he knew there was a remote that would trigger the explosion, but in the end, he couldn't kill innocent people. When whoever was controlling the bomb saw that he was trying to warn us, they detonated it."

Musa blanched. "He tried to warn you?"

"Yes. You didn't know?"

He shook his head. "I did not find his note until too late. It explained everything. Why he did it and where to find his brother. But he made no mention of his plan to not follow through."

"It may have been a last-minute decision," Gavin said.

Caden nodded. "That's what I think. And Rayi was all right?"

"Yes. He was released shortly after Abdul left for the hospital. Traumatized, but physically unharmed. He will be okay." He adjusted the baseball cap.

"So, they let Rayi go before they knew Abdul defied their orders," Travis said.

"Yes, and he and my wife are under heavy guard at a secret location at the moment."

"So, you came all this way to tell me this?" Heather asked.

"I did. But also because I wanted to apologize in person. My stance on my country's cultural beliefs and treatment of women and children is well known. I have many enemies and it seems they have found a way to get to me—through my children. Once, laughter filled my home in spite of the turmoil in my country, the stress of my job, and my outspoken views. But now there is just the sound of my wife's sobs. I was hoping that if I met you, talked to the woman who was with Abdul in his last moments . . . well, I suppose I was hoping it might bring some closure in addition to everything else."

○ ○ ○

"Closure is a good thing." Heather's heart pounded her own rhythm of grief, the memories swarming, invading the semblance of peace she'd managed to find over the last few months.

"Sounds like you've made some serious enemies," Caden said. "Can you think of anyone specific? Have you had any threats that really stand out?"

Musa's features clouded. "No. And I have gone over and over it with that fine-tooth comb you Americans are fond of. I have come up with nothing. I mean, yes, of course, there have been threats, but we took precautions. Mostly we had been concerned they'd try to kill me, but instead, they went after my sons. They watched them, paid off their bodyguard, and grabbed them on their way home from school." He scoffed. "And no one saw a thing."

Someone saw something, but no one wanted to come forward. Heather frowned. "You've done some investigating on your own, I'm sure."

"I have." He smoothed his mustache. "I cannot sleep or eat or function some days. The death toll for children in Afghanistan is the highest in the world. Of course, we know this. Everyone knows this. But it does not make the pain any less. I must know who killed my son." His eyes hardened. "And I *will* find out one way or another."

"Was the shirt special?" Heather asked.

He blinked. "I'm sorry, what?"

"The shirt he was wearing the day he died. Was it special to him?"

"No. Not that I know of. I had never seen it before. Why?"

She shook her head. "I have it. I kept it. You can have it back if it would . . . help . . . in any way."

Musa tilted his head and studied her. "You kept his shirt?"

"I . . . yes . . . but don't ask me to explain, please. I can't."

Once again, the man's emotions nearly overcame him, but he fought them back with visible effort. "I . . . no. It is special to you, I can tell. Keep it. Do not let his memory fade. Remember he died a hero, not a terrorist."

"I'll remember," Heather whispered. A tear traced down her cheek, and she swiped it and straightened her shoulders. "Thank you for coming."

"I am sorry I scared you. I just had to be careful."

"I understand. Now."

"Your English is very good," Travis said.

"I had many tutors growing up. My father wanted me to go into banking, not politics. He thought it very important for his son to speak English. Abdul spoke it just about as well as I do."

Caden tapped the table. "Just a moment if you don't mind. I've thought of another question."

"Yes?"

"How'd you know Heather would be here at the hospital? If you're not involved in trying to hurt her, how did you know to find her here?"

Musa shrugged. "It was an educated guess. Her friend Asher James is in this hospital. It only makes sense that she would show up at some point to see him."

Heather flinched. Talk about predictable. "So, you've just been waiting for me to arrive."

"Yes."

"But we came in the back way."

"And as I was walking, I spotted a small caravan of security in the parking lot. I simply waited and saw you coming in. Some things can be attributed to—how do you say—dumb luck, no? I waited to see what floor you got off on and followed." He frowned. "Although that is not the room I expected you to go to, so I lost track of you for a while. I have been wandering the floor, looking for you. You are here to see someone else?"

"It's a long story." Heather drew in a deep breath, her mind processing everything she'd just learned. She pulled her phone from her pocket. "Could I have your number?"

"Of course." Musa gave it to her and she tapped it into her device.

When she finished, she looked at Travis. "Well, that solves one problem but raises another."

"Yeah, I was thinking the same thing."

"If he's not the one who's been after me and behind the attempts on my life . . ."

"Then who is?"

CHAPTER NINETEEN

With tons of questions but no answers, Travis led Heather, Caden, and Gavin to Asher's room, only to find him dressed and sitting on the edge of the bed.

Brooke's eyes widened when she saw them. "We're just getting ready to leave. What are you guys doing back here?"

"It's a long story," Heather said. "I'll fill you in later."

Asher's gaze connected with Gavin's. "Have you heard?"

Gavin frowned. "No, what?"

"Benny Silver committed suicide."

"What? When? How?"

"Six weeks ago. Shot himself in his basement up in Michigan."

Gavin pressed the heels of his hands to his eyes. "Aw, man. And we're just hearing about this now?"

"I know."

"Who's Benny Silver?" Travis asked.

"Wait a minute," Heather said before anyone could answer Travis. "I remember him. He was the one involved in Gina's husband's friendly fire death, wasn't he?"

"Yeah."

Heather glanced at Travis. "I treated him at the hospital for something before we left on our sandboarding trip. I do remember he was really down and asked one of the psychiatrists to come in and do an evaluation."

"Apparently, he was battling depression over the friendly fire incident," Asher said, his voice soft. He rubbed his eyes, then dropped his hands. "I can't believe we're just now hearing about this. Usually the grapevine is much quicker. My buddy Matthew Irwin called to check on me and told me he'd just found out from—" He waved a hand. "Well, it doesn't matter. No one found him until last week. His neighbor said she'd noticed a smell coming from the house and at first didn't think anything about it. Then said it eventually faded, but a flock of vultures kept coming into the yard. She went to investigate, looked in the basement window, and saw him."

Travis shuddered. "How awful. Where did everyone think he was?"

"Still overseas. He never told his family he was coming home. His sister is beside herself, and Benny's parents . . ." He shook his head. "It's bad."

"Oh my—"

"Does Gina know?" Travis asked.

"Sarah and one of her shadows are on their way to tell her now."

"Any more sightings of the man they saw following them?" Heather asked.

"No, nothing yet."

"Well, this day just keeps getting better and better," Gavin muttered.

The sadness in Heather's eyes cramped Travis's heart. He gripped her hand briefly and she shot him a tight smile.

"All right," he said, "I think it's time for Heather and me to head back to my place. Anyone want to make sure we're not followed?"

"I'll help," Asher said quickly. At Brooke's ferocious glare, he ducked his head. "Or not," he mumbled. "Maybe next time?"

Brooke looked at Heather. "If he was the only one available to help, it would be a no-brainer, but I think he needs to sit this one out."

"Of course." She lifted a hand to rub her eyes. "I'm sorry. I feel like such a burden."

"What! No." Brooke hurried to wrap her friend in a hug. "That's one thing you'll never be." She pulled away and patted Heather's shoulder. "It's just the doctor was very specific about what Asher could and couldn't do if he wanted to leave the hospital, and Asher promised. Didn't you, sweetheart?"

"I did."

"And Heather will be perfectly fine in the care of Travis, Gavin, and Caden, will she not?"

"She will," Asher agreed. "Absolutely." He lifted his head and met each man's gaze. "But if you need me, Brooke will be fine with it."

Gavin patted the man on the shoulder. "I think we've got this covered."

Asher nodded, and Travis led the way out of the room toward the elevator. Travis's phone rang the minute the doors swooshed open. "Hold up, it's Ryker." He swiped the screen. "Ryker? How are you doing?"

"Not good. My dad beat up the doc."

The teen's harsh words laced with panic slammed him. "Did you call 911?"

Three sets of eyes locked on Travis.

"Yes. He's got a bad laceration on his head. Maybe a broken rib or two. I don't know."

"Where's your dad?"

"I . . . I don't know that either." The teen coughed to cover up a sob, but Travis heard it loud and clear.

"Take a deep breath, Ryker," he said. "Tell me the details."

"I'd just gotten back from a run to the medical supply store. I entered through the back of the clinic and heard a yell, then a loud crash. When I ran into the doc's office, my dad was beating on him."

"Oh man . . ."

"I yelled at him to stop and he came after me."

Travis closed his eyes, envisioning the scene playing out. "Are you okay?"

"Yeah. I pushed him off of me and out of the doc's office. After I locked the door, I grabbed the phone and called 911. We're at the hospital. I couldn't get him to wake up, Travis. What if he dies because of me? What if—"

"Stop right there. This isn't your fault. Tell me where you are." He had to be in the same hospital.

"I'm in the ER. Oh, you've got to be kidding me," Ryker muttered.

"What is it?"

"Child Services is here." He let out a harsh laugh. "If they think I'm going with them to some strange home, they're out of their minds."

"Just tell them they can work on a placement for you, but you want to stay with the doc. I'll come sit with you, okay?"

"It's my fault," he said, his voice low.

"It's not."

"My dad came looking for me and he—" Ryker broke off and Travis waited, his heart pounding an empathetic ache for the hurting teen. "Earlier, he'd told me to stay away from Dr. Colson, and I told him to mind his own business. He lost it when he saw my bike there. I'd driven the doc's truck to get the supplies."

Travis pressed the button on the elevator and the others followed him inside when the doors opened. "Hang tight. We're coming down."

"Coming down? Where are you?"

"Upstairs."

A grunt. "Get away from me, man."

"Sorry?"

"Some social worker is trying to tell me I need to go with him. I'm not going."

"Tell him I'm coming. You can stay with me."

Heather raised a brow at him, but a small smile curved her lips, and the look in her eyes said his impulsive offer had been the right thing to do.

The elevator opened, and Travis led the way down the hall, with Heather hurrying along beside him. Gavin and Caden stayed with them.

Travis pushed through the heavy door and stopped when he saw Ryker sitting in a chair, a young dark-headed guy not more than five years older than Ryker standing to the side.

"Hey, you okay?"

Ryker's head snapped up. "Travis. You came."

"I said I would."

"Yeah, but . . . yeah." His eyes moved to Heather, then Gavin and Caden. "Thanks."

"I'm Mickey O'Reilly with CPS," the young man said.

"Who called you?"

"The hospital. Apparently, they're familiar with Ryker."

Ryker's glare should have incinerated the man. "I'm not going with you. I'm seventeen."

O'Reilly held up a hand. "It's not up to me. It's the way the law works."

"I'll just run away, so why don't we save us all the paperwork and trouble?"

O'Reilly frowned. "Look, I'm sorry, I don't want to do this either, but it's my job."

"Look," Travis said, "he hasn't been removed from his home, so technically he's not in the system right now. He can come stay with me and I can protect him."

"I'm sorry, I can't do that."

Caden cleared his throat and flashed his badge. "Actually, I'm going to take this young man into custody. He's a crucial witness in a case I'm investigating—and may need protection from some pretty bad people—so I'll take it from here. We'll let you know when he's ready for you."

O'Reilly let his gaze touch each person before landing back on Caden. He opened his folder, scribbled something on a piece of paper, and handed it to Caden. "I'll need your signature on this."

○ ○ ○

Heather's heart beat a happy rhythm when the caseworker left the hospital. She had a feeling he could get into some major trouble for walking away like he did, but for now, Ryker was in good, safe hands.

Caden turned to the teen. "You want to stay with Travis?"

Ryker looked at Travis, then back at Caden. He gave a short, small nod. "Yeah. That would be nice. Thank you." He hesitated. "Were you serious when you said I might be in danger, or was that just for the CPS dude's benefit?"

"I'm serious. I don't know if you're in danger or not, but I don't want to gamble with your life and assume you're not. I wasn't there when you helped Heather, and I don't know if those guys saw you. If they did, then yeah, the threat could be a very real thing. I think we'll err on the side of caution here." He frowned. "And since we're already watching out for Heather, we'll simply keep you in the same place and make sure there isn't any backlash coming your way."

"Makes sense to me," Travis said. "I've got plenty of room at my place."

"What about the doc?" Ryker asked.

"We'll wait until we get an update on him before we leave."

The teen's shoulders wilted. "Thank you."

They found seats in the waiting room, and Heather studied the teen, wishing she could distract him from the scenarios he was playing in his head about the doc. She slid over next to him. "Hey."

"Hey."

"Can I ask you a question?" She took his shrug as permission to continue. "What happened to your mom?"

"She overdosed when I was about seven and a half."

Again the ache in her chest flared for this kid. "How have you turned out so awesome?"

He hesitated only a fraction at the abrupt question, then offered her another lift of one bony shoulder. "I don't know about awesome, but if you mean how did I avoid going down the same path as my dad, then I have to give the doc credit for that. I was ten when my dad broke my arm. Of course, I didn't tell anyone that he did it, but I think the doc knew. He was really kind and patient. I asked questions throughout the whole process. From X-ray to setting it to the cast. He asked me if I was interested in medicine. I said yeah."

"And the rest is history?"

Ryker hesitated and Heather waited, letting him decide if he wanted to finish the story or not. "Something like that," he finally said, his voice low. "At the time, I just wanted to know what to do for it when it happened again, but over time, yeah, I found myself drawn to medicine—and the doc. Mostly the doc."

"I see."

His eyes lifted to hers. "Yeah, I'm sure you do."

"Why'd your dad break your arm?"

He looked away, letting his gaze settle on the hands clasped between his knees.

"Ryker?"

He cleared his throat. "Um . . . because I wanted a birthday cake."

Heather bit her lip and blinked back tears for the little boy who'd just wanted a cake. "A cake?"

"My mom had made me one for my sixth birthday," he said, "and I remembered it tasted so good. But more than that, I felt loved that day. Like someone was happy I was on the planet and I was worth celebrating." He shrugged. "I guess on my tenth birthday, I wanted that feeling back so I asked my dad if I could have a cake. He said he wasn't spending any money on a stupid cake.

I started crying and he hit me. I crashed into the coffee table and broke it—with my arm."

Heather wanted to throw up. Memories assaulted her. Being pushed into a wall by her father. His heavy fist slamming against the side of her head. His ability to twist her arm in such a way as not to break it but cause excruciating pain. She shuddered. One thing she could never understand was the ability to hurt a child on purpose. "I'm sorry, Ryker."

"I am too. The doc showed me how a real man is supposed to act, so I'm grateful for that." His eyes slid in the direction of the operating room. "He has to be all right, Heather. I don't know what I'll do if he's not."

She reached over and clasped his hand. "I know."

They fell silent and Heather offered up a prayer for the man who meant so much to the kid sitting next to her.

The minutes ticked past. Thirty minutes later, Caden looked up from his phone. "All right. It's arranged. I've got a couple of buddies who are going to follow you back to Travis's place and stand guard. There's a BOLO out on Donnie Little, who was last seen at a convenience store about an hour from here. Local authorities are on the move looking for him. We're also delving into his background to see if there's anything that would indicate where he's trying to disappear to. We're monitoring his wife's cell phone, and so far, there've been no calls from him."

Finally, the door opened, and the doctor stepped into the waiting room. Ryker shot to his feet. "How is he?"

"He had some internal bleeding, but we've gotten that under control. He'll be good and sore for a while, but he should be just fine."

A long breath escaped Ryker and his fingers curled into fists at his sides. "Thank you."

"You feel all right about heading to the ranch now?" Travis asked.

"Yes. Yeah."

"Do you need to get anything? A bag from the cabin or your father's house? We can escort you there to pick up whatever you need."

"No—" He froze.

"What is it?" Travis turned to see a large man striding toward them.

"That's my father and he—"

"You get yourself home, boy!" Donahue lurched toward the group, his eyes bleary, balance not quite steady.

"—looks drunk." Ryker planted his feet to face the man with a granite jaw, clenched fists, and blazing eyes. "You beat up the doc."

"Because he's got no business interfering in our lives." The slurred words accompanied the sickening smell of alcohol and foul breath. "He's making you think you're something special and you're gettin' too uppity for your own good."

Ryker launched himself toward the man, and Gavin caught him, while Caden moved lightning quick. Before Heather could blink, he had the man's hands behind him and cuffs around his wrists.

Heather grabbed Ryker's fist and squeezed. He blinked and the red rage that had been in his eyes faded to a deep sorrow. "Check him for weapons," he told Caden in a low voice. "He'll have *something* on him."

Gavin let Ryker loose and the teen kept his distance from his father. Security hurried over and Caden explained the situation, then patted Ryker's father down. He pulled a small pistol from his coat pocket. "What do we have here?"

"Everyone carries," Donahue said. "Lots of snakes around here."

Caden looked back at Ryker. "Does he have a CWP?"

"No, he has a record."

"Okay, then I'll detain him and turn him over to the local cops. They can arrest him on assault charges and carrying without a permit. I'll make sure they add drunk and disorderly to it too."

Ryker pulled his old phone out of his pocket. "I'll call the sheriff."

That seemed to jolt some sobriety into the man. "Ryker! You're going to put your old man in jail? You'll just have to bail me out, you moron."

Ryker turned his back to his father. When he hung up, he nodded to Travis. "I'm ready to leave when you are."

"Ryker? What are you doing? You seriously doing this?" Donahue sounded more sober at this point—sober mixed with shock and a touch of desperation.

Ryker ignored the new tone in his father's voice and kept his gaze locked on Travis. "I'll be waiting outside for you."

"I'm going to make you pay! You'll regret this!"

The sheriff chose that moment to enter the hospital. His eyes widened slightly at the scene before him, and he huffed a disgusted sigh. "I was two blocks over at the diner. Thanks for interrupting my meal, Donahue."

He led the protesting man away, and Ryker scrubbed a hand down his face. "I can't help him, can I?" he asked Heather.

"He doesn't want to be helped right now. Until someone's willing to be helped, then no, you can offer and offer, but—" She broke off as her own words slapped her in the face. She caught Travis watching her, a soft, knowing expression on his features. She grimaced and shot him a smile. "But maybe one day he'll realize how much you tried to help him, how much you *still* want to help him, and he'll finally let you."

Ryker's gaze bounced between her and Travis, then back to her. He gave her a smile identical to Travis's. Heather resisted the childish impulse to stick her tongue out at the two of them. Barely.

Travis placed a hand at the small of her back and escorted her toward the exit.

Caden fell into step with them. "I don't think we should be obvious about you leaving the hospital. But when you pull out of the parking lot, an unmarked vehicle will fall in behind you at a discreet distance to make sure no one else is following. Once you're back at the ranch—and we're sure no one followed you—we'll have a couple of officers keep watch on the place. And you."

Heather kept her groan to herself. Squelching her resentment at the need for all the help, she made a vow. When the person responsible for causing all this drama was captured, she was going to request the pleasure of slamming the cell door herself.

CHAPTER

TWENTY

When they made it back to the ranch with no one shooting at them, attempting to run them off the road, or blowing anything up, Travis released a small breath of relief. Even the fact that the snow had started up again didn't faze him.

After a stop at a superstore for clothes and toiletries for Ryker, they'd made good time. Instead of going to his parents' home, though, he pulled into his driveway and they all got out.

"You live here?" The awe in Ryker's voice was unmistakable.

"Yeah. It's a work in progress, but I'm having fun doing it."

"It's awesome, man."

"Thank you." Travis shot a smile at Heather. "You don't mind moving over here, do you? With Ryker, there aren't enough bedrooms over at Mom's."

"Of course, but I don't mind staying with your—"

She broke off when he shook his head. "I'd rather keep you close by. I'm almost one hundred percent sure that no one knows you're staying here, but I'd rather not have you that far away in case anything were to happen." He shifted. "Um . . . but if you're not comfortable with that arrangement, I can let Ryker stay here and we'll just—"

This time he was the one who broke off, as she placed a finger against his lips.

"It's fine, Travis. I'll walk over and get my stuff." She held up the satellite phone he'd given her. "And I'll keep this on me at all times."

"I'll help you after I get Ryker settled in a room."

"It's a small rolling suitcase. I think I can handle it." When he frowned, she pointed. "Look. Guards. People with guns who know how to use them. This place is protected better than the White House."

"Not quite, but I see what you mean."

She waved and headed toward his parents' home.

Travis turned back to Ryker, who was still looking around him in awe. "You ready to check out your room?"

The teen bit his lip and nodded. "Yeah," he whispered. "Thanks."

Travis watched Heather enter the house, then turned and led the way up the front porch to the door. He didn't bother locking the house most days simply because he didn't need to. He pushed open the door and stepped into the foyer. New paint smell still lingered, and Travis drew in a deep breath. Stairs straight ahead led to the second floor. "There are two bedrooms up there. Pick whichever one you like best. I'll let Heather have the one down here."

"I'll sleep anywhere."

"The bedroom is good." Travis clapped the teen on his shoulder. "Past the stairs is the great room. On past that is the kitchen and eating area. Then a small hallway with the guest room on the left and the master on the right. If you need anything to eat or drink, the refrigerator is full."

"I don't know what to say."

"You don't have to say a word. Pick out your room, then come on down."

Ryker took off up the stairs just as Heather stepped inside, pulling her small bag behind her. When Ryker disappeared into the room to the left of the stairs, she shot Travis a small smile. "Have you always collected strays?"

He laughed. "Strays? No. But I do like helping people. I always have. Maybe that's why God puts me in the position to do so."

"Well, you're good at it."

"Good at it?"

"Yes. You're pushy about it, but not overbearing."

Another chuckle slipped from him and he led her to the bedroom that would be hers. "I'm glad you don't think I'm overbearing."

She placed the bag just inside the door and he waited while she took in the room. "It's lovely. Such a pretty shade of blue."

"I thought it was a peaceful color." Pleased that she approved, he led her into the living room where she walked to the mantel and ran her hands over the wood. "You made this, didn't you?"

"I did. I've always found woodworking to be an escape. A stress reliever, I guess."

"You're very talented."

Travis could feel the heat rising in his cheeks, but her praise freed something inside of him. "You don't think it's a silly hobby or a waste of time?"

She blinked. "What? No, of course not. And if someone told you it is, then they need their head examined. This is art."

"Thank you." He couldn't help the husky quality to his voice and cleared his throat.

"Who told you that it was silly?"

"A woman I dated a couple of years ago. For a while I wondered if she was right."

"Rest assured, she was very wrong."

"I appreciate that. It galls me to admit she really did a number on my self-esteem. Made me feel less because I don't wear a suit to the office or drive a black Mercedes."

"You don't need any of that stuff. Trust me, she didn't deserve you and you're well rid of her."

He stepped over to her and took her hand. “I’m sorry this is happening to you, Heather, but I’m not sorry that I’m getting to spend a lot of time with you.”

Her gaze locked on his. “I feel the same way, but . . .”

His heart stuttered. “But?”

“I like you, Travis. A lot.”

“I’m still hearing the ‘but’.”

“But I’m . . .” She sighed and the conflict in her eyes tore at his heart.

“You’re what, Heather?”

She shook her head. “This may be a premature statement, but I’m going to go ahead and say it. The truth is, I have a lot of emotional baggage.” She paused. “It might just be too much to ask of anyone to take that on. Too much to ask of you. You deserve so much better than that.” A grimace creased her features. “I’m not saying this very well and I may be completely out of line because I might be reading you wrong, but—” This time it was his finger on her lips that stopped the flow of rambling words.

He raised a brow. She was seriously worried that she wasn’t good enough for *him*? “That’s it?” He dropped his hand. Her words gave him courage.

She frowned. “What do you mean, that’s it? Yes, that’s pretty much it.”

“First of all, you’re not reading me wrong. Second, do you think I’m blind or stupid?”

Her jaw dropped. “Of course not. Quite the opposite actually.”

“Then let me decide what I think I can handle. And just so we’re clear, you haven’t inflicted anything on me.”

“Except a killer?”

Her dry tone made him smile. “Okay, well, other than that. But, seriously, don’t you think we can only go up from there?”

She shook her head. However, the slight curve of her lips gave him hope. “I’m just asking for a chance to get to know you more.

And let you know me. If you're in interested in that. If you're not, then I won't say another word."

"I'm interested," she said, her voice soft. But the shadows in her eyes said she was still worried.

Footsteps on the stairs made him pause. "To be continued."

He turned to see Ryker enter, phone pressed to his ear.

"Okay," Ryker said, "thanks for letting me know." He hung up and ran a hand over his eyes. "The doc is doing better," he said. "And my father goes before the judge tomorrow morning."

"Do you want to be there?" Travis asked.

"No. Not this time." Sadness flickered before he forced a smile. "Hey, do you mind if I go exploring a bit? I'd love to check out that barn."

"You ride?"

"Yeah. A buddy of mine from school had horses, and his parents used to pay us to muck out the stalls and stuff. After we were done, we'd go riding."

"Then go explore and enjoy yourself, just keep an eye on the weather. It's not horrible right now, but it's supposed to get worse."

"Thanks, man." He shoved into his coat, gloves, and hat, and spun toward the front door.

"Hey," Heather called.

Ryker turned back with raised brows.

"Just . . . be careful and don't pull those stitches out."

He grinned and was gone before they could blink.

"Well," Travis murmured, "he seems to like it here okay."

"What's not to like?"

Travis's phone buzzed and he snatched it to glance at the screen. "It's Asher."

"If it's nothing private, can you put it on speaker? I want to hear his voice."

He did. "Hi, Asher, you're on speaker with Heather and me. What's up?"

"I just got a strange call from Jasmine, Benny Silver's sister."

"Okay."

"She wanted to know if Benny had any enemies, anyone who'd want to see him dead."

Travis raised a brow at Heather.

She frowned and shook her head. "The only time we talked was when he was in the hospital, and he didn't say much. I just picked up on some possible depression. Why?"

"Because the autopsy just came back and the ME said he didn't kill himself. He was murdered."

○ ○ ○

Heather gasped. "Murdered!"

"The ME said upon initial inspection at the scene, she couldn't see all of the details. It wasn't until she was doing the autopsy that she came across what looked like defensive wounds on his hands. Fortunately, it was cold in the basement where he was killed, so decomp was slowed down."

"So, the sister called you?"

"Yeah, I told her if she needed anything, to let me know. I mean, I know there's nothing I can do, but it just seemed like the right thing to offer. Anyway, when she called a little bit ago, she said she knew it was a long shot, but the cops were asking her for names of anyone who might have had it in for Benny. She had no idea, so she called me to see if I had any insight or if I could give her some names of other soldiers to talk to."

"And?" Heather asked. "Do you have any insight?"

"No, none. But Jasmine said the medical examiner was going over his body very carefully looking for forensic evidence now. And a crime scene unit is heading back to his basement to see if they can find anything."

Heather frowned. "Isn't it too late for that? I mean, you think anything would be left?"

"You never know. I'll keep you updated."

She pursed her lips. "Okay, thank you, Asher. It's good to hear you sounding so well."

"I'm fine, Heather. Or at least very much on the way to fine. You watch your back."

"I am. Thank you."

The front door opened, and Ryker stepped inside. He brushed snowflakes from his hat and pulled his gloves off. "Man, it's getting cold out there, but the horses are awesome. Your sister's in the barn working with one of them. She said to tell you she might need your help with Herman. She didn't say much, but I could tell he wasn't doing too great. What's wrong with him?"

"He's one of the older horses and has been battling cancer. Over the past couple of weeks, he's been going downhill fast, and Sandra's probably going to have to put him down. They've already got the hole dug for his grave, but Sandra's been hanging on to him as long as possible. I guess it's time."

"Aw, man. I'm sorry. That's a tough thing to have to do."

Travis let out a long sigh. "Thanks for letting me know. And Sandra will be glad for any help you want to give her. I know you want to keep working for the doc."

Ryker nodded, then blew out a low breath. "Well, I don't have to worry about it until he's back at work and that may be a few weeks, so I'll just play it by ear if that's all right."

"Perfectly all right."

"In the meantime, I don't mind helping with the horses." A yawn hit him. "You okay with me taking a nap?"

"Of course," Travis said.

Heather gave an agreeing nod. "Sounds like a good idea. You really should take it easy. You're still healing, remember?"

He pressed a hand against his side. "Kinda hard to forget, but thanks." He paused. "Thanks for everything." He took one step, then stopped and turned to Travis. "If you have to go help Sandra with Herman, let me know. I want to help."

"You don't have—"

"I know I don't. I want to."

"Sure. I'll let you know."

Ryker jogged up the stairs as though completely healed, and Heather shook her head. "If that's taking it easy, I've got to come up with a different description."

Once he was gone, Heather dropped her head into her hands. "Murdered?" she whispered through her fingers and looked up at Travis.

"Yeah."

"What's going on?"

"I don't know. I really don't know." He paused. "I'm going to let Caden know and see if he has any thoughts on this."

"You do that." She chewed on her lip. "I feel like everything is circling back to something that happened in Kabul."

"What makes you say that?"

"Just a feeling, I suppose. I can't even think of any one thing that happened that would have led to all of this. The attempt to blow up the hospital is the big one, though." She hesitated. "I wonder how Gina's going to take this news. She was so angry about Brad's death, but never once did I hear her say anything against the soldiers responsible. It was just a stupid, tragic accident."

"You want to be the one to break it to her?"

"Unless Sarah already has." She stood and paced from one end of the room to the other. "I'll call her and see what she says."

"Good idea. The phone in my office is untraceable. You can use it."

"Untraceable?"

"I work from there occasionally and I don't want some of the people I call having my number—or the ability to track me down."

Well, that made sense. "Also, do you have a computer I can use? I really need to check in with my boss at the hospital as well as scan my emails."

"Yeah, sure. It's in my office next to the phone. Also secure and untraceable. Password is the first two letters of the kids' names from oldest to youngest, then their ages, youngest to oldest."

She blinked. "Travis, you don't just give out your password to your computer."

"I wouldn't give it to anyone, but it's you. And I have no problem with you having the password." He headed for the kitchen. "I'm going to grab a soda. You want anything?"

Heather was still trying to wrap her head around his words. "Um, yes, please. A water would be great."

"I'll be right back."

"I'll be in your office calling Sarah and checking my email."

And fighting her exploding feelings for the man who always seemed to say the right thing at the right time.

The door to Travis's house burst open and Heather flinched, then relaxed when she saw it was his nephew. "Martin? Everything okay?"

"No, where's Uncle Travis? Mom needs him in the barn."

"He's in the kitchen. Is it Herman?"

The boy nodded, tears in his eyes. "She's going to have to put him down and she wants Uncle Travis there. Then they'll have to haul him out to the pasture to bury him."

The ranch was beautiful, but this was one example of the harsh realities that came with it.

"I'll help too," Ryker said from the top of the stairs.

Heather didn't bother to protest. If he ripped the stitches open, she'd close them back up.

He descended while Martin darted for the kitchen. "I heard the door slam open and came to see what was going on."

Because no abused kid could ignore a loud noise in the house he lived in. Loud equated to trouble in just about every instance.

Travis hurried from the kitchen, followed by Martin. Travis caught her eye. "You'll be all right here by yourself?"

"I'll be fine, Travis. Do we need to review the security you have here?"

"No. No, we don't. You're right. No one's coming on this property unless they're invited."

"Exactly. Go help your sister."

"Could take a while. It's snowing a little harder too."

"I'm aware. Does she need me to help with the other children?"

"They're with my grandma," Martin said, inching toward the door.

Travis grabbed his Stetson with a glance back at Heather. "I'll text you updates."

"Perfect."

Once they were gone, Heather made her way to his office and stopped in the doorway. She felt like an intruder in the very masculine space but shrugged off the sensation and rounded the desk. With a wiggle of the wireless mouse, she brought the screen to life.

And smiled.

His desktop held a picture of his nieces and nephews piled on top of him. "Cute." She typed in the password and navigated to the internet browser. While her email was loading, she picked up the handset and dialed Sarah's number.

"Hello?"

"Sarah? It's Heather."

"Oh, Heather. I didn't recognize the number. Are you okay?"

"Yes, listen. Asher just told us that Benny was murdered."

"I know. It's awful. I'm still reeling."

"I'm assuming Gina knows?"

"No, not yet. I've called her a couple of times, but she's at work and not picking up."

Heather frowned and rubbed her eyes. "Okay. Will you let me know when you talk to her? She's had such a hard time with Brad's death. This may really throw her. Bring up his death all over again. Before I left Kabul, she told me Benny had called her a few times to check up on her after his discharge." He'd been part of the unit who fired the round of bullets that killed Brad. "I'm just worried about her."

"I'll keep trying her."

"Yeah, me too. Thanks, Sarah."

Heather hung up and clicked on the web browser bar. She entered her social media information and her profile details popped up.

And she smiled. Her guilty pleasure. Her time waster. Her secret that she'd never in a million years admit to Travis Walker. But she'd missed posting over the last few days, and her fans had apparently missed her. When she'd discovered that she really enjoyed medical dramas, she also realized she hated the inaccuracies. So, she started blogging about the errors in the shows and described in detail what would actually happen in the given situation. It hadn't taken long for her blog to explode, gaining new readers by the day. And Heather loved it.

For the next few minutes, she read the comments and then simply posted that she was dealing with some personal issues but would soon be back. "Keep posting your questions," she muttered aloud while she typed the words. "I promise to answer them in the order listed."

She clicked on Facebook and started scrolling, catching up on the lives of friends and coworkers.

And Brad Wicks, Gina's husband. His mother had written a blistering post about how he just wanted to grow up and serve his country but had instead been killed by that very country. She'd put up pictures from when he was a child. Then a teen. His wedding day. Heather read one of the posts:

> It's a shame a mother has to take things into her own hands to see that justice is done and her son's death doesn't go unpunished.

"What in the world?" Heather whispered. She clicked on each picture. And came to the video of her in the operating room, working on Abdul.

> And this one. Really? Trying to save a would-be murderer? Why does he get medical attention when he tried to kill people like my son? Shame on this doctor. Shame on you, **Heather Fontaine**.

The woman even had the nerve to tag her in the post?

A chill settled over Heather as she went on to the next picture. One of Benny Silver's obituary.

> At least he can't kill anyone else's son.

The chill turned to ice when she clicked the next picture.

> And here, this horrible, horrible woman. My son's *wife*. The woman who was supposed to love him and watch out for him. She encouraged him to join her in that wretched country where he died. And she gets to live. That's just not fair—and that needs to change.

Heather noted the post had been written an hour earlier. She reached for the phone and dialed Gina's number.

○ ○ ○

Travis inhaled the familiar scent of barn—horse manure, hay, saddle oil, leather, and more. Sadness and grief. Herman had been in the family for almost twenty-five years.

Sandra had insisted Herman stay in the barn, his home for the last year and a half. He now lay between the rows of stalls on a massive tarp, sides heaving with his efforts.

Once he was gone, Travis would have to drag him behind the tractor to the gravesite. And the packed snow would help the tarp slide along the ground. The wind had picked up in the last thirty minutes and whistled around the building while the temperatures continued to drop.

Travis's heart cramped as he watched his sister sit next to her beloved friend and say her final words. Tears streamed down her face, and Travis fought his own emotions.

Herman butted her knee gently with his nose and gave a low whinny.

"How do I do this, Travis?" Sandra whispered. She stroked the animal's nose. "All of a sudden he's having a better day. I can't put him down while he's like this, can I?"

The horse definitely was *not* having a *better* day. "Sandra, he has cancer." He sat next to her and pulled her into a hug. She buried her face in his shoulder. "I know it's hard," he said, "but he's not going to get better. Look at him. He barely made it out of the stall before collapsing. You have to do this for him." His eyes locked on the vet waiting quietly. Patiently.

"It's okay, Sandra," Ian said. "You're my only client today. Take as long as you like."

"Sandra," Travis said, "*look* at him. He's hurting and he's counting on you to help him."

Her fingers stroked Herman's jowl, moved over his muzzle, then up to his forehead. The horse huffed and shifted as though trying to get up. And failed. Sandra drew in a shaky breath and nodded to the vet. "Okay. It's not going to get easier by dragging it out. And Travis is right. He's in pain. It's time to do the right thing."

Ryker had distracted Martin by asking the boy questions about one of the other horses. However, when the vet moved, Martin hurried back to Herman's side and dropped to his knees next to his mother. He wrapped his arms around the horse's neck. "Bye, Herman," he whispered.

Sandra gripped his shoulders. "We'll just hold him while he goes to sleep." She settled the horse's head against her thigh and turned her gaze to Travis. "You'll go with us to bury him? Joe already had his grave dug out and the tractor waiting to push the dirt over him."

"Of course." He texted Heather a quick update while Ian efficiently placed the IV in the horse. Just as he sent the text, his father texted and asked for an update. The man and two of the ranch hands had taken a trailer to a livestock auction in Williamston early that morning in an effort to beat the snow. They'd have to wait until roads were cleared to get back home. He'd offered to postpone the appointment because of the plans to put Herman down, but Travis had told him he could handle everything at the ranch. In the middle of updating his dad, Heather's text pinged across his phone.

She offered her sympathies. A second text from her said,

I have a lot to show you when you get back here. I think Gina's in danger. I called her and told her to come here immediately before the roads get too bad. She said she thinks she can make it. I hope that's all right. I'm sorry if I should have asked first, but I just thought it was urgent.

Travis frowned. Of course it was all right, but what had she found to indicate that Gina was in danger?

I'm also getting ready to call Caden and fill him in. Maybe he can send someone to escort her and make sure she's not followed.

All right. I'm only going to be gone for another thirty minutes or so.

No worries. I'll catch you up when you get back.

Travis finished texting his father, then notified the guards of Gina's imminent arrival. He tucked his phone in his pocket and turned his attention back to the situation at hand. His heart broke for his sister and nephew. And himself. "Where's Joe?"

"He was taking a half day to come do this, but his boss called him in to a last-minute meeting. Mandatory."

"Of course."

"Not everyone owns their own company, Travis." Her eyes flashed at him. "Don't judge him."

"I'm not."

"You are."

Okay, he was. And the man *had* taken care of having the grave dug. "I'm sorry."

More tears spilled over her cheeks and she shook her head. "No, I'm sorry. I'm hurting and—" She glanced at the vet, still waiting patiently with the syringe. The IV was in, along with the meds to send Herman into a relaxing, pain-free twilight sleep. Sandra nodded. "Let's send Herman on to that rainbow bridge so he won't suffer any longer."

"Is there really a rainbow bridge?" Martin asked.

Sandra smiled through her tears. "I don't know," she said, "but God created Herman to live his life on earth with us as a temporary arrangement."

"Like he loaned him to us?"

"Yes. That's a good way of looking at it. Or gifted him to us. Either way, God trusted us to take care of him, so I fully believe that God has a plan to take care of Herman once he dies. Whether that includes a rainbow bridge or not, I don't know, but God's got Herman in his hands regardless of what that looks like."

Martin nodded, a single tear traveling down his little-boy cheek. He bit a trembling lip, then looked at Ian. "I think it's time to give Herman back to God so he can make him feel better."

Ryker choked on a sob and turned away.

Travis couldn't stop his own tears from spilling over.

CHAPTER TWENTY-ONE

Caden sat at his desk in the office and tapped the keyboard, looking for information on Benny Silver. It wasn't his case or even his business, but for some reason, he wanted to know more. The guy had an exemplary record and no blame had been laid at his feet in the friendly fire incident. It was just a tragic accident involving miscommunication and bullets. A deadly combination.

"You're deep in thought," Zane said. His desk faced Caden's.

"Thinking about how everything connects."

"How does it?"

"It doesn't." He rubbed his eyes. "But it has to. Doesn't it?"

Benny and his unit had been clearing a building and found a hostile. Bullets had been exchanged, and in the end, Brad Wicks and Stuart North had been wounded. Stuart had died en route to the hospital. Brad made it to the operating room, where he'd succumbed to his wounds shortly thereafter.

The investigation had determined that the bullets that had killed Brad and Stuart had come from Benny's weapon. Had the man panicked in the chaos? Shot at anything that moved? It was possible, but usually friendly fire incidents were a result of miscommunication or an unexpected move by someone else on the team. Not panic. Unfortunately, since the man was dead, they'd probably never know for sure.

His phone rang and he snagged it. "Caden here."

"This is Sheriff Osborne in Kent County. I had a message to call you if we got anything from forensics with the murder of Benny Silver."

"You found something?"

"Yeah. A couple of days ago. Sorry it's taken me so long to call, but we've been going full steam ahead with this investigation. I'm now ready to catch you up. We got a hit on a hair found at the scene. The lab here did a rapid DNA test, and it came back a match to a guy by the name of Donald Little."

Caden sucked in a fast breath. "Are you kidding me?"

Zane's head popped up and his eyes narrowed.

"So, you know the name?" the sheriff asked.

"Oh, yes, sir, I sure do. He's wanted here in connection to a kidnapping."

"Well, well, how about that? Little has quite the record. Assault and numerous other charges."

"I'm not surprised. Sheriff, Benny was killed about six weeks ago, right?"

"Something along those lines, yes. Why?"

Just a couple of weeks before someone hired Little to kidnap Heather. "I'm simply trying to put together a timeline for things happening on this end with Little. Thank you for calling. I'll let you know if we manage to find the man."

"That would be appreciated."

Caden hung up and called Travis. He got his voice mail. "Travis, call me when you get this. Donnie Little's DNA was found at the scene of Benny Silver's murder. I'm thinking that's not a coincidence. We need to know what links Heather to Benny Silver and if something happened in Kabul between those two." He hung up and turned back to his keyboard. There had to be something else and he was determined to find it. His next call would be to Heather to ask that very question.

Just as the screensaver morphed into his work screen, his phone rang again. "Caden here."

"It's Heather."

At the sound of her voice, he straightened. "I was just getting ready to call you. Everything all right?"

"No. I don't think so. I came across something on Patty Wicks's social media. She's Gina's former mother-in-law."

"Let me get the page pulled up and I'll take a look." He clicked his way to the woman's page and noted that she didn't have very good privacy settings. Which worked for what he needed. He scrolled to her latest post and read. Then whistled. "Wow. That's intense."

"Exactly. She tagged me in the post, which, of course, drew my attention to it. This time she mentioned not only me but Gina in her rant. She's escalating, Caden."

"I can see why you're concerned."

"Gina's on her way to Travis's home to stay here just in case Patty decides to take a leap off the deep end and go after her." She paused. "Caden, do you think she could be the one behind everything that's happened to me? It seems far-fetched, but . . . logical, too, in a way. Maybe."

"I don't know, but it bears investigating. I'll start getting warrants for what I need, like her financials and more." He'd also contact a few people who knew her and get them to fill out a questionnaire. One could learn a lot about a person's state of mind by listening to what their friends had to say. "You stay put until you hear back from me, okay?"

"I'm not going anywhere."

"And keep your phone on you."

"I have a new number. Travis gave me a satellite phone just in case I'm in a spot with no signal."

Caden wrote the number down as she quoted it. He'd enter it into his phone as soon as he disconnected with her. "I'm going to get a warrant to search her house and get her financial and phone records ASAP. We'll see if she's got a GPS on her vehicle too. Hang in there, Heather. This is a good, solid lead."

"I'm so glad."

"Although I've got to say, regardless of what his mother thinks, Brad looks really happy with Gina. Especially the one of them on their honeymoon."

"Honeymoon? I didn't see that one."

He checked the post stats. "Looks like she just added it a couple of minutes ago. We'll have Patty Wicks in custody shortly."

"Thanks, Caden, I appreciate this. Do you think you could make sure Gina gets here safely?"

"I'll see to it."

"Oh, and any word on Donnie Little?"

"Yes, that's what I was going to call you about. The sheriff investigating Benny Silver's murder called. He said they'd found a hair at the scene. Thanks to one of those rapid DNA tests and Donnie being in the system, they got a hit. It's his, Heather."

"*Donnie Little's?*"

"That was my reaction too. So, I need to know if you can link anything that happened in Kabul to you and Donnie Little."

She went silent. "No." She sighed. "I can't think of anything. I mean other than Benny Silver was the one who killed Brad, and Brad's mother is very bitter about that. Is there a link between her and Donnie? Could she have sent him to kill Benny?"

"I thought about that and am going to start searching for a connection between the two of them."

"I'll keep thinking too."

"If anything comes to mind, call me. Also, late yesterday, we had a hit on an ATM in Raleigh, North Carolina, but by the time officers arrived, he was in the wind again. Don't worry, we'll get him. Just keep your head down."

"I am. I know I'm not your only case, but I'm grateful for all the attention I'm getting."

"Right now, my focus is on you. I'll be in touch."

"Bye."

He hung up and met Zane's inquisitive stare. "I think we're getting ready to find us a kidnapper and a possible accessory to murder." He told him about the conversation with Heather and showed him Patty Wicks's social media page.

"I'd say that's pretty incriminating."

"Ready to take a ride and track this woman down?"

"I am. Maybe she can tell us where Donnie Little is, because I've still got squat on his location."

"He'll turn up. And when he does, we'll grab him." Before he hurt anyone else.

ooo

While Heather waited for Gina to arrive, she researched Donald Little. The fact that his DNA had been found in Benny Silver's house was mind blowing. There had to be a connection—and truthfully, something was niggling at the back of her mind, but for the life of her, she couldn't pull it out. Maybe it was just the idea that Patty Wicks could have hired him to kill Benny. But what did that have to do with her? She blamed Benny for her son's death, for sure. But did she also blame Heather for being unable to save him? It made sense in a weird kind of way. But why the whole kidnapping thing?

The more she searched, the more her head pounded. Ignoring the tightening over her right eye, she continued to click from one page to the next. "More like one dead end to another," she muttered.

Donnie seemed to have no connections whatsoever with Gina's mother-in-law, but that didn't mean there wasn't one. Just that she couldn't find it with her limited skills. Then again, if the man was a hired killer, it wasn't likely he was going to advertise that on social media, right? Maybe Caden or one of the FBI analysts would have better luck. Most likely she was wasting her time bothering to search.

Heather left Donnie Little and Patty Wicks on the back burner of her mind and rewound to the conversation she'd had with Musa. She couldn't help but wonder if she'd missed something. Some question she hadn't asked. *Something.*

Still thinking, she pulled up her contact list on her phone and found Musa's number and dialed it. After the fourth ring, the call went to voice mail. "Musa," Heather said at the tone, "this is Heather Fontaine. I hate to bother you. Don't know why I am, really. I just wanted to speak to you one more time about Abdul and the day of . . . well . . . the day he died. I'm sorry to ask you to rehash it, but I would appreciate a call back when you have the time." She gave him the number, then hung up and sat there, her mind churning, her left leg bouncing.

With an impatient sigh, she forced her leg still and texted Travis, asking for an update whenever he had a moment. His reply came within seconds.

Herman is gone. We're going to have to move him. Loading him up to take him out to bury him. Thankfully, Joe had the grave already dug.

I'm so sorry. Sorry for Sandra and your grief, but glad Herman is no longer suffering.

Same here, thanks. Will touch base soon.

Heather stood to pace while she rewound her thoughts to the night she'd fled her home and friends. That night was the beginning of everything. Before then, Musa had been watching her—not a stalker after all—so what had triggered the break-in that night? Or was it all just a stupid coincidence that it had happened at that particular time?

She went back to Benny Silver. Another question nagged at her. Something she should remember, but the thought refused to let her grab hold of it. Something about Benny and a medical issue. She'd seen him in the hospital, but for what? And why?

The doorbell rang and Heather jerked, the fleeting thought gone. She opened the front door. Gina's curious dark green eyes met hers, and the relief that pulsed through her at seeing her friend made her realize just how worried she'd been. "Hey there. Come on in." Heather escorted her into the den area. "Did you have any trouble getting here?"

"No, the roads had a few slick spots, but it wasn't too bad. Going to get worse, though. Probably pretty fast."

"Did you bring an overnight bag?"

"I did. I left it in my car for the moment." Gina's gaze traveled the room. "This place is amazing. I had no idea Travis lived out here."

"This is the first time I've seen it too."

"I told you there was a special look in his eyes whenever they landed on you." Gina grinned.

Heather could feel the heat rising at Gina's words and knowing look. She couldn't help the smile that curved her lips, even as she dreaded telling the woman what she knew. This was her friend, a woman who'd helped her save lives in the operating room time after time. How could she tell her that her mother-in-law was a monster? A bigger one than she'd ever dreamed. "Well, I'm not going to argue about it this time."

Gina laughed. Then sobered. "Okay, so what's going on? Why would you think I'm in danger?"

"Have you not seen the social media posts your mother-in-law's putting up?"

With a groan, Gina rubbed her head. "No, I haven't checked it lately. I got so tired of her hate that I haven't logged in."

"Well, I'm sorry to be the one to show you, but . . . come look."

"What is it?"

"She's all but made threats against you, Gina."

Gina's eyes widened. "Threats? Are you serious?"

"Unfortunately. Has she ever said anything to you about blaming you for Brad's death?"

Heather led the way into Travis's office and rounded the desk to seat herself in front of the computer once more. She wiggled the mouse, typed in the password, and the Facebook page she'd left open popped up. After refreshing it, Heather stood and motioned for Gina to stand beside her so she could see the screen.

For a moment, Gina simply frowned. "Yes, she's made threats. A number of times. To my face. She blames me for talking him into one more tour."

"What do you mean?"

"Brad wanted out. I didn't." She rubbed her eyes. "I was doing good work there. At least I thought I was. I know now that it was all for nothing, but—"

"All for nothing? What?" Heather gripped her friend's hand. "Never. We made a difference. We saved lives. *You* saved lives."

"At the expense of Brad's!" Tears welled and spilled over. She dashed them away with impatient swipes. "It wasn't worth his life."

Heather could understand her feeling that way, but she sure wouldn't relegate the work they'd done to having no value or being worth nothing.

Gina shook her head. "I'm sorry. What do you have to show me?"

"Sit here and you'll see."

Heather moved, allowing Gina to slide into the chair. She stared silently at the screen while she clicked each picture and read each caption below.

"Caden said she'd added more pictures since I last looked at it," Heather said, watching over Gina's shoulder. As each picture slid past, Gina grew more tense. The last picture flickered briefly on the screen, and Gina gasped and shut the page. She whirled to face Heather. "I've seen enough. I'm going to delete the page as soon as I can get to my phone."

"Wait," Heather said, "go back—" Her ringing phone cut her off. She glanced at the screen. "I have to take this."

"Sure."

"Your room is upstairs on the right. Across from Ryker's."

"He's here too?"

"Yes. Not here in the house at the moment, but . . . it's a long story. Let me grab this call and then I'll explain."

"Sure. I'll just go get my stuff."

Heather waited for Gina to leave, then swiped the screen. "Hi, Musa, thank you for calling me back." She sat back in front of the computer and opened the screen again. She'd seen something in that last picture that she wanted another look at.

"What can I do for you, Dr. Fontaine?"

"I hate to ask, but I keep thinking about the shirt that Abdul was wearing that day. Do you know anything about that?"

"Yes, Ravi told me," Musa said. "And I have thought long and hard whether to tell you about it. Which is why I said nothing."

Uh oh. "Why wouldn't you want to tell me?"

"Because it is special to you. It makes you think of Abdul and . . ."

"And?"

A sigh filtered through the line to her. "And I do not want to take that away from you."

"Please," Heather said, "just tell me."

After a brief pause, he said, "The shirt was given to him by the person who took Rayi. He was told to wear it. He was told he *must* wear it. That it was part of the deal to release his brother safely."

Heather's heart thudded a pained beat. The killer had forced Abdul to wear the shirt. So, what was the significance of that? "I see."

"Anyway, is there anything else you need?"

Footsteps outside the office door caught her attention and she stood. "No, thank you for calling me back."

"Of course."

They said their goodbyes and she hung up, then strode into the hallway to see Gina at the bottom of the stairs. "The bedroom looks like it will be perfect. I'm just going to take this up there."

"Okay, do you need any help?"

"I've got it, thanks."

Gina slipped up the stairs, and Heather returned to the computer. Wiggled the mouse and waited for the page to appear on the screen.

She frowned and zeroed in on the honeymoon picture—the one that she'd gotten a glimpse of when Gina had clicked on it.

And there it was. "How can that be?" she whispered to the empty room.

She blinked and looked again. The picture hadn't changed. Brad Wicks was wearing the shirt that Abdul had on the day he'd attempted to blow up the hospital. The one Musa had just told her his son had been forced to wear as part of the deal.

CHAPTER TWENTY-TWO

Travis worked the controls of the tractor to lower the horse into the grave. Sandra and Martin and the vet stood to the side, watching, shielding their faces from the whipping wind. From this side of the pasture, Travis had an unobstructed view of the front of his home, and he'd noticed the red pickup truck drive onto the property. He also noticed the chains on the tires. Good for her. At the entrance to the property, one of the ranch hands had verified the driver's identity before sending her on to the house.

Gina.

Good. Since this was taking much longer than he'd planned, having another person in the house with Heather eased his anxiety a fraction. As much as the ranch hands would do their best to protect those on the land, the place wasn't trespasser-proof. It was still possible for someone to gain access to the land without being noticed, just not to Travis's home. Which was where Heather was, so that was all that mattered for the moment.

Once the horse was in the hole, Travis maneuvered the controls once again and pushed the dirt over him. Over and over until there was a rounded lump covering the area.

He'd just shut off the engine when he spotted his mother racing toward them. Dread coated his insides at the look on her face. She stopped at the edge of the fence and waved to Sandra, who broke away from Martin and Ian and ran to meet her. His mother said something to his sister and handed her a cell phone. His mother headed back to the house—probably because she didn't want to leave the younger kids alone too long. Sandra ran along behind her, phone pressed to her ear.

Travis stepped out of the Bobcat and went to Martin. "Wonder what that's all about?"

"I don't know. But I heard Gigi say my dad's name."

"I'm going to get out of your hair," Ian said.

Travis shook the vet's hand. "Thank you for everything."

"Of course."

Ian headed to his van, and Travis placed a hand on Martin's shoulder to direct him toward his parents' house. Now what?

○ ○ ○

Heather couldn't stop looking at the picture. She dialed Caden's number again.

"Caden here."

"It's Heather again."

"You okay?"

She paused. Sighed. "I don't know. I think I'm grasping at straws."

"But?"

"But . . . I've just come across something, and I think I'm putting this all together." Terrified she was right, she gripped the phone tighter. "The last picture Mrs. Wicks posted was a picture of Gina and Brad on their honeymoon. He's wearing the shirt that Abdul wore that day he was supposed to blow up the hospital."

"What? How can that be? How do you know it's the same shirt?"

"Because of the paint stains. The shirt is navy blue, and it has white paint stains on the left shoulder and down the front. They kind of look like teardrops. There's no mistaking it."

"Then how did a kid in Kabul get his hands on that shirt? And why?"

"That's what I want to know. And I have an idea. Do you have Benny Silver's medical records?"

"Sure do. Once Silver's death was ruled a homicide, the sheriff didn't let any grass grow under his feet. He got warrants for everything. One of those things was medical records. He was trying to trace a path to who Benny had come into contact with just before his death."

"What about his medical records from Kabul?"

"Yep. That was all included. What's up?"

"I'd be interested in seeing those," Heather said. "I don't suppose you could send them to me."

He chuckled. "No, I can't."

"I figured."

"But if you'll tell me what you're looking for, I might be able to find it."

"I think Benny was in the hospital the day of the attempted bombing." She pressed a hand to her head. She was going to need her migraine meds if she let herself get too worked up—and right now, she needed all of her wits about her. "Can you just tell me if he was there on September twenty-eighth?"

"Sure . . . uh . . . let's see July twenty-fourth, sinus infection. Placed on antibiotics and given a nasal spray. August first, infection in his hand, August fourteenth, follow up on the infection. September eighteenth, flu shot. September twenty-fourth, appendicitis. Yep. He was there."

"He was there," Heather said. "That's it," she whispered. "I knew there was something I was trying to remember ever since someone said he'd been murdered. September twenty-fourth, Benny Silver had surgery on his appendix. I took it out."

"Heather, what are you thinking?"

"That Gina's mother-in-law somehow managed to arrange for the bombing because she knew that Benny was there." But that didn't even make sense. What made sense was too horrible to think about.

A low breath escaped Caden. "That's a pretty far stretch. How would she know about that? It was an emergency situation."

"I know."

"How long was he in the hospital?"

"Over a week. He'd developed complications and an infection." She closed her eyes and thought. "He was admitted on the twenty-fourth, moved to the recovery tent on the twenty-fifth, and the bombing occurred on the twenty-eighth. That means he would have been there four days before Abdul showed up."

Caden was silent. "I still don't think it's possible to set something up that fast and from this kind of distance. She was here in America while everything else was going on in Kabul. Like I said, that's stretching it."

"Yes. Yes, it is. Then she hired someone to do it."

"That's possible, I suppose." A pause. "Okay, this is going to be a far-fetched thought, but . . . what about Gina? It was her husband who was killed by the friendly fire. I think we have to look at her as a possible suspect in this. That and the fact that Gina was actually in country and could set it all up."

"They could be working together," Caden went on.

"I don't believe so," Heather said. "Brad's mother hates Gina. I'm thinking she might have thought Gina was going to be at the hospital that day as well. She was supposed to work, but we convinced her to ask off at the last minute to go sandboarding with us. Brad had been gone only about a month, and I could tell she was struggling. I asked the others if she could go, and they all agreed it was a good idea."

"Again, we know whoever was in your house was working with someone. Maybe the mother-in-law. But . . . I'll be honest—right now, I keep coming back to Gina."

So did she. But . . . "Again, I don't see how." She paused. "However, she did leave the party early. A short time before I did. And . . ."

"And?"

"She's the only one who could have given Brad's shirt to Abdul,

Caden. It was there, in Kabul. I saw Brad wearing it not long before he died. How do we explain that one away?"

"Unfortunately, I don't think we can."

Heather shivered and walked to the office door. She shut it and locked it. "She's here, Caden. I brought her here to Travis's home." She swallowed and pressed a hand to her stomach. "I feel sick. I've done exactly what I didn't want to do, and that's possibly put his family in danger!"

"First, you need to get away from her and we'll put the family on alert. Travis has guards there who will help. I'm texting him right now."

Silence descended and Heather pressed her fingers to the bridge of her nose.

"Heather, you still there?"

"Yes."

"Can you get out of the house? Signal for some help?"

"Maybe." She went to the window. A blanket of white covered everywhere she looked. "I'm in Travis's office with the door locked." Heather paced behind the desk. "What do I do, Caden? This is crazy. It can't be Gina."

"But what if it is? You can't take any chances. We need to clear her before you do anything else. Hold on a second, will you?"

"Sure."

Quiet murmurs reached her. While she waited, she went back to the window and unlocked it. It wouldn't be any trouble to climb out. She slid the window open and cold air rushed in.

"Heather? I just got Patty Wicks's financials. Let me take a look."

"Of course."

She paced while she waited. He finally returned to the line.

"It might not be Gina after all," Caden said. "Her mother-in-law has had some significant withdrawals from her savings and she even cashed in a life insurance plan. Could be how she paid to have people do her dirty work."

That made sense. "How do I tell Gina this?"

He hesitated. "Let's play this safe. You don't say anything to Gina. Not unless you have someone with you. Don't be alone with her."

She didn't plan on it.

"Travis isn't answering my texts," Caden said. "I'm going to call him as soon as I hang up with you."

"Hold on." She glanced out the window. The wind had really started to blow as the trees in the distance were bobbing and swaying. "Travis is talking to his mother. He's got Martin with him." The two started hurrying toward his mother's home.

A knock on the door almost made her drop the phone. "Heather?" Gina's voice came through the wood door.

"Just a second," she called. Lowering her voice, she said, "Caden, Gina's at the office door. I'm going to sneak out the window and see if I can get Travis's or one of the guards' attention."

"I'm calling 911 and sending some local officers out there."

"No. Not yet. We may be overreacting."

"I'd rather do that than leave you in the vicinity of a possible killer."

Yeah, so would she.

"Heather? You in there?" Gina called.

"Stay on the phone with me," Heather said to Caden. Then raised her voice once more for Gina. "Yes, I'm still on the phone. Be there in a minute."

"Okay." She waited for Gina's retreating footsteps before darting to the window and shoving it open. She swung a leg over the sill and pulled herself out.

Just as she turned, she caught a brief glimpse of movement to her left. A hard hit to her wrist sent the phone tumbling to the ground. Heather cried out and she grabbed her hand, pulling it to her chest.

She spun to face Gina, who was holding a weapon, the black muzzle of the barrel centered on Heather's face. Without a word—or moving the weapon from its target—Gina slowly knelt and grabbed the phone from the ground. She tapped the screen. "It's on mute." She held it out to Heather. "Put it on speaker and say goodbye like everything's fine or I'll start shooting people. Understand?"

Heather gave the brief thought to blurt out she was in trouble, but Gina's dead-serious look convinced her if she did, someone would lose his life. Heather tapped the screen. "Caden?"

"Heather! What was that? I heard you scream."

"I . . . uh . . . tripped climbing out of the window."

"You okay?"

"Peachy."

Gina waved the weapon at her and Heather flinched.

"Caden, I've got to go. Um . . . Travis is heading this way and I need to fill him in on everything." Heather never took her eyes from Gina's.

"Okay," Caden said slowly, "so I don't need to call him?"

"No."

"Then let me know if there's anything I can do."

"I will. Bye." Heather tapped the screen to disconnect the call. She'd briefly considered trying to get away with leaving the call connected but was glad she didn't when Gina turned the phone to check it. With a jerk of the gun, she motioned Heather away from the window, then stepped forward to drop the device inside. "Close the window," she said.

Heather did so with shaky hands. The wind chilled her, her fingers going stiff with the cold.

Struggling to find a way to alert someone without getting them killed, she scrambled through various scenarios at lightning speed. And came up with nothing. When she turned, she faced the weapon once more.

"I know you know," Gina said.

"Well, I wasn't positive. Not until now." She was proud of her even tone and lack of any discernible fear.

"You locked the office door. Why else would you do that unless you suspected something?"

"Caden suspects something too."

"But he doesn't know for sure."

No, he didn't. "We thought it was your mother-in-law. She took out a lot of money for some reason. We speculated it was to pay for everything."

"The money is for a shrine to Brad. An entire building in her backyard that she can visit and remind herself of everything she's lost and blame those she considers responsible."

Heather shut her eyes for a brief moment. How very sad. She opened her eyes and locked them on Gina. "So, what now? Travis will be back at any moment, and there are three guards patrolling the grounds around this house. Do you really think someone won't come help me?"

"The first person who realizes something's wrong gets a bullet. They might get me in the end, but maybe that's for the best. However, I'm willing to bet no one else wants to die today."

"If you wanted to die, you wouldn't be working so hard to avoid getting caught."

Gina started to protest, then shrugged. The terror Heather had experienced when she turned to face the gun was nothing in comparison to the horror that swept through her envisioning Gina hurting someone else—especially one of the children. "So . . . what now?"

"We take a ride."

"But the roads are going to be awful in a very short time."

"And if anyone tries to stop us," Gina said as though she didn't hear Heather's words, "you convince them that everything's okay. If they're not convinced, they die. Am I clear?"

"Crystal."

o o o

Travis had hurried into his mother's home to find Sandra on the phone, looking like she was on the verge of tears.

"Are you sure?" she'd asked. "Are you positive?" She'd hurried down the hall, her voice fading as she went, but he caught something about, "Let me grab some things for the kids and . . ."

Travis looked at his hovering mother. "What's wrong?"

"Joe was in an accident and he's headed for the hospital in an ambulance."

"An accident? Is he okay?"

"Yes. He said he had a cut on his head that probably needed some stitches. They're also going to do a CT scan to make sure there's nothing more serious going on. He's insisting he's fine, but you know Sandra. She won't be satisfied until she sees him herself."

"Of course."

"I'm going to take her to the hospital. He's at Mission." His mother bustled around grabbing her coat, gloves, and hat. "Can you help me get the kids into the van?"

"Mom, the roads might be okay right now, but they're going to be icy very soon. I'm not sure it's a great idea for you to be driving on them. And no, not because I think you're old or incompetent. I don't even want to drive on them when they get like that."

She hesitated, then said, "I have to. Now. Before it gets any worse. Joe put chains on the tires yesterday, so we'll be fine getting there. We'll stay in a hotel tonight if we have to. We can all wear the same clothes two days in a row without the world ending."

Travis almost protested once more, but then thought about Heather and resisted. It might be better if the kids were gone from the ranch. "I know Sandra's going to be impatient about getting there, but just go slow, okay?"

"I promise."

"And if it's too bad, turn around and come back."

"Travis, darlin', the longer we stand here, the worse it's going to get."

"Right."

Once everyone was loaded into their car seats and his mother was in the driver's seat, Travis headed back toward his home, only to stop and frown. Gina's red truck was headed down the drive. From his position, he couldn't see if anyone was in the passenger seat, but a bad feeling developed in his gut and grew with each spin of the wheels taking her away from the property. He snatched his phone from his pocket, noted he had three missed texts and three missed calls. All from Caden. In all of the hurry to get his family situated, he'd had to ignore the phone. Now, he wasn't sure who to call first. He settled on Heather and dialed the number even as he hurried toward the house.

When her phone went to voice mail after the fourth ring, he picked up his pace. He couldn't figure out why he was so out of sorts. Everything looked fine and no one had raised an alarm. He rounded the corner of the house and headed for the back door. Johnny Kaufman sat on the front porch, his Stetson shadowing his face.

"Hey," Travis said, "where did Gina go?"

"She said she'd forgotten something and had to run home."

Travis frowned. "Alone?"

"No. Your girl went with her. Said she didn't want the other woman to be alone."

And just like that, fear shot straight through to his heart and gripped him by the throat. "No! What? Why didn't you stop them?"

"They were insistent that everything was fine, and they'd be back later tonight."

"No, no, no!"

A Jeep appeared on the dirt drive, coming from the direction of the main road of the property.

"Chris!" Travis ran to meet him.

Travis's ranch manager braked to a stop, left hand on the wheel, his right in a cast from elbow to wrist, thanks to a battle with an ornery bull.

"Did you see them?" They would have had to get past Chris at the end of the drive.

"Yeah. I tried to get her to stop and wait for you, but Heather insisted they needed to go and all would be fine."

That didn't sound right. Something was way wrong. He jumped in the Jeep. "Why didn't you call me?"

"Tried. You didn't answer."

"Just go! We've got to stop them." Thankfully, someone had outfitted the vehicle with snow chains.

Chris gunned the Jeep, spun into a U-turn, and barreled down the snow-covered drive. It wasn't icy yet, but if the weather held true to what the forecasters called for, it wouldn't be long before driving would be hazardous. The wind already rocked the Jeep with a strong force. Travis called Caden.

"'Bout time you called me back," the man snapped. "Is Heather okay?"

"I don't know. That's what I'm trying to find out. She just left here with Gina. Chris and I are trying to track her down."

"What do you mean, she left with Gina? She was trying to get away from Gina by climbing out of your office window!"

Travis winced at the shouted words, then froze when they registered. "What are you talking about?"

"She called. We put it all together."

Caden launched into his explanation, and Travis felt his blood running colder and colder with each word the man uttered. Chris spun the wheel and sent them careening onto the snow-covered asphalt that would take them toward town.

"And now you've let her get in the car and drive off with Gina?"

"I didn't let her!" Travis raked a hand over his head. "Are you serious? Gina?" He never should have brought Heather to the ranch. He'd gotten distracted with his family issues. He'd been arrogant in his belief that he could help her. He'd been so sure she'd be safe here with the ranch hands and . . . him.

"Yes! Gina!" Caden's shout grounded him. No time for recriminations. It was time to find Gina and Heather and end this once and for all.

"I'll call 911 and get the cops on the way."

"I've already sent them, looked up Gina's vehicle, and sent them her tag number. Hopefully, we'll have them in custody soon."

"What was Gina thinking? Why was she after Heather?"

"I think it has to do with that shirt that the would-be hospital bomber in Kabul wore. Gina's husband was wearing it in a picture on social media."

"And Heather put it all together. That shirt connected Gina to the kid in Kabul."

"Exactly. She's got to be behind everything."

"I still have a ton of questions."

"Let's get Heather back so we can get some answers."

Travis stared at the empty road in front of them and despaired once more of that happening.

CHAPTER TWENTY-THREE

Heather gripped the seatbelt Gina had told her to put on. Not out of any concern for her safety, but most likely as a restraint. Gina held her weapon in her lap, her left hand still aiming it at Heather while she drove with her right. The roads had turned icier and she had to go slow even with the chains.

"Where's the shirt?" Gina asked.

"In my closet."

"Don't lie to me! It wasn't there."

"How do you know? Was that you in my room the night of the party?"

"No."

"Then who? Sam or Donnie?"

Gina cut her a sideways glance. "Donnie."

"The shirt was there. It's just in a box in the top right-hand corner."

"Of course it is," Gina muttered.

"How do you know him?"

"He was a friend of Brad's. And just as angry as I was that Brad was killed the way he was. We were talking one night, and I told him that Benny didn't deserve to live. He needed to die."

"So, you tried to kill him by forcing a kid to wear a bomb,"

Heather whispered, her stomach turning at the bitter hatred pouring from the woman. A woman she had trusted. That she had considered to be a friend.

"I did. If I'd had more time, I could have probably found a suicide bomber who would have done it voluntarily, but you can't just put an ad in the paper for one of those, can you? And I needed to do something fast. I was at a café one afternoon and saw the family on the street. I could tell the older boy adored the younger. I figured he'd do pretty much anything for him."

"Including die."

"Yes. But we see how well that worked out, don't we?" She shook her head and her jaw twitched. "Do you know what it took to set that up? All of my careful work and planning, and he didn't follow through. If I hadn't already released his brother, I would have had him killed too."

"You were with us on the trip. You'd just gotten back. You had no time to release anyone."

"Money talks. You know that as well as I do. It only took a phone call."

True. Unless Gina gave a name, she'd never know who'd been willing to do her bidding. "Just like it took a phone call to detonate that bomb."

"I couldn't believe it when I stepped out of the tent and saw him warning you. If I'd been two seconds later, he would have had that bomb off of him . . ."

"So, you just pressed the button."

"I did."

The woman was a monster. But she hadn't always been that way. She'd fought as hard as Heather to save patients.

Heather shut her eyes, trying not to envision everything Gina was saying.

"Anyway, when I said Benny Silver needed to die, Donnie asked me how much it was worth to make that happen. I told him to name his price. It took quite a bit of Brad's death benefits."

"You paid him money you got from the Army for Brad's death?"

"I did. Once Donnie told me it was done, all was well. I was moving on, finally had some peace that Benny was dead and Brad was avenged. And then the night of the party, I overheard you talking about that shirt. Brad's favorite. The one I gave him the day he asked me to marry him. He loved that shirt, and I thought it fitting that his murderer would be killed by the person wearing it. I thought it had been destroyed when the bomb went off. I saw him take it off, but I . . ."

"You were watching."

"Of course. And I saw him take the shirt off and warn you, but—"

"But you were so busy blowing up a teenager, you didn't notice he'd dropped the shirt."

Gina slapped the wheel and Heather jumped. "Don't say it like that."

"How do you want me to say it, Gina?" The woman didn't answer, and Heather let out a shuddering breath. "No wonder you left the party early."

"I was in shock, panicked. I had to figure out what to do. One thing I knew, I had to find that shirt and find it fast. It was the only thing that tied me to that kid—to the bombing. If you flashed that shirt around or even wore it, and someone remembered it was Brad's—" She stopped and shook her head. "I couldn't take the chance."

"So you called your friend Donnie to come help."

"And he was more than willing—for a price, of course."

Heather processed the fact that Gina wasn't even trying to hide what she'd done. Which meant Gina didn't plan to let her live much longer. "You set all of this up. This elaborate . . . whatever . . . just to find that shirt?"

"I had to get it back."

"That kid had a family who loved him, and you used him like he was nothing." It was unfathomable.

"Shut up! Just shut up! I need to think!"

Heather sat silent for a moment. She needed to think as well. The longer she stayed in the car, the farther away she'd get from Travis and help. They were no longer on the ranch property, but if she calculated their location correctly, they were on the road that ran parallel to the north side of the ranch.

She rested her arm on the door next to the window and let her hand dangle near the handle. She'd have to hit the lock button with her thumb and pull the handle with her other hand. Unfortunately, Gina was driving too fast now for Heather to risk it. If she broke a bone during her escape, it would be for nothing. Hopefully, the snow would soften the landing. "How long have you been planning all of this?"

"All of *this*? Just in the last few days. Revenge against Benny Silver and that blasted hospital that let Brad die? Since the day I learned it was friendly fire."

"Brad's death was an accident, Gina. A tragic, awful accident."

"Which doesn't make Brad any less dead or make his mother hate me any less, does it?"

"No, it doesn't." She was coming down to the now-or-never timing. She had to get out of the car. A plan had formed, but would it work? *Keep her talking. Distract her.* "Donnie was waiting in my closet that night, wasn't he?"

Gina laughed. A harsh, humorless sound that scraped up Heather's back like fingernails on a chalkboard. "Yes. He texted he couldn't find the shirt, so I told him to grab you and bring you to me. I'd get you to tell me, then Donnie would . . . take care of you while I went and got the shirt." Her lips tightened and she shot Heather a narrow-eyed glare. "Only you ran. What tipped you off?"

"The clothes on my couch were moved. They looked off, along with a few other things. The big thing was my bedroom door was almost shut. Barely cracked. I always leave it wide open. My nerves were screaming at me that someone was in there. So I ran."

"Of course you did."

"One of the big things was the picture on my refrigerator. Donnie had drawn little red dots on all of my friends' foreheads."

"He did what?!"

Heather raised a brow. "Yes. Between that and the cracked bedroom door, I wasn't hanging around to find out what was going on."

"What an idiot."

"That's the pot calling the kettle black, isn't it?" Before Gina could respond, Heather thought of another question. "You put the trackers on the cars."

"I had to find you. I figured one of them—probably the lovesick Travis—would lead me to you."

Heather's heart clenched at Travis's name. She could only pray he was looking for her. Again. Gina's betrayal burned and fury bubbled beneath the fear. But it all made sense. Everything pointed to someone who knew her well. She just hadn't been able to pinpoint anyone who could have that much evil in them. "You were supposed to be at the cabin, but you never showed up. Why not?"

"I had just started that stupid job that I had to take because all of my money went to hiring people to take care of things for me. I was getting ready to leave when my boss came in and told me he needed me to work an extra shift." She huffed a short laugh. "I tried to get out of it, but he said if I didn't stay, not to bother coming back. I stayed. I called Donnie and he was angry, but when I mentioned I couldn't pay him if I didn't do the shift, he changed his tune pretty quick."

Heather leaned forward slightly, like her stomach hurt, but in truth, was hiding the fact that she'd released the seatbelt.

"What are you doing?"

"My stomach is in knots. Are you surprised? I'm a little stressed."

When Gina glanced at her, Heather looked out the windshield. "Watch out!"

Gina stomped the brake and jerked her head back around. The

chains grabbed the ice and the truck skidded but slowed enough. Heather jammed her thumb against the unlock button and pulled the handle. Going with the motion of the suddenly slowed vehicle, she threw herself from the seat. She hit the snow-covered asphalt hard, but nothing broke. She rolled to the edge of the road, scrambled to her feet, and dashed into the woods.

Gina's screams echoed behind her, as well as the woman's exit from the vehicle and the crunch of her footsteps over the snow and brush. However, Heather kept going, not looking back, focused on getting away. Heart pounding, adrenaline pumping through her, she aimed for Travis's ranch and prayed she was going in the right direction. When he'd shown her around the property, he'd pointed out the property lines—including the road Gina had been on.

Once again, she placed one foot in front of the other, begging God to protect her. Travis had to know she was missing at this point. Didn't he?

Oh, please, know I'm missing.

"I'm going to kill you!"

Over the blowing wind, Gina's shout echoed too close. Heather's footprints would lead Gina right to her if she didn't do something. A childhood game of hide-and-seek in the snow flashed through her mind. She had nothing to lose. She ran in one direction, then backtracked in her footprints and darted behind a massive tulip tree, planting her back against it. The brief snow squall that had lessened visibility was letting up. Maybe the wind was a blessing in disguise—she could only pray the swirling new snow made it harder to see her footprints.

While her heart thundered in her chest, she pulled in three deep breaths and listened.

Nothing but the wind.

Gina must have stopped to listen as well.

Okay then. That was good, right? That meant Gina had lost her. Maybe?

Heather darted to the next tree. Then the next. The trees weren't too thick in this area. From her current hiding spot, she could see the pasture. But she couldn't make it all the way across there to the house without Gina having the opportunity to put a bullet in her back.

The crackle of underbrush kept her moving.

"Stop now or I'll go down to that house and shoot everyone in it!" Gina's enraged shout spurred Heather on.

No she wouldn't. Gina couldn't take the chance that Heather would manage to slip away and find a phone. Like the one in the barn. Or the bunkhouses.

Heather ran along the tree line, surprised she wasn't gasping for breath at this point. Maybe it was the adrenaline, maybe it was the knowledge that if she stopped, there would be no hope for escape. Whatever the reason, she headed for the nearest path that would lead her up and hopefully to a place where she could hide.

When she found the trail, she scrambled along it, dislodging rocks and other debris in her climb, sometimes slipping and having to catch herself. Her hands felt like blocks of ice, and she quickly huffed a warm breath of air on them before continuing her way up.

She made a point to deviate from the path every so often in order to stay behind the protection of the trees. However, she could still hear Gina behind her in spite of the wind.

When she reached the top, she stopped, looked back. Gina raised the weapon and aimed. Heather dropped to the ground and rolled off the path behind a tree. *Please, Jesus, help me.*

Sweat trickled down her temples, and she swiped it away while she assessed her location. At least her exertion was keeping her body warm.

Twenty yards away she spotted something that gave her an idea. But she'd be exposed trying to reach it. Then again, would Gina risk the sound of a gunshot that would bring ranch hands to investigate?

With renewed energy, she pushed off the ground, praying she

could make it to the cave near the ledge and get out of sight before Gina realized where she was.

○ ○ ○

Of all the stupid—

Donnie slipped through the underbrush, fighting the freezing wind and watching the unsuspecting Gina follow Heather. The more he walked, the more his rage grew. The double-crossing wench. Making him hike through a blasted ice jungle, treating him like he was no one once she got what she wanted from him. This was *not* what he'd signed up for. If she'd just paid him like they'd agreed, he'd be sitting on a Caribbean beach somewhere, soaking up some much-needed sun.

Why hadn't she given him the money? He'd done everything she'd asked. Including dealing with the explosives. And leaving Sam for dead. He still felt kind of bad about that. Not so much for Sam, but for Tammy. But a simple phone call to the hospital to check on him had revealed Sam was recovering and under strict supervision.

At that point, Donnie had known the game was up. At least for him. Sam wouldn't mean to blow the whistle on Donnie, but he'd thought it was all a game and that would be his story—and he'd tell them all about Donnie Little, the man who'd asked him to play.

Once he'd figured law enforcement would eventually put everything together—including his involvement—Donnie had to come up with another plan. The one he'd settled on was slipping over the border to Mexico with his money to live a life of leisure. He'd envisioned doing a little deep-sea fishing or opening a dive shop. He'd turn his life around, maybe meet a woman who didn't nag him to death. He'd miss his kids, but maybe he could have a few more. Raise them right. With the money Gina owed him, it had been a distinct possibility.

Now his dreams smoldered like a pile of ashes. Thanks to Gina and her stupid self.

He'd thought she was different, but no . . . she was just like every other female on the planet. Looking out for herself—and cheating him out of his payday.

He'd thought he could trust her. She'd paid him for offing that guy, Silver, in Michigan, but he knew she wasn't going to pay him for this one. He bit off a curse. The little two-timing backstabber. He'd get rid of Heather Fontaine, then take Gina to the nearest computer. Once she'd transferred the money she owed him—and maybe a bit more, he'd get rid of her too. It might be the one time he actually enjoyed the kill. He'd wrap his hands around her throat and watch the life fade from her eyes.

He kept an eye on her as she stormed after Heather, who had scaled the side of the steep cliff like a billy goat, reached the top, and then disappeared behind a copse of trees.

Donnie picked up the pace. The last thing he needed was to lose them.

CHAPTER TWENTY-FOUR

Travis didn't think his blood pressure would ever return to normal. They'd lost her again. Travis listened to Caden map out a plan to find her. The man had already passed on the vehicle make and model, along with the license plate, to the chopper he'd requested. Assuming it could even make it into the air with all the snow.

So far there'd been no sign of Gina's vehicle. "How did she just disappear like that?" She should have been on the road in front of them. Gina might not have law enforcement training, but she did have military expertise—and a weapon. And that made her a deadly foe. "Turn around," he said.

Chris glanced at him. "What?"

"Turn around. She must have somehow doubled back."

"But wouldn't we have seen her?"

"Depends on where she turned around. We've been going this way for the past fifteen minutes. If she was ahead of us, we'd have caught up to her by now."

"I don't know," Chris said. "She's got chains on her tires just like us. She might be going pretty fast."

Travis thought about it. It was a valid observation, but . . . he didn't think so. She'd turned off somewhere, probably in order to throw off anyone who might be after her. "Turn around. We're going to go back and check the side roads. You want me to drive?"

"I got it. It's the one thing I can still do around here." One-handed, Chris expertly spun the Jeep around, chained tires crunching on the still accumulating snow, to head back the way they came, while Travis mapped the area in his head. There were two ways she could have gone, driving from the direction of the ranch.

"Travis, you there?" Caden's voice jerked his attention back to the phone.

"Yeah. Tell the chopper to head back toward the ranch. There are two roads that go near the ranch. Highway 29 goes behind it and Harrison Road runs perpendicular. If she's headed back that way, she's on one of those two roads—or one of the side streets. But all of the side roads come out on those two main roads. I'm thinking she may have turned off this main road just in case she was followed."

The chopper would be able to spot the vehicle a lot easier than he and Chris. Maybe. If she'd pulled into a garage or under any kind of shelter, she'd be virtually invisible from the sky. The thought sent waves of worry and fear through him. He was banking on Gina not wanting to get as far from the ranch as possible. Going in the other direction than Chris saw her go.

Caden passed the information along, then came back to Travis. "It's heading back that way, but he's reported the wind is really blowing him around and he's going to have to put her down."

Not what he wanted to hear. "I understand. Just . . . tell him to find her first."

"I don't think that's going to happen. I think we should meet you at your ranch, and we'll start formulating a strategy to find her just in case the chopper has to land. And I think it's going to. Like now."

He didn't like it, but . . . "Yeah. Fine. We should be back in the next twenty minutes or so."

His phone buzzed and he took a quick glance at the screen.

The security camera he'd installed on the ledge had sent him a notification. Heather's face came into view and Travis blinked even while his heart leapt into overdrive. "Hey, hold up, hold up. I know where she is!"

"How's that?"

"She just told me." He gave Caden a quick explanation of the camera in the cave as he pulled up the app and turned on the talk feature. She had her back to the camera, but he could hear her gasping for breath.

"Heather," he said in a whisper.

She spun to face the camera, eyes wide and frantic. She held a finger to her lips. Then mouthed, "Don't talk."

Travis muted his side but could still listen to Heather. "Talk to me," he muttered. "Where's Gina?"

"How long until someone can get there?" he asked Caden. "We're at least twenty-five minutes out, thanks to driving the wrong way."

Caden grunted. "I'm probably forty minutes from you. I'm on my way, but travel is getting worse. The wind is whipping, and I just got word that the chopper had to get away from it. Zane's on the phone with local authorities and they're saying the same thing about the roads, but they're sending out to the location. Is she alone? Safe for the moment?"

"Appears to be. But she's afraid and didn't want me to talk. She obviously got away from Gina. She's hiding from her, Caden."

"Which means Gina's looking for her."

Heather went completely still, tilted her head, then her eyes went wide and she ducked out of sight of the camera. He barely refrained from calling out to her. Then his phone pinged once more as Gina stepped into view.

◦ ◦ ◦

Heather had found a small, shadowed niche toward the back of the little cave. At least she was protected from the gusts of wind that occasionally found their way in. She tucked her hands between her thighs, trying to warm them enough to get some feeling back in them, and pressed her back against the cold rock wall. She forced herself to take slow, silent breaths.

"I know you're in here," Gina said. "You might as well come out. I'm not going away."

Oh, she was going away. Hopefully for life. Heather prayed she lived to see it happen. Gina's footsteps echoed in the area. About thirty yards deep, Travis's cave was wider than it looked from the entrance. Roomy and dark, it had seemed like the perfect hiding place. She'd hoped the falling snow would cover her tracks as she darted in, set off the alarm, then popped back out to keep going. But Gina had been too quick. Quicker than Heather had anticipated. It had been a risk, but Heather had had no choice if she was to let Travis know where she was.

"Heather, come on. I'm cold and I know you have to be too. I just want to get this over with. Give me the shirt and I'll disappear. I'll change my name, get plastic surgery, whatever. I won't hurt you—or anyone else—if you'll just give me the shirt. Please."

Heather wondered when she'd had "stupid" tattooed on her forehead. Gina had just revealed her plan for after she killed Heather. Unbelievable. The woman fully expected to escape and disappear.

"Come out now!" Heather heard a thud. Had Gina stomped a foot? "Why are you dragging this out? It's not like you're going to change the outcome."

Wind whistled outside the opening behind Heather, and she shivered when snowflakes skated across her face. If she could just stay quiet until Travis arrived with help . . .

"Fine, have it your way." Gina started walking toward Heather's hiding place, and her muscles clamped down.

"Gina!"

Travis's voice echoed in the cavernous area and Heather flinched. Gina let out a small scream and spun. Heather darted forward and tackled the woman. Together, they hit the hard-packed mud flooring and the gun spun from Gina's hand.

A fist caught Heather in the solar plexus, and she gasped, the breath whooshing out of her lungs while pain radiated through her core.

Heather shot a blind, desperate punch at Gina's face and clipped her chin. The woman's head snapped back, slamming into the ground, giving Heather the chance to scramble away. She reached for the weapon, closed her fingers around it.

Pain streaked through her head and neck as Gina's fingers curled in her hair and yanked her head back. Heather cried out, but her grip on the gun only tightened.

She swung the weapon around and caught Gina in the forehead, opening a gash, sending the woman screeching backward.

Heather whipped the gun up and aimed it at her former friend. "Stop! Stay there or I'll shoot you!"

For a moment, Gina didn't move. Her harsh breathing filled the cave.

Heather waved the gun toward the entrance. "Let's go."

Where were Travis and the others? Unable to get to her because of the weather?

"Where is he?" Gina cried. "I heard Travis. Where is he?"

Heather ignored her. "Travis? Can you hear me?"

"I can," he said, his voice tinny and small coming from the minuscule camera, but at least she could hear him. A sob clawed at her throat and she choked it back. "Where are you?"

"Trying to get to you. Are you okay?"

"I've got the gun and we're coming down."

"No, just stay there. It's gotten a lot icier in the last little bit. We're coming to you. Should be there in about five minutes."

Gina hesitated, her gaze swinging from the little camera to Heather, fury building in her eyes. "You're kidding me. There's a camera?"

"Yes. And everyone knows. Give it up."

"So that's why you were so eager to climb that hill." She paused and rubbed a hand down her face. "Well, I guess I'll just have to stick with plan B. I'm going to disappear." She stood.

Heather held the weapon steady. "Stop. I may be a doctor, but I went through the same training you did and you know I know how to use this."

"Then you'll have to shoot me, because I'm walking out of here before anyone else shows up." She started toward the entrance and Heather blocked it, keeping the weapon on Gina's midsection. Gina stopped and backpedaled, her eyes locked on the space behind Heather's shoulder. "What are you doing here?"

Heather almost spun but stopped. "I'm not falling for that." Gina was doing the same thing Heather had done in the car. Right? Pretending to see something in order to distract her. But Gina didn't avert her gaze and the color had leeched from her face.

The hairs on the back of Heather's neck stood up. She slowly turned and froze. Donnie Little stood at the entrance, his malevolent gaze and deadly gun held on Gina. He switched both to Heather when he spotted the weapon in her hand. "Drop it."

"Or what?"

His eyes flickered, his finger twitched, and Heather dropped to the floor. She hit hard, her hand with the weapon bouncing. The gun flew from her fingers and skidded to the edge of the ledge. Unable to grab it, she rolled back into the niche where she'd first hidden from Gina, just as Donnie's gun spat its bullet.

The crack of the weapon reverberated through the cave. Her ears rang. Distantly she thought she heard Travis yelling her name.

She definitely heard Gina screaming.

Heather raised her head to see Donnie with the gun back on Gina. "I want my money, you traitor."

"Are you crazy? The cops are going to be here any second!"

"Nice try."

"I'm serious. There's some kind of camera thingy and they know we're here."

"Well, leaving works for me. After I get rid of that one." Again, the gun pointed in Heather's direction.

She ducked back down. "Don't shoot me! I have money too! If that's what you want, I'm worth more alive than dead."

Travis, where are you?

○ ○ ○

Terror had exploded within Travis's chest when Donnie had stepped into the line of sight of the camera. Then the gunshot, the screams, and no visibility of Heather. Not knowing if she was hurt had nearly sent him into cardiac arrest. Then he'd heard Heather holler and relief pounded through him. Briefly. He was sure Donnie had more than one bullet.

"Donnie!" he yelled. "Put the weapon down!"

No answer. .

"Travis?" Caden's tense voice came through the phone line. "What's going on? Tell me what you see."

Travis put the app on mute so those in the cave couldn't hear him. "Donnie Little is there now. I heard a gunshot and screams. Heather and Gina are out of camera range, but I can see Donnie holding the gun on them. And he looks very unhappy." He glanced at Chris. "Do you dare go any faster?"

The man shook his head. "Not if you want to stay on the road and avoid sliding into a ditch and delaying us even more."

Travis sent up prayers while he watched the camera.

Why was it when he needed to get somewhere in a hurry, the weather worked against him? He prayed for Heather's safety, for the truck to stay on the road, and for Donnie to be indecisive.

"How did Donnie find them, Travis?" Caden asked. "She had a police escort for the most part. Someone watching her back. Any thoughts?"

"A few. I think Donnie must have planted a tracker on Gina's car like she had him do to the others. I'm guessing she provided the ones that went on the other cars, but he brought his own to the party. What kind of tracker did Gina have on her vehicle? Was it the same as all the others?"

"Uh . . . I'm not sure. I don't think I ever saw hers or the others. I just checked to see if they had one. They all reported back that they did."

"We need to know that. Can you find out?"

"Hold on."

He was holding. Mostly his breath. So far, all was quiet in the cave, but Donnie was walking slowly and getting ready to step out of view of the camera. He tapped the mute button once more to allow his voice to be heard. "Donnie! Donnie, can you hear me?"

"I hear you, but I'm not talking to you." Donnie's arm drew back and he slammed the grip of the weapon into the camera. It went dark.

"No!"

"What is it?" Caden's sharp question penetrated his helplessness.

"He broke the camera. I've lost eyes and ears."

"Local law enforcement is still trying to get there, but the winds are high and visibility is low. Not to mention the icy roads."

"I'm aware." He was in the same situation. But the ranch driveway came into sight. Finally. And then he had an idea. A quick glance into the back of the Jeep told him it might work. "Go on past it," he told Chris, "to the top. I'll hike from the road down to the part of the cliff that's over the ledge, then rappel down."

"Gear's back there. You think you can do that?"

"I think that's the only way."

"I'm not going to be much help with this arm."

"We'll figure it out."

Chris pressed the gas, going faster than either of them was comfortable with, but deciding it was worth the risk.

"Travis?" Caden was back on the line.

"Yeah?"

"The tracker is slightly different. Similar, but definitely different."

Everything started to make sense. "Before I lost sight of them in the cave," Travis said, "Donnie said Gina owed him money. I think he planted that tracker before Gina found out about the T-shirt."

"And when it went missing, he simply put another one on her car?"

"Yeah. And *that's* how he found them at the ranch."

CHAPTER TWENTY-FIVE

Heather huddled in the niche listening to Donnie and Gina argue—Donnie demanding his money and Gina begging him to put the gun down.

"Donnie, you know I'm going to give you the money. Please, stop pointing that at me."

"Oh, I know you're going to give me the money? Aren't you the one who told me I needed to disappear?"

"Yes, because I didn't want you to get in trouble! But we've got to get out of here."

"Not before I find out how much money she's talking about. Now shut up."

Gina went quiet and Heather trembled, trying to figure out how she was going to get away from them. They blocked the only exit. The only one that wasn't a ten-story death drop.

"Get out here," Donnie demanded.

"Don't shoot me and I'll give you every cent." Would it work? Buying time to escape? Only one way to find out. *Please, God . . .*

Heather glanced around the edge of her hiding place. The temperature had dropped and the cold seeped through her sweatshirt. Gina's back was to Heather and she stood in front of Donnie, who had his back to the entrance. The shattered remains of the camera lay on the cave floor.

An idea formed. A crazy, risky idea, but it had worked earlier with Gina and now might be her only hope. She stepped out of the niche and moved deeper into the cave, distinctly aware of the gun resting on the ledge behind her. She was tempted, oh so very tempted, to try and get it, but it was clear Donnie would shoot her if she made one move he didn't like.

Now, she was banking on Donnie's extreme greed and curiosity about the money she had promised him. If she could get out of the cave, she might have a chance. He scowled at her but didn't shoot. "How much?"

"Two-hundred fifty thousand."

He blinked. "Where?"

"In my savings account."

"Prove it."

"I need a phone to access the account, but once we have a signal, I can show you the balance."

"Then let's go."

Where was Travis?

He aimed the weapon at Gina. "And if she's got that, I don't need your measly twenty grand."

Gina shrieked. "She's lying!"

"I'm not," Heather cried, "but don't shoot her!"

When Donnie hesitated, Heather rushed, arms outstretched, right into Gina's back. The hard shove sent her slamming into Donnie, who windmilled backward and hit the ground with a thud. Heather darted past them, aiming for the exit.

A hand clamped around her ankle and she cried out. Went down, sprawling next to him. Panic clawed at her, but she controlled it, as she kicked out with her free foot and caught Donnie on the forearm. He hollered and squeezed her ankle in a vise grip.

Gina scrambled off of him, kicking and screaming. He brought the gun up, aimed it at Gina, and fired. Gina dropped and Heather couldn't stop the cry that escaped her. Then Donnie whipped the weapon back to Heather.

Another pop sounded and Heather gasped, waiting for the pain. Instead, Donnie jerked back, his hand going to his shoulder.

Which freed Heather's leg.

And yet, Donnie didn't drop the gun. He staggered to his feet, lifted the weapon, and aimed it at . . . Travis!

Heather launched herself forward into Donnie's knees. He gave a hoarse shout and fell once again.

Travis landed on top of him. "Run, Heather!"

Heather scrambled away from them.

The two men rolled over and Donnie aimed a punch at Travis's head. Missed and connected with the cave floor. Travis bucked and wrapped a leg around Donnie's. Flipped him and gained the upper hand.

But the more they struggled, the more they inched toward the ledge. Heather searched for a weapon. Gina's gun was near the edge of the ledge, but where had Donnie's gone?

Panting, searching, she couldn't find it. Did he still have it? More rolling right to the edge. This time with Travis on top. "Travis! Get the gun by the edge!"

He reached for it and Donnie took advantage of the moment to swing a punch that caught Travis on the chin. His head snapped back and Donnie rolled out from under him and snagged the gun. Dragging in heaving breaths, the man turned it on Travis, who kicked out and connected with the hand holding the gun. The gun spun over the ledge and dropped out of sight. Donnie screamed his rage and sprang at Travis, who tried to spin away. But Donnie managed to grab Travis's calf. Travis kicked once more, his boot scraping the man's face. Donnie reared back, lost his balance, and went over the ledge . . .

. . . pulling Travis with him.

ooo

"No!" Heather's cry echoed through the cave as she leapt over Gina and darted to the ledge. Sobs ripped from her throat and she dropped to her knees, not wanting to look down and unable to stop herself from doing it.

The wind whipped her hair around her face, but the snow had stopped falling. She could see Donnie on the ground below, his neck twisted at an odd angle. Her frantic gaze scanned the area around him. But Donnie was the only one she could make out.

"Travis!" She choked off a sob. "Travis! Where are you?"

"Heather!"

His strangled voice came from beneath her, and she gasped, going to her belly and inching out to see him. "You're alive! Oh, thank you, God. Thank you." She couldn't tell what he'd managed to grab hold of, but his swinging feet gave her hope. "Hold on. Don't fall! Don't you dare fall!"

She thought she heard him say something like, "Not planning on it."

Heather ran back to the entrance of the cave and grabbed the rope he'd rappelled down with. Too short. "Hey! Who's up there? Hey!" A head poked over the top of the incline, and she recognized the guard that had been patrolling the entrance to the ranch. "Chris! Travis went over the ledge! I need you to throw down another rope. You're going to have to pull him up."

His eyes widened.

"Now!"

He disappeared. Her terror for Travis mounted with each passing second. How long could he hold on? "Hurry!"

Two seconds later, Chris returned. "Watch out! That's all I got. Hope it'll reach. The other's still tied to my Jeep."

The rope landed at her feet, and she scooped it up, hands trembling, fingers once again numb from the cold. "When I yell, you need to start pulling him up!"

"I'll be waiting!"

The wind blew hard, causing her eyes to water and her breath to catch in her lungs. She took precious seconds to run back into the cave, yank Gina's gloves from her hands, and pull them over her own.

Quickly, she returned to the ropes and tied the one Chris had thrown down to the one already tethered to the Jeep that had held Travis when he rappelled down. She tied a double fisherman's knot—thank you, Jeffrey Steadman—then pulled on it, using all of her body weight to test it. It held. Holding the other end, she ran back to the cave. Gina hadn't moved. She was probably dead, but Heather couldn't stop to check. Not yet. She made it to the ledge and threw the rope over. "Travis, grab the rope, then tell me when to pull!"

Within seconds, the rope went taut. "Now!"

She ran to the entrance. "Now, Chris! Now!" After the longest two seconds of her life, the rope pulled taut and started moving.

She heard Travis grunt and soon his head appeared level with the edge. His gloved hand slapped at the rock and he held on, dangling, but he had a good hold on the ledge. Heather hurried to grab the material of his coat in both hands. And pulled again. The rope attached to the Jeep moved more and the upper half of his body made it over the ledge. "Come on, come on."

And then he was all the way in, his head in her lap. For a moment, he lay gasping. "I think I dislocated my shoulder."

"Hold on and I'll look." She ran to the entrance. "He's up, Chris! He's up!" She hurried back to Travis and went to her knees beside him. "Let me look."

He flinched away from her reaching hands.

"Travis, you almost died. Now is not the time to be a fraidy cat when it comes to doctors. Now pull on your big-boy pants and let me look at it."

He huffed out a choked laugh and nodded. "Fine."

Heather ran her hands over the shoulder, feeling bones and moving the joint. "It's not dislocated, but you no doubt sprained it."

"I'll take it. Man, that was terrifying."

"Yeah," she whispered, then let the tears flow. "Why do I always cry when I'm around you? I never cry."

Using his good arm, he pushed himself into a sitting position and tucked her next to him. "I can't believe that just happened."

"How did you not . . . how did you manage . . . how?"

"He had my leg when he went over. I managed to grab that piece of rock that juts out. I knew it was there and just reached for it, praying. And I snagged it with one hand. It stopped the fall and Donnie swung into the side of the cliff . . . and let go."

Heather could envision it and swallowed the nausea that his words induced. "I don't want to think about it, but I'm probably going to dream about it. It's a toss-up as to which nightmare I'll have now."

Travis gripped her tight and she buried her face in his neck, inhaling his scent.

"I know the feeling," he said.

"Travis! Heather!" Chris's shout reached them. "Somebody let me know what's going on. The cops are here."

"About time they showed up," he muttered.

Tucking his wounded arm against him, Travis rose and held out a hand. She let him pull her to her feet. Her legs trembled but held her. They walked to the entrance, the temperature dropping the closer they got. "We're okay, Chris!"

"Hold on a second." Heather returned to the woman who'd tried to kill her numerous times and knelt next to her. She pulled one of the gloves off and placed two fingers on Gina's throat. "No pulse. She's gone." Tears battered her lids and she drew in a deep breath, trying to get control of her emotions, wondering why she was grieving so hard. But she'd loved Gina like the good friend she'd been. *Thought* she'd been. And her betrayal—and death—left her raw. "So much bitterness. So much hate," she whispered. "She had so much potential, Travis. She was an excellent nurse and probably saved as many patients as I did in Kabul."

"She was a very lost soul," he said.

Heather stroked Gina's hair away from her face. "I wish it could have ended differently for you, Gina. I wish you would have let someone reach you, that you would have asked for the help you needed." She sniffed as she rose and let Travis tuck her under his good shoulder. "I wish I'd seen the depth of her pain," she said. "Was I too wrapped up in my own stuff? Was I that blind?"

He shook his head. "I don't think so. I think she knew exactly what she was doing and there was no deterring her. No one saw it because she truly didn't want to be helped. She was too clever, too cunning, in maneuvering all the pieces in her twisted desire for revenge and her desperate need to find the one piece of evidence that could connect her to that bombing. No wonder she was so good at chess. She was always thinking three moves ahead."

"Somehow, she set up Rayi's kidnapping, managed to get Abdul to almost blow up a hospital, and who knows what else? Unbelievable." She paused. "Donnie and Brad were best friends. He was just as angry as Gina was about Brad dying in the friendly fire incident. I think he also was a little bit in love with her. When she expressed the desire for revenge, he went along with it. Mostly because she promised to pay him, but partly because he wanted to impress her. I think. I don't guess we'll ever know for sure now. I just know when she betrayed him, he didn't hesitate to kill her."

"Well, he definitely left an impression." Travis drew in a deep breath. "Now, let's figure out how we're going to get down this cliff without breaking anything."

She squeezed his hand. "You'll figure it out."

"Travis Walker? Heather Fontaine?"

The shouts came from outside the cave.

"In here," Travis called.

Two members of the SCSAR team stepped inside. Under the large letters on their jackets read South Carolina Search and Rescue. Never had she been so glad to be rescued. "Hey, you two ready to get out of here?" the one in front asked.

"Yes. Please." Heather held out a hand to Travis. "I'm ready to go home."

He clasped her gloved fingers and brought them to his lips. "I'm right behind you."

"Can we build a fire in that big fireplace of yours when we get back from the hospital?"

"Hospital? Um . . . no hospitals. And no doctors—except you. I'm okay with you."

Heather smiled. "And I'm okay with you, Travis Walker. Let's go."

CHAPTER TWENTY-SIX

Four weeks later

Heather sat on the couch in Travis's living area, her head snuggled against his good shoulder, fingers wrapped around a mug of hot chocolate. A fire burned brightly in the fireplace opposite them. "People will be here any minute now," she murmured.

"I know." He kissed the top of her head. "I almost can't believe we made it to this point. It still feels surreal or something."

"Yes. It's been a very strange four weeks. I'm still a little unsure of what to do with myself."

"I know one thing you can do."

She tilted her head up, met his gaze, and smiled. "What's that, cowboy?"

His lips settled over hers and she cupped his chin to kiss him back, secure in his warm embrace. He tasted like chocolate and whipped cream—and icing? She pulled back slightly. "Travis?"

"Yeah?"

"When you got the hot chocolate, did you happen to get into anything else?"

He frowned, but his eyes slid from hers. "What are you talking about?"

"Cake."

"Um . . . well . . ."

"You snitched a piece, didn't you?"

"No way. I wouldn't do that. You sure do have a lot of balloons in there. And the streamers are just the right touch."

"Stop trying to change the subject. If you didn't eat a piece of the cake, then you skimmed the icing."

He grinned. "I might have done a little skimming."

"Travis Walker, that cake is not for you!"

"I know, but are you kidding me? This house smells like nothing but sugar and cake. It was just sitting there, practically begging me to sample it, so I did. No one will ever know, I promise. I smoothed the little area over really well."

"You're hopeless."

His knuckles gently scraped down her cheek and he kissed her nose. "I'm hopelessly crazy about you, Heather Fontaine," he whispered. "You know that, right?"

"I'm beginning to believe it. The more you kiss me, the more I'm convinced."

"I'm more than happy to keep convincing."

She laughed and he kissed her again.

With his forehead against hers, he stared at her, making her want to squirm. "Why are you looking at me like that?"

"Were you ever bitter?"

She blinked at his suddenly serious tone. "Sorry?"

"About how you grew up? The way your father is and the way he treated you?"

She sighed. "Wow, what brought that on?"

"I'm . . . curious, I suppose. I see what happened to Gina and how she let Brad's death take over her entire life, her attitude, everything. And then there's you."

"It's not just me. Most people who suffer trauma don't turn into killers, but . . ." How did she explain? "Okay. Was I angry? Yes. Did I ever wish I was someone else who had loving parents? Yes. Bitter? Maybe. Yes. I think that went with the anger."

"What changed that for you? Because I look at you and I don't see an angry or bitter person. You've let it go."

"Well, I'm sure part of it was the fact that when I realized the anger was controlling me and not the other way around, I decided that would never do. That's also when God and I were developing a relationship and he was showing me some things about myself. Like to have the kind of future and life I wanted, I needed to release that anger, the unforgiveness, and the hatred. I make it sound easy, but I promise, it wasn't."

"But you did it."

"With some divine help, yes."

"Gina couldn't do it."

"You were right, back in the cave, when you said Gina wasn't open to doing it. We tried to help her, tried to form a real friendship with her, but she didn't want our help. If there's one thing I've learned from you all, it's if someone doesn't want help, it's hard to give it."

"I wasn't giving you a choice."

"I know." She laughed. "Trust me. But deep down, even though I had a hard time admitting it, I wanted your help. And I wanted Caden's help in getting that video down. Thank goodness, it's gone now, by the way."

"I noticed and I'm glad." He hugged her and she closed her eyes to simply enjoy the moment.

"Travis?"

"Yes?"

"I'm glad you were the one to come after me."

He leaned back and lifted her chin to stare into her eyes. "I'll always come after you, Heather. I'll never leave you to face trouble alone."

"Thank you," she whispered through a tight throat. She cleared it and he ran a thumb over her cheek.

"Okay, now for the serious stuff," he said, setting her back from him.

Heather's heart thumped. Serious stuff? "All right."

"I have a question for you that you never answered."

She frowned. "What's that?"

"Your time-waster. I know you have one. So, what is it?"

Heather almost wilted. Serious stuff, huh? She could feel the heat moving from her chest into her neck and finally her cheeks. "I guess I do. Maybe. I mean, it's kind of one, but it helps people too. It's really a stress reliever."

"You're killin' me, woman. Spill it."

She laughed, then gave a little groan. "Okay. I watch medical shows on television and then dissect everything they do wrong—and right—and write a review on my blog. I have quite a few followers—mostly writers."

His jaw dropped and she ducked her head. He lifted her chin to meet his eyes. "That's incredibly fascinating. You like medical shows but feel like you shouldn't because they're beneath you. So, this is your way of justifying watching them."

"What? No, I don't think they're beneath me!" When he raised a brow at her, she giggled. "Okay, guilty. Silly, isn't it? Although, some of them are really well done, even if they don't get all of the medical facts right every time. So, yes . . . I enjoy them."

Laughter poured out of him and she grinned. Then narrowed her eyes. "Now, it's your turn."

"What?"

"Why are you so antsy around doctors?"

He groaned and dropped his head into his hands. "It's stupid."

"Travis, you might as well tell me. I'm not going to let this go, you know."

"It's Sandra's fault. She used to make me be her patient when we were kids and she used to pinch me when she 'gave me a shot.' And if I ever actually had to go to the doctor, she would tease me that I'd have to get a shot."

"How mean."

"She was a brat, but I've grown to love her." He paused. "How many followers?"

A car door slammed. "They're here," she said.

"Yes, they are." His eyes glittered with sudden excitement and he stood to go open the door.

Before he could get there, Brooke swung it open and stepped inside, stomping her boots on the mat. "Hey, y'all, I've got the chips and dip."

"And I've got the drinks," Asher said from behind her. "Sarah and Gavin just drove up, and I think Ava is a few minutes behind."

"Awesome," Heather said. "This is going to be so fun." A dark blue SUV pulled into the drive. "And that's Dr. Colson." She slipped out the door and ran to hug the man. He smelled of peppermint and citrus soap. "I'm so glad you felt well enough to come."

"I wouldn't miss this for the world. I'm still a little dependent on this cane when I get tired, but I'll be able to toss it soon enough."

Heather led him inside, then looked out the window. Ava drove up, followed by Caden. She turned to Travis. "Our gang's all here. Now we just need your family."

He waved his phone at her. "They're on the way."

Sure enough, within three minutes, she spotted Joe and Sandra's van, followed by Travis's parents in their golf cart.

"Ryker's in the van, right?" she asked.

"Supposed to be." Travis whistled and everyone quieted. "Thank you, guys, so much for coming today. The guest of honor is here and will be walking in at any moment."

"We're ready," Sarah said.

Caden's eyes widened as he glanced around. "Did you buy every balloon in the city?" He batted one that floated past his face.

"Just about," Heather said. She peered out the window once more. "Here they come!"

Everyone fell quiet. The door opened. Sandra stepped inside carrying baby Lisa. Jackie, Davey, and Martin followed, their excitement palpable. And then Ryker's lanky frame filled the entrance.

"Surprise!"

The one word, yelled in unison, filled the home.

Ryker gasped and stepped back right into Joe. The man put his arm over the kid's shoulder and maneuvered him forward.

Heather grinned. "Happy birthday, Ryker."

"But . . . but . . . what?"

Heather laughed and Travis stepped forward. "Welcome to your surprise birthday party."

Ryker's throat worked and his gaze touched on each and every person, finally landing on his doctor friend. He rushed forward to hug the man, who patted him on the back. "Happy birthday, son."

"I don't know what to say. It's not my birthday yet."

He did look a tad dazed. Heather grabbed his hand and ushered him into the spacious kitchen where the others had gathered around the island.

And the twelve cakes. Ryker spotted them and gaped. "What . . . ?"

Travis plunked a Stetson on his head. "This was Heather's idea, but we all helped."

"I helped ice the heart-shaped cake," Jackie said.

"And I licked the bowl," Martin chimed in.

Everyone laughed, then fell silent as Ryker took it all in. "I don't know what to say. No one's ever—" Tears filled his eyes and he sniffed, then shook his head. "Oh man. Thank you. I . . . just . . . wow. Thank you."

"You said the last cake you had was for your sixth birthday," Heather said. "I wanted you to have a cake for every one that you missed since then."

Ryker turned and hugged her, burying his face in her hair. "Thank you. You're going to have me crying like a baby."

"That's all right. We'll all probably join you."

He chuckled and drew in a deep breath.

"When are we gonna eat the cake?" Davey asked.

More laughter filled the kitchen, and Ryker hefted the kid onto his back, then Travis handed him a brightly wrapped package. "For you."

"Open it!" Jackie fairly danced with her excitement.

With Davey hanging on like a monkey, Ryker opened the gift as if it contained a priceless treasure. A fine tremor ran through his hands. "I haven't gotten many gifts before. I don't know what to say."

Heather's heart broke once again for the teen. "Well, you can come to expect it from now on."

Ryker finally pulled the paper from the box. And gasped. "A phone?"

"We figured you could use an upgrade," Travis said.

He simply stared, his mouth working. They'd rendered him speechless. A tear slipped over and tracked its way down his cheek. He swiped it and cleared his throat. "Thank you. Again."

Dr. Colson stepped forward. "There's one more thing."

Ryker waited while the doctor pulled an envelope out of his pocket. Dr. Colson passed it to Ryker.

"You got in. On a full scholarship. I've already sent my endorsement. All you have to do is accept the invitation and show up for the first day of class."

And that was it for Ryker. A sob erupted from him, and he bolted to the man who'd practically raised him. Ryker wrapped his arms around the doctor and held on while he wept.

Travis slid an arm around Heather's shoulders and she buried her face in his chest.

But not before noticing there wasn't a dry eye in the room.

"So," Davey said, "are we just gonna cry all day or are we gonna eat some cake?"

○ ○ ○

Two hours later, with Ryker hooked up to his new phone and Travis promising to pay the bill as long as Ryker was in school, Travis took Heather's hand and they slipped outside to the warmth of the barn.

The moment they stepped inside, Travis shut the door, pulled her close, and kissed her. He put everything he felt for her into that kiss, and by the end, all he could manage to say was, "I love you, Heather."

He heard her swallow. "I love you too, Travis."

He hugged her once more, then let her go. "We can go back to the party now. I just wanted to kiss you."

She bit her lip. "Travis, I . . ."

His brows creased. "What is it?"

"It's not anything you don't already know, but I come with a lot of baggage. I still wake up screaming some nights. Far less than I used to, but . . ." She pursed her lips. "I'm stubborn and like to be in control and I still don't ask for help very easily."

"And I'm . . . hmm . . . I'm easygoing, never lose my temper, and am an all-around perfect guy." He paused while Heather's jaw dropped. "Oh, wait," he said, then stopped. "Never mind, that's all I can think of."

Heather blinked. Then laughed. That deep belly laugh he'd heard only once in all the time he'd known her. The fact that he'd been the one to bring that laughter to the surface warmed him all the way to his toes. Tears leaked from her eyes and she shook her head. "Oh, Travis, you're so very good for me. And to me."

"Does that mean you'll let me stick around for a while?"

She smiled and more tears gathered even though she didn't let them fall. "I think that can be arranged."

He kissed her again, long and slow and sweet. "I don't think I'll ever get tired of that," he whispered. He knew he wouldn't.

"Then you're in good company."

More laughter. One more thing about her he'd never get tired of.

"I'll tell you a secret," she said, "but you've got to promise you won't let on that you know."

"A secret about what?"

"Asher and Brooke."

He raised a brow. "What about them?"

"They're pregnant."

"What?" His shout sent her into a fit of giggles.

"I caught Brooke puking in the bathroom the other day and flat-out asked her, but she wants to wait a little longer to tell everyone."

"Why?"

"Because she's not very far along," Heather said, "and I suppose she wants to make sure everything's okay. But she said I could tell you since she knows I can't keep secrets from you."

His heart puddled into the soles of his shoes. He was completely besotted with this woman. "Thank you for telling me. It'll be hard, but I won't say anything, I promise."

"We'd better go see if there's any cake left. I'm afraid Davey's going to have quite the tummy ache tonight."

"I think he was on his fourth piece when we left."

"Fortunately, I know someone who can help him out with some prescription meds if he needs them," Heather said.

He wasn't ready to let her go just yet—or share her with other people—but he figured it was probably a good idea, considering he'd like to simply sweep her up and hurry her off to the nearest reverend and be done with it. But he'd wait. She was worth waiting for.

He opened the barn door for her and cold air gushed in, but Travis didn't feel it. With the warmth of Heather's love and the promise of a future with her filling him, he sent up prayers of thanks and wrapped his arm around the shoulders of the woman he loved as they headed back to the house. Together.

READ ON FOR AN EXCERPT FROM
BOOK 4 IN THE

DANGER NEVER SLEEPS

SERIES

CHAPTER
ONE

Thursday afternoon in May

Today, the watching ended and the killing started.

Anticipation arched through him. The man in the ski mask turned his gaze from the front door of the luxury home to the end of the street. For ten days, he'd hidden and observed—and learned—the routine of the household and even the neighborhood.

Right on time, the mail truck turned onto the street and began its stop, deliver, go. Stop, deliver, go.

As soon as the vehicle moved on to the next house, the man's gaze swung to the front door once more. And there she was. In her midfifties, the woman of the house took care of herself. She ate healthy with the occasional sweet indulgence, and she jogged two miles every morning. On Wednesdays, she volunteered at her grandchildren's elementary school.

He could have snatched her off the street during one of her runs, but he couldn't take the chance that a doorbell camera would catch him. No, this was better. They had an alarm system, but no cameras.

She slipped out onto the porch, down the walkway, and to the mailbox. For the past two weeks, she'd done the same thing every day at approximately the same time. Other than the Wednesday break in routine, it was like she had nothing else to do but work out at the gym, jog the route in her neighborhood, and wait for the mail. What a sad, sorry life. But that wasn't his problem.

Just off the wraparound porch, the seven-foot fir tree to the left of the door hid him well. His heart thudded, but he'd prepared himself for the adrenaline rush. His right hand curled around the grip of his weapon. The suppressor added weight to the gun, but he hardly noticed it. He'd had fifteen years of preparation and training, research and planning.

She was on the first step, then the second, then walking to the door.

As she twisted the knob, he stepped from behind the tree and clapped a gloved hand over her mouth. A muted scream escaped her, and he brought the weapon up to the base of her skull. Whimpers escaped through his fingers. She shook so hard, he thought he might lose his grip.

He shoved her through the door and kicked it closed behind him. "Where's your husband?"

He kept his voice low. A sob ripped from throat and harsh breaths gushed from her nose. He released his grip so she could answer.

"He's not here."

"He is, because I know you're supposed to be leaving in an hour for your holiday in Turks and Caicos. The suitcases next to the door tell me he's getting ready to load the car. So, if you want to live to enjoy your trip, you'll get him in here."

"He's—"

"Darling?" The voice came from the balcony overlooking the foyer. "I'm almost ready. Was there any mail? I'm expecting—" He stopped, gasped. His hands gripped the railing and his gaze met the man's. "What do you want?"

A smile curved beneath his mask. "Hello, Maksim. Come on down."

"Don't hurt her." The husky baritone held fear—and . . . something else. Resignation?

"Well, now, that depends on you, doesn't it?"

"I'm coming." The man hurried down the winding staircase, stopping at the bottom. "Please. Let her go. I'll do whatever you want. Do you need money? I have ten grand in the safe."

Money? He almost snorted. Money was the last thing he needed. He kept the weapon on the woman's head. "Turn slowly," he told her without taking his eyes from her husband, "and reach into my left-hand pocket. Pull out the object." She didn't move and he narrowed his gaze on the man at the bottom of the steps. "You might want to convince her to do as I ask."

"Darling, do as he says, and it will be all right."

The woman whimpered and turned, her eyes downcast. She reached for his right pocket.

"My left," he snapped.

She jerked her hand away, then slid it into the left pocket of his blazer.

"Good. Pull out the photo." With shaking fingers, she did so. He nodded to the husband. "Come get it."

Maksim's brows dipped farther over the bridge of his nose, but he did as ordered without having to be told twice. When he held the picture between his thumb and forefinger, he looked at it—and swayed. "I see."

"I'm sure you're starting to."

"Max? Make him let me go." The woman whimpered and the intruder tightened his grip.

"Who are you?" Maksim whispered.

"I think you know that answer."

What little color the man had in his face drained away as his suspicions were confirmed. "You're Nicholai, aren't you?"

"I am."

"How did you find me?"

"It's a long story. And not one I have time to tell. I have one question and if you know the answer, you will live."

Maksim's eyes lifted to meet his. "Let me guess, you want to know who the man is."

"No. I know who he is. I want to know who the child is."

The woman had gone completely still, with only an occasional tremor shuddering through her.

Maksim stood still, studying the picture. When he looked up, fear was written in his blue eyes. "Why?"

"It doesn't matter why," Nicolai snapped. "Who is it?" He dug the suppressor harder into the woman's head. She shrieked, the sound grating against his eardrums.

Maksim stepped forward, hand outstretched. "Please!"

"Who. Is. The. Child?" Nicolai asked, his voice low. Calm. Controlled. "Don't make me ask again."

"His daughter."

A daughter.

A thrill like nothing he'd ever experienced lit up everything inside him. His enemy had a daughter.

"Well, well," he murmured.

His original plan immediately shifted. He had a lot of thinking to do, but he'd stick with it for now. It was the end that would change.

The daughter would be the last to die.

Nicolai fired his gun and the woman slumped. She was dead before she hit the ground.

The husband screamed. "You promised!"

"Exactly. I made a promise and now, I'm keeping it." He aimed the weapon at the man.

"How did you find me?"

"Some people just can't throw anything away."

Maksim swallowed. "The files?"

"The files. Now, it's just you and me. We have a lot to talk about before you die."

"A death that will be slow, no doubt?"

"The slowest."

Maksim bolted into the hallway. Nicolai blinked. Okay, he hadn't expected that, but he knew this house as well as its owners, thanks to the blueprints he'd acquired. He followed his target to the closed office door. Maksim might try to call for help, but no calls would go through. Nicolai had made sure of that.

He didn't bother trying the knob, but simply lifted his foot and kicked the door in on the first attempt.

Maksim sat behind his desk, pistol to his chin, blue eyes teary. Determined.

"No! Don't you dare!"

Maksim never blinked. He pulled the trigger. A red mist coated the window behind him. Nicolai screamed his fury before he grabbed the nearest bookcase and shoved it to the floor. Then the next and the next and the next. Until he slumped to the floor amidst the chaos to catch his breath and reconfigure the plan.

○ ○ ○

Ten days later
Saturday morning

FBI Special Agent Caden Denning stood outside the upper-middle-class home with his phone pressed to his ear. "There's a security system, Annie. This is a very nice neighborhood with a lot of cameras, but first see if you can get anything on the home system." Annie's skills at the Bureau were legendary. Hacking into an alarm system that recorded footage would be child's play for her, and time was at a premium. "Officers are going house to house asking for footage," he said, "but I want inside the home cameras now. I don't want to have to wait for the powers that be to give it to me."

"Of course," she said. "And I know it's early and missing a lot of data since you haven't even seen the crime scene yet, but I'll run this murder through ViCap and see if it matches any other murders of entire families. Depending on what shows up, we can add the other information as we get it."

"Perfect."

Caden shoved his phone into his pocket, pulled the little blue booties over his shoes, and signed the crime scene log an officer held just as a black Jeep Wrangler pulled to the curb. His partner, Zane Deveraux, joined him on the porch, coughing into a tissue. The man's nose was red, his lips chapped, his hazel eyes bloodshot with dark circles beneath them. Morning stubble graced his face and his dark hair looked finger combed.

"Dude, are you on some undercover assignment I don't know about?" Caden asked him. "That's one heck of a disguise."

"I wish. I think I'm officially sick."

"Sorry, man. I can take this if you need to go home."

"I'll be fine, just don't get too close."

"You don't have to worry about that." The last thing he needed was a cold—or whatever affliction the man had.

The foyer inside the home held a set of stairs to the second floor. From his position in front of the door, Caden could see straight ahead into the den. The living room was to the left, the dining room to the right. Even though he couldn't see it at the moment, he knew the kitchen with a large island was connected to the dining room. "Who found them?" Caden asked.

The officer looked up from the log. "The neighbor. She and the wife—"

"Angelica," Caden said, his voice low.

"Right. Angelica. They go walking every Saturday morning. When the woman—Angelica—didn't show up at their usual meeting spot on the curb, the neighbor came looking for her. The front door was open, so she walked in."

Caden groaned. "Walked in to see—"

"Yeah." The officer nodded. "She ran screaming to her husband who called us. Paramedics almost had to sedate her she was so hysterical. They finally got her calmed down."

"That poor woman."

Bracing himself, Caden forced his covered feet forward and entered the den. He spotted the victims and let his chin drop to his chest while grief slammed into him.

Zane blew out a harsh sigh, coughed, and pinched the bridge of his nose. "I'm sorry, man."

When Caden had heard the last name and saw that the father was military . . . For a brief moment, he'd hoped it wasn't his friends. Then he'd been given the address and all hope fled. He squeezed his eyes tight. He didn't want to see this.

"You want to take a pass on this one?" Zane asked.

"No." Caden opened his eyes and studied the family huddled together on the couch. "Staff Sergeant Michael Fields, his wife, Angelica, and their two youngest children, Brian and Ellen, ages eight and ten." Each had one bullet to the forehead. The nausea swept through him and he fought the swirling grief to focus on the building rage. He could manage the anger. "Where's Mickey?"

"Who?"

"Their oldest son. He's fourteen or fifteen, I think. He's named after his father, but everyone calls him Mickey."

"I'll get someone looking for him." Zane turned to the nearest officer and requested he ask the neighbor about the teen.

"I go—went—to church with them," Caden said. "Brian sat on my lap last Sunday during the children's sermon." He swallowed hard, forcing the memories to the back. "Who would do this?" he asked, not expecting an answer.

"Robbery doesn't appear to be a motive," Zane said. He nodded to the elaborate media system nestled into the wall unit. "That would bring in a lot of cash."

"So, why?" Caden muttered. Another rhetorical question. Until they took apart this family's lives, they wouldn't speculate.

Zane continued to frown and turned his eyes from the scene. "Adults are bad enough, but kids . . . they get to me. I'm going to be seeing them in my nightmares for months."

"I know. Same here." It would probably be more like years.

Caden's phone rang. Annie. He swiped the screen. "That was fast."

"I had an almost immediate hit in ViCap. There are two other murders that I can say initially match yours."

"Tell me."

"In both families, each person was murdered with one gunshot to the head. They were all seated on the sofa, kind of huddled together. Scenes were middle- to upper-middle-class neighborhoods."

"Where?"

"First one was San Diego, California, last month. Second one almost two weeks ago in Houston, Texas. I've pulled the photos and other information from those two scenes and sent them to you. That's all for—" A pause. "Hold on, Caden, we might have something more for you."

We?

Within a minute, she came back. "Okay, Daria's got more information for you." Daria Nevsky, a new analyst with mad skills in all things technical. "And, as of twenty seconds ago, she'll be your go-to on this one. Gary's handed me something else to work on." Gary Smith was her supervisor.

Caden went still. Daria had worked on other cases with him, but . . . "This is a big one, Annie. You think she can handle this?"

"Without question."

Her complete lack of hesitation settled his momentary twinge of anxiety. "Fine."

"Truly, Caden, she's better than I am. I'm putting you through to her. Hold on."

Better than Annie? Not likely.

The line clicked. "Caden?"

"Yeah." Man, she sounded too young to be as good as Annie said. Not that age had anything to do with skills or being a good agent, but still . . .

". . . has a camera in the den facing the sofa, so I'm sending the footage to your phone. You can watch it yourself."

"Wait, you actually got something?"

"Yes. Our speech reader even got some of the words from Mr. Fields's lips before, well . . . before."

Before Michael had been shot. He just prayed he'd been the last one to die and the kids hadn't seen—

"Caden . . . Caden?" Daria's voice pulled him back.

He blinked the images away. For now. "I'm here."

"Did you get the video?"

He checked his phone. "I did." Along with everything Annie had sent him.

"I added the captions to it so you can see what the words are."

"Impressive."

"I aim to please. Unfortunately, the camera in the kitchen area wasn't working, so I'm not sure what happened after you see the gun fly back into the living area."

"What?"

"Just watch it. It's self-explanatory. Call me if you need anything else. I've also texted you my direct line."

"Thanks. I'll be in touch." With that one conversation, she'd managed to reassure him she was up to the tasks ahead of her. Caden hung up and filled Zane in.

His partner rubbed his head. "Three cases?"

"Yeah. And at the moment, it looks like they could all be connected. Too many similarities not to be, even without the full workup of this scene."

"Then it's got to be the same person or persons doing this." Zane's hoarse, flat words pierced Caden's carefully constructed emotional barrier. "I hate to say it, but . . . I think we've got a serial killer running loose in this country."

"Possibly." Caden kept his voice calm, detached, even as his heart thudded hard enough to hurt. *Focus.* "Serial killers don't usually have a territory this wide. Three different states? And opposite ends of the country?"

"True. Not that it's impossible, but I'm not sure I buy it. He could definitely be classified as a serial killer, and I'm willing to bet these killings aren't random. There's a connection somewhere that made these people targets."

"I agree."

"So, once again, we circle back to motive," Zane said. "When we find out the connection, we'll figure out the motive."

"Exactly." Caden rubbed a hand over his chin. "So, this is it. We don't leave here until we know what we're dealing with."

"Yeah, because if we don't, what you wanna bet, there's going to be a fourth?"

"I agree." He looked up as the officer Zane had assigned to find Mickey approached.

"No one seems to know where the teen is," the man said. "The neighbor had the kid's number. I've called it, but it went straight to voice mail." He handed Caden a piece of paper with the number on it.

"Thanks." Caden texted the number to Daria and asked her to track the phone. He looked at Zane. "We're going to need to set up a task force."

"I was thinking the same thing." His partner coughed and pulled a pack of tissues from his pocket. "Be right back."

Caden let his gaze scan the room, ignoring the chatter of the other officers coming from the open front door. He stopped at the mantel. Pictures lined it. Mostly of the children. Some of the family. And one of another family he'd seen somewhere.

Zane returned with a bottle of water. "Sorry. Had to take some Motrin and blow my nose. Seriously, how can your nose feel stuffed completely full and when you blow it, noth—"

"I don't need the details, dude." Caden nodded to the iPad Zane still held in his other hand. "Let me see those pictures from the first crime scene again, will you?"

Zane pulled them up. "Why?" He popped a cough drop.

"Scroll through them. I'm looking for something in particular."

His partner swiped one picture after another.

"There," Caden said, grabbing the tablet from his partner. "Stop."

"What do you see?"

"The same picture on that end table in the Baileys' home is over there on the mantle." He pointed. A do-it-yourself Christmas photo in a small black frame sat on the stone mantle next to others like it. An antique clock behind the pictures had ticked away their final minutes.

Zane raised a brow. "You and that memory of yours," he muttered. "Okay, then. Family number one and family number three knew each other. Well, there's part of a connection. Family number two probably knows one and three. But how? Or is that a stretch? Is there any evidence in family number two's home to suggest a connection?"

"Those are really good questions. Could be a college fraternity or sorority. We have to look at both spouses' connections to each other."

"Let's watch the footage. Maybe that'll help.

Caden tapped the link to the video. They watched as it began to play.

The picture was clear.

As was the barrel of the weapon aimed at the family.

Unfortunately, the killer's face was not.

Beyond the gun, seated on the couch, were Michael, his wife, and the two younger children. All four of them looked terrified. Mingled with Michael's terror was fury. The man was a fighter. He held himself still, only out of fear for his family. How had the killer managed to get the drop on him?

"That's freaky," Zane said. "I feel like I'm watching this from his point of view."

Caden paused the video, turned, and pointed to the wall behind them. "That camera up in the corner near the molding. It almost blends right into the wall. The killer might not have realized it was there."

"I don't know. He keeps his back to it."

"You think he wanted us to see the footage?"

"Who knows, man? Let's get this over with and watch to the end."

Caden ignored his anxiety at what he knew was coming and pressed play. Daria's captions popped up on the screen.

"I'll give you whatever you want, just let them go," Michael said. He stopped speaking as the killer responded, words too muffled for the speech reader to pick up. Then Michael's lips moved once more. "You want me to say what?"

The tip of the gun turned on his wife. She cowered over Brian, and Michael held up a hand, yelling, "Stop! I'll say it. 'Trusting a liar will only get you killed.' There. I said it. Now, let them go."

The gun jerked. Four times. And it was over.

But no. It wasn't.

The gun flew back into the room and landed on the floor just within range of the camera. A foot appeared in the frame for a brief second before disappearing. Someone had walked in the door and sent the gun flying?

Caden blinked, swallowing hard. "Mickey made it home," he said, his voice low. "He walked in the front door as the man was killing his family and he acted."

"Kicked the gun out of the guy's hand?"

"Yeah."

"Then what?"

"I don't know." Caden's mind played out several scenarios of what could have happened next. None of them good. All of them stomach turning. He drew in a shuddering breath.

Caden swallowed twice and sighed. He handed the iPad to Zane, walked outside, and lost his breakfast in the nearest bush.

CHAPTER TWO

It hadn't taken long for them to be discovered.

Nicolai, dressed in a grey T-shirt, blue jeans, baseball cap, and sunglasses, ignored his throbbing knee and watched from across the street. No one paid him any attention as he blended in with the other neighbors who'd stopped their Saturday morning routine to gawk at the unfolding scene.

The cell phones were out in force, no one wanting to miss a moment of the excitement in their otherwise boring routines. The killer made sure to stay out of the line of sight of those cameras. Positioned toward the back of the crowd, he leaned against the nearest tree, pulled the ballcap lower, and crossed his arms. He also had a good view of the busybody neighbor who'd found the family. She'd disappeared into the ambulance when the paramedics had arrived, then two officers had joined her in the back of the vehicle. No doubt grilling her about what she'd seen. The killer wasn't worried. She hadn't seen him. A short time later, she'd rejoined the neighbors still watching the action.

She spoke to each person she knew, and he prepared himself to duck away if she came at him. For now, she seemed content to speak to the older gentleman on the other side of the tree.

Law enforcement had been in the house for a while, wondering who the monster was who'd kill an entire family. Especially kids. He frowned. He could understand their horror. He'd admit the kids were the hardest, but they were part of the promise.

I'll kill them, I'll kill them all. I promise.

Just three more families and his mission would be complete, his promise kept. His grandmother was wrong. Vengeance didn't belong to God. It belonged to *him*. And it tasted sweet.

"Terrible shame, isn't it?"

He almost came out of his skin when the man to his right spoke and the killer realized the words were directed at him. He cleared his throat. "Uh . . . yeah."

"So, who are you? I know everyone who lives around here but don't think I've seen you before."

"Oh, I was looking at that house for sale on the corner, saw all the excitement, and thought I'd stick around to see what was going on."

Thank goodness he'd spent some time coming up with a plausible story should something like this happen.

"Oh, well, it's a great neighborhood. Don't let this keep you away. We've never had any trouble like this before."

"Of course, of course. Thank you for letting me know." He paused. "So, you've lived here a while?"

"Yep, me and the missus built one of the first houses back here."

"And you know the family, of course?"

"Yeah. I'm just glad the older boy wasn't home when it happened."

"Heard someone mention that. He'll probably head somewhere he feels safe."

"Probably."

"Can't believe he just ran off. Guess shock can make you do things out of character."

"Of course it can," a familiar voice butted in. Nicolai stiffened when he recognized it belonged to the nosy neighbor. "That poor boy," she said. "I just pray he turns up soon. Or heads straight to the nearest police station." She sighed. "Knowing him, though, he'll head to that dojo. I think he'd move in there if given the option."

"Naw," the other man said, "my guess is he'll head to his grandparents' house. They're close."

Nicolai shoved his hands into his pockets and clenched his fists while pasting a smile on his lips. He doubted the kid would go to either place, but if he had to put money on one or the other, he'd guess the dojo. "Well, I guess I'll be on my way. I have a realtor to talk to about a house."

He slipped away with the woman's questions floating behind him. But he wasn't quite ready to leave yet, he simply wanted to get away from the two chatterboxes. It wasn't hard to find another spot in the crowd to blend in. Officers questioned the neighbors and took their names and contact information. Each time an officer got close to him, he simply moved behind someone else.

For the next two hours, he watched, careful to stay out of the way of the panning phone cameras. With his position at the rear of the crowd, he wasn't worried one bit about being caught on video.

He sighed and worked his jaw with a wince. That kid had taken him completely by surprise. He'd known he took karate at the dojo, but he'd severely underestimated the youngster's skills. He wouldn't let that happen again. He could admire him even as he killed him.

Regret pierced him at the thought. He *did* wish he could let the cops know that he took no pleasure in the killings. It was just something he had to do. A promise he'd made and had to keep. And if he didn't keep his promise, what kind of man did that make him?

When the cop had puked into the bushes, it had bothered him. He had no agenda with the officers. They were just doing their jobs.

And he'd done his. It was time to go. He turned on his heel and winced at the shooting pain in his left knee. That was one complication he hadn't needed, but it wouldn't keep him from doing what he'd come to do. He limped across the front yard to the stolen car he'd parked at the neighborhood pool. He was ready for all of this unpleasantness to be finished. He missed his home, the peaceful lull of the water lapping against the sides of his boat. But . . . a promise was a promise.

Unfortunately, the oldest son of Michael Fields was still alive and that had to be rectified as soon as possible.

Acknowledgments

As always when it comes to this stage in the book process, I'm terrified I'm going to forget someone who is fully deserving of being acknowledged for their contribution to the story.

It goes without saying that I first say thank you to my Lord and Savior, Jesus Christ. With every book, I tell him that I'm not sure I can do it again. And with every book, he pulls me (sometimes kicking and screaming, but mostly prayerfully) through it. He talks me off the ledge and calms the panic attacks and reminds that he's called me to do this. So, thank you, dear Jesus, for not giving up on me and for letting me deliver one more story. May it reach the reader who needs to see you on the page.

Next, I'd like to say thanks to my wonderful and amazing family. I certainly could NOT do this without you.

And then there are the others who invest themselves in me and my stories. My critique partners and fellow writers who unselfishly brainstorm and offer insights and scenes when my brain is on the fritz—Lynn H. Blackburn, Colleen Coble, Robin Carroll, Pam Hillman, Voni Harris, Carrie Stuart Parks, Edie Melson, Emme Gannon, Erynn Newman, Alycia Morales, Linda Gilden, Molly Jo Realy, Tammy Karasak, and Michelle Cox. Thank you for letting me borrow your brains and always for your prayer warrior spirits. I love each you.

Thank you to Barb Barnes, who more than earns her money with my stories. You are simply amazing and I love you dearly, my friend. ☺

Thanks to Tamela Hancock Murray, my agent, who works so diligently on my behalf. You are much loved and appreciated!

Thank you, Andrea Doering, my Revell editor, for continuing to believe in me and my stories. You are awesome and I wouldn't be here without you. Thank you for sticking with me through all the ups and downs. ☺ Thankfully, more ups than downs!

I don't want to let another book go by without mentioning my thanks to Rel Mollett. Thank you for all of the social media posts and newsletters and contests you've orchestrated, written, and posted! You free me up to write, and that is invaluable.

Again, thank you to the readers who buy the books. Without you, I couldn't do what I do. You are loved and appreciated!

Thank you all, and I hope you enjoyed the book! Come find me on social media on Facebook at www.facebook.com/lynetteeason and Twitter: @lynetteeason.

God bless you all.

Lynette Eason is the bestselling author of *Collateral Damage* and *Acceptable Risk*, as well as *Protecting Tanner Hollow* and the Blue Justice, Women of Justice, Deadly Reunions, Hidden Identity, and Elite Guardians series. She is the winner of three ACFW Carol Awards, the Selah Award, and the Inspirational Reader's Choice Award, among others. She is a graduate of the University of South Carolina and has a master's degree in education from Converse College. Eason lives in South Carolina with her husband and two children. Learn more at www.lynetteeason.com.

INTENSITY. SKILL. TENACITY.

The bodyguards of
Elite Guardians Agency have it all.

Revell
a division of Baker Publishing Group
www.RevellBooks.com

Available wherever books and ebooks are sold.

"For any reader looking for 'edge-of-your-seat' thrills, this series is the perfect gift."

—Suspense Magazine

THE **HIDDEN IDENTITY** SERIES

Revell
a division of Baker Publishing Group
www.RevellBooks.com

Available wherever books and ebooks are sold.